THE MORNING PAPER

The teenager on the bicycle tossed the papers lazily, landing one in Martin's yard.

"I'll get your paper," Jan chuckled.

"Get back here!" Martin called, crouching naked behind a lawn chair.

Before he could stop her, she was running out into the yard, the dew glistening on her bare skin. She picked the rolled package up as the boy shrugged and rode on, seeming not to care, as though he saw such sights every day.

Martin felt anger at the newsboy's nonchalance. After all, Jan was beautiful.

She stood in the yard's center, watching the boy continue down the street, throwing his wares once more. She waved at his back, then faced Martin. In his panic he gasped at the way the light caught her, making her into a wretched-looking caricature of herself for just a moment. His lungs sighed out every previous desire as her skin suddenly seemed to be a covering of dry, brown leather, her hair ragged sprouts of weeds on a bald head. . . .

He blinked, drawing a deep breath of relief as his eyes cleared and she became as beautiful as ever, snickering to herself lewdly. . . .

Books by Ron Dee

Blood
Succumb

Published by POCKET BOOKS

SUCCUMB

RON DEE

POCKET BOOKS
New York London Toronto Sydney Tokyo Singapore

This book is a work of fiction. Names, characters, places and incidents either are products of the author's imagination or are used fictitiously. Any resemblance to actual events or locales or persons, living or dead, is entirely coincidental.

An *Original* Publication of POCKET BOOKS

POCKET BOOKS, a division of Simon & Schuster Inc.
1230 Avenue of the Americas, New York, NY 10020

ISBN: 0-671-87110-2

First Pocket Books printing April 1994

10 9 8 7 6 5 4 3 2 1

POCKET and colophon are registered trademarks of Simon & Schuster Inc.

Cover art and design by Gerber Studio

Printed in the U.S.A.

This is for Mark, whose "Saturday Mornings" diatribe and earnest critical dissections have been of more assistance than he might guess (it finally sank in, Chomper): To commemorate those trials we've overcome and to rest in peace those to which we've each succumbed.

To give peace to that piece of mind.

Is all that we see or seem, but a dream within a dream?

—E. A. Poe

The rope was not there. He had believed that there would be a companion at the bottom of the rope who would satisfy him for ever, and now he was at the bottom, and there was nothing but the noises and visions which meant nothing. The rope was not there. . . .

—Charles Williams
Descent into Hell

SUCCUMB

1

Martin sat, one leg hung over the arm of his chair, staring at the black TV screen. Down the hall he could hear Leigh's voice faintly intone a departing salutation to God, in Jesus' name, backed by squeakier voices that belonged to Cissy and Will. Then the floor thudded with each child's noisy stomps, and he imagined the scramble for bed being made.

"Good-*bye,* Mommy!" shrieked Will in a voice combining excitement and nervous fear.

"Good *night,* Will," Leigh corrected.

"Will you eat breakfast with us in the morning before you go?" begged Cissy's brisker voice.

"I'll even make it," Leigh replied. "Get to bed now and go to sleep."

Martin sat, staring at the black screen that mirrored the emptiness of his life; waiting, listening to his wife lovey-dovey the children. He loved both rug rats, too, but tempered that attachment with how they had irrevocably changed the course of his life. They made him stagnant in a job he didn't dare leave and had all but overtaken the dreams he barely reached for. His ambition of rock 'n' rolling was overwhelmed by the necessity of supporting his budding family and by his finding he must take his university courses seriously. Jim and Darrell, his pianist and drummer, waited patiently as his appearances at the weekly nightclub sessions became monthly and then grew more infrequent. They finally formed a new group, and though they let him play as backup guitarist once or twice, it was only a gesture.

He was no longer one of them. The years went past, and his hair was chopped shorter and neater. His hours were regulated by the outside world they all abhorred. Though none of them were ever actually hippies—those long-haired dissidents were being crushed by disco fever even as he turned eighteen—he, Darrell, and Jim had been their indirect offspring. Then his marriage to Leigh and the responsibilities it entailed, especially with her pregnancy, made him the first to break away and become one of the suit-and-tie establishment.

A dog in the back yard. In bed by eleven and up in the morning, at the office from eight to five. A house to buy, a family to raise, and bills to pay. Vicious circle. Once you were in, you were trapped and couldn't get out.

Cissy was born, and they struggled. Leigh went to school, and they struggled harder; then they bought this house, way over their budget, so Leigh got her job, and they struggled still more.

Will was born.

They struggled, but they bought beyond necessity when Leigh's promotion made the money easier, and his own long hours made his guitar become dusty in the closet. He spent his spare seconds before the TV, slightly humiliated that Leigh was doing more to support the family than he was. When he quit his job as a music tutor and part-timer at the grocery store for a position at Dex Sales he went to night meetings to study their computer programs, and he left the years he spent in school unused, and he struggled . . . *alone.*

He had given up his dreams and was trapped, and though he struggled, that grappling was a fly's battle with an elephant. In the end he lost.

Shuffle. Bump. Shuffle. Sigh.

Martin did not move.

Leigh crossed the room. "God, I'm tired."

Martin closed his eyes.

"I hope those two won't be any trouble while I'm gone, Marty. If they get to be too much, Mother offered to watch them." She hesitated, touching his shoulder. "Martin?"

He looked at her, examining her from the straggly blond bun at the top of her head to the cheeks that were flushed for a better reason than any he had; then he let his gaze rest on the softly rounded figure beginning to be marred by wifely fat. Her face was apologetic but didn't hide the excitement she wouldn't express in words: She wanted to go.

"Martin?"

He raised an eyebrow.

"I gave the house a good cleaning, so if you just pick up after yourself, it shouldn't be much trouble to keep it livable."

His mouth was dry. "You're really looking forward to this, aren't you?"

"Kind of."

"Just 'kind of'?" His eyebrow arched higher, and he thought of the guitar.

She furrowed her forehead indecisively, then giggled. "I don't know. It's kind of exciting. . . ." She closed her mouth and shrugged, then walked past him to a chair at the room's other side, lowering herself into it. "It's something new."

"Yeah." He looked at his feet. She wanted to go.

"Don't do this, Marty," she whispered. She showed her plaintive gray eyes, and her tight lips emphasized a trembling mouth. She leaned forward, stretching the green paint-stained work blouse she put on after getting home. He did his best not to let it remind him of the time when it been fresh and new. The first time she'd worn it they had taken a drive, leaving Cissy with Grandma. Leigh's mother.

He winced, remembering that day. He'd taken that fresh clean blouse off her, and they'd undressed in that old deserted house out in the country. He'd wanted to stay in the open air, but she had been paranoid at the thought of being seen.

It had been so good back then.

She was still talking, and he looked back up.

"It'll only be until Monday, and maybe being apart will kind of clear the air." Her mouth turned in a hopeful smile. "It'll give you a chance to work on that old T-bird and watch those movies I don't like. You could even get out your old guitar and play it. It's been a long time since you've done that. Maybe you could call up Jim and Darrell and have a jam session. It—it'll be kind of a vacation. I'll finally get a chance to travel . . . and you—"

"Great vacation," he muttered, "for you."

"For both of us," she insisted.

"Right." Martin closed his eyes again, feeling the tension even in this brief exchange. Their marriage was slipping. Ten years, five of steady sliding, and she was leaving on a vacation.

"Well"—she shrugged—"you don't like to go places anymore, anyway."

His thin eyebrows met on his forehead.

"I mean, you don't like to go out of town, Marty. I'm sorry, but I don't really count going to antique car shows as anywhere, or even going to those loud concerts." She shut her mouth, shaking her head. "It'll do us both good." Her round eyes were hopeful. "Maybe we'll learn to appreciate each other again."

He didn't reply. The days of their romance were so far away he could hardly remember why he'd married her. The dissipating physical attraction of their youth was practically lost in the overly familiar swell of her breasts and thighs—an infrequent meal for an appetite deadened by too many such chicken dinners.

"Ready for bed?" she asked suggestively, pursing her lips.

He still didn't reply, wondering if Jim or Darrell had finally been captured, too, and snared in the harness of marriage, house payments, and children.

Cissy and Will. He smiled a little. Despite the rest of it, they at least made life a little better. He *did* love them. He loved and sometimes envied them. But if he had to do it all again . . .

"Come on, the TV screen isn't all that exciting, is it?" She giggled again. "What's showing? *Dark Side of the Moon?*"

"You said Tom was going to Dallas with you, didn't you, Leigh?" He crossed his legs, hearing his annoyance in the slow rustle of his blue slacks. The pleasantness faded from her cheeks.

"You know he is. It's his presentation, Marty. He had to really wangle so I could go with him. He knew I wanted to do a presentation, and he's just helping me out. It's the chance I need. With the experience, I could get into line for a better position." She looked around the worn furniture and shook her head. "This stuff won't last forever, and someday we may want to find a bigger house."

"Did you ever wonder why?"

"What?" Her mouth dropped open to match her puzzled eyes. "Wonder what?"

Martin didn't look at her. He thought of the fateful night when she'd told him about expecting Cissy and the gallant chilvary that had brought about his immediate proposal. When they were married in the university chapel the next week he had given up his swinging bachelorhood to the crushing responsibility of the establishment's simplest trap. He had made himself faithful to one woman, a girl he'd met and loved after she told him how she admired his ability on the guitar and then shared the magic in her bag of Colombian.

And he'd made her pregnant. Except for that, their fateful first night was almost an exact replay of similar evenings shared with many others.

He frowned, for the first time in years remembering a woman he'd briefly known right before he met Leigh. Her name had been Sally. He had been with her only one night, and she'd disappeared. Leigh had still been with him when he awakened and had virtually moved in with him, swelling belly and all.

"Wonder what, Marty?"

He remembered how he'd been entranced by Leigh's sweet body at the beginning. Looking at her now, he swallowed. "Didn't you ever wonder why Tom"—he sneered—"why Tom wanted *you* to go with him?"

"I"—she smiled weakly—"it's not what you think."

He crushed his fingers into the chair's fabric, having to imagine Tom's likeness, since he'd never met the man. He conceived of a cross between a dark, muscled athlete and a smarmy Cary Grant. "Well, have a fucking great vacation," he muttered.

She shook her head, spreading her hands. He heard her loud gulp. "Marty . . . I just meant it might be good for us to be apart for a few days. To give us time to think. It's been so hard for us both these past months. Something always seems to be coming between us. I want it to be like it used to be. I want you to take time to relax by yourself. You need it. I need it. We've both needed to do that—"

"If you have time to relax," he spat. "You'll be awfully busy. Especially with Tom, huh?"

"Marty!"

Her lips were trembling again.

"Have a great vacation *fucking,* I should have said!"

She stared at him. "Marty, this is a job. I just meant it might be good for us to spend some time away from each other. We've been arguing so much"—her voice quavered —"just like now."

"I thought you said we need to talk it out. You were so damn big about us both going to talk to that damn preacher." He cleared his throat loudly and picked up a package of Winstons, knocking a cigarette into his hand and running his forefinger along it. That was another thing the great net of the establishment was trying to hook him into. Religion. But so far he'd managed to steer clear of accepting it. The knowledge made him smile, and he knew he was still a little free. He could dream a bit, even if he knew those dreams would never come true. He thought of the mysterious Sally again. He could only vaguely remember what she had told him: "Your dreams are you. You are your dreams. You can't ever lose your dreams because they are yourself. You are your dreams. . . ."

Fucking right. Like wow, man. Far out. Despite the years and changes since he'd licked her tiny nipples and listened to her spaced-out voice, he'd never forgotten that. He had forgotten her, but not what she said. He smiled loosely at

Leigh. "Yeah, you wanted to talk it all out and bring me to see some counselor at that frigging church."

"You didn't want to talk with Brother Halverson," Leigh whispered. "He's a good man, though. He understands, and he cares. He could help you, Martin. He could help *us.*"

Martin huffed, clicked his Bic lighter, and held it under the cigarette hanging between his lips. He crossed his legs the other way and snorted.

"Martin, please. I just want to try."

He took a long drag of smoke and wrinkled his nose when he let it out, tasting it as it coursed through his nostrils and tickled the tiny hairs. He closed his eyes again, thinking of that girl Sally and what she'd said . . . of Maggie, Jo, and Tonia before her.

He had exchanged them and his freedom for Leigh and this house.

The room was silent.

Leigh's chair squeaked, and he heard her feet on the carpet. He felt her breeze as she passed him. Swish, swish. Silence. A door slammed shut.

Martin opened his eyes, swallowed, and licked dry lips. The TV screen was still dark, and as empty as the room. As his heart.

"Leigh?" he whispered, then he stood up. He dumped the long ash onto the clean floor, then scuffed it into the carpet bristles. Somewhere inside himself the long-lost romance they'd shared still made him care, but always like this . . . too late. Even now it wasn't always bad, and there were nights when they still laughed together and held each other close . . . and there were still those Saturdays when they took the kids on outings, though they were less and less frequent.

"Leigh?"

Silence; the silence of a slasher film when the last living character makes his way through a house full of the dead, the silence bearing the hollowness swallowing his life. A life begun with grand ambition, sidetracked by his dazed belief in love and subsequent quixotic chilvary, finally met by the concrete brutality of the real world. Though he tried to combine them, he repeatedly found himself forced to lower his expectations. Dreams of perfect life, perfect wife, peace, and, finally, love itself turned into the craving for a perfect job, cash position, and comfort. It was entrapment by a world he had never wanted, picking away the youthful fantasies until they were only half-remembered dreams.

Martin picked his feet up lightly, passing through the hallway adorned by the pastel photo portraits of Cissy and Will, their pictured likenesses growing steadily younger until he reached the room he shared with the woman who'd borne them. He listened to the settling house with closed eyes and stood outside the closed barrier to that room for a long minute, then rested his hand on the doorknob, wanting to open it and apologize to Leigh. Despite the fervor he put into his words, he knew they were untrue and only spoke of his longing for an excuse to escape.

His fingers rubbed the brass knob.

Twisting it, he pushed the door open and looked in to see her undressing. He studied the familiar curves of her hips, trying to imagine and remember.

"Leigh," he began slowly, sucking on the cigarette for strength. "Leigh, I—"

She stood still for a moment, then faced him with averted eyes. Red blotches marked her streaked cheeks, and he saw the pain in her damp eyes. "I . . . I don't need this, Marty. Get out of here!"

"I—"

They stared at each other, and her shoulders slumped. A loud sniffle escaped her, and she wiped her face with the back of her hand, turning to toss her bra on the floor and drape the nightgown over her head. She pulled back the waterbed's quilt. "I'm tired, Marty. I'm going to bed. It's going to be a very long day for me tomorrow, and I want to do well. I don't"—her voice tightened and she balled her fists—*"I don't need this.* This is just why I think it will be good for us to be away from each other."

"Leigh, I'm sorry."

The long blue cotton gown hung over her like a monk's

habit, and her face showed a monk's sternness now. "Not tonight, Marty," she told him quietly. "Not *now.*"

He knew what she meant, hesitated briefly, and turned back, closing the door behind him. He had known it would be like this.

And her refusal helped excuse his lust for escape.

2

Leigh made breakfast as promised, then left for her office in the Town and Country wagon. She gave Martin a peck on the cheek on her way out the door. She didn't look back.

He thought of that as he drove the kids to the baby-sitter, not playing his usual games with them.

"You're Dr. Frankenstein and I'm the monster," snarled Cissy, grabbing hold of Will between them on the front seat. "I'm going to eat your brains!"

"Dad!" shrieked Will, grabbing Martin's arm.

"Goddammit—" The car lurched, tires squealed, and Martin fought to regain control. The silver Fiat next to him honked its horn wildly, and for a moment Martin was afraid they were going to collide.

Instead he pulled the wheel hard to his right, feeling like a desperate sailor in the midst of a violent storm.

Crunch.

"Oh, shit," he gasped, hitting the brakes. Another horn blasted behind him, and he cringed at the sound of more squealing tires that were not his own, seeing the big Monte Carlo in the rearview mirror. He frowned at the driver's raised middle finger, but instead of shafting him back Martin just blushed.

"Ow!"

He looked down at Will. The little boy had slid onto the floor, and Cissy was kicking him. "Get up, stupid-head," she shouted.

Sweat ran down into Martin's eyes. He watched the Monte Carlo at his rear cut into the left lane and speed around him, still honking as the driver leaned toward him with his insult. Martin waved back humbly and looked at his children. "Are you guys okay?"

Cissy grinned. "Boy, Daddy, you were just like James Bond!"

"Will?"

He struggled back up to the seat with flashing eyes. "She kicked me, Dad. I fell down."

"He's not hurt. He just acted like he was in one of your horror films, Daddy." Cissy slapped Will's arm as he sat back down. "He's a pud! He doesn't even like to watch 'em!"

"She hit me!" he shrieked again. "Dad!"

Other cars stopped behind Martin were honking now. This time he did turn and shoot the bird to them. It made him feel better.

"Cissy doesn't like those horror shows either, Dad—not even James Bond!"

"Do to!"

"Liar!"

"That's enough!" Martin yelled. He waited until they were both still, then moved slowly ahead, wincing at the way the car pulled to the right. He knew he'd fucked the alignment.

The two children began whispering their insults to each other, but Martin ignored them, thinking instead of the way Leigh had left him to watch over them. She was gone on her trip and expected him to keep up his own job, keep the house clean, and keep the kids in line besides.

Halfway downtown Martin turned onto a street of houses much smaller than his own, older homes that had seen better days. He passed the rows of tall trees and peeling paint, then pulled up into a driveway. Cissy and Will got out fast and ran to the front door of Lisa Murrow's house. Lisa, an overweight divorcée with three kids of her own, opened it as he followed and smiled at his glum face. The kids ran past her.

"Want a cup of java?" she asked, touching his wrist with her hot, damp hand.

He looked at her. She might have once been attractive, one of the schoolgirls who wouldn't even consider his invitation for a date. But now her face was buffered in fat that seemed out of place. She resembled a badly misused car held together by chewing gum and baling wire. There was no telling where her hips separated from her torso.

"Come on, Marty. You're early this morning, and you look like someone who just got robbed. What's wrong?"

"Nothing," he said, but he didn't try to walk away.

"I can tell that's not true." Lisa laughed, drawing him into her house. "Want to tell me about it? Married men should talk to other women besides their wife, you know."

"I have to get to work." He watched Cissy and Will sit down in front of the TV with five other children. "And you have to get some of the kids to school, don't you?"

Lisa looked over her shoulder. "Maybe we can talk tonight, then, huh? Cissy said Leigh was going to be gone for a few days. Is that the problem?"

His eyes roamed her again. She had almost certainly been very pretty once. And she was easy to talk to.

"I'm good at daddy-sitting, too," she whispered, winking.

"Yeah?" he found himself asking.

"Yeah. Sit anywhere you want, Martin, but preferably on my face."

Even though the thought of seeing her naked made him want to shudder, he almost considered the offer.

"We can talk more when you come to pick the kids up," she offered. "I guess we're not in a hurry, are we? We have all weekend."

All weekend. But surely he could do better than her.

It took him longer than he believed it should to decide she wasn't worth risking his marriage. He waved back at Cissy and Will, then turned to his car, not replying.

3

"'Wanna take a bath?'"

Martin sipped beer from the sweating can and kept his eyes closed, envisioning the body of the woman behind that voice.

"'Wanna take a bath?'"

He sighed, letting the invitation caress him.

"'Wanna take a—'"

Pop. Pop. A synthesizer chord hummed, jarring open his eyes. Pink Floyd spilled softly from the speakers, then boomed, wiping even the memory of the sultry invitation —Toni Tenille's soft words?—from his thoughts. He let his fingers touch the strings of the guitar he held in his lap.

Pop, whir. Silence.

"Sorry about that," broke in a smooth voice as Martin hastily reached to lower the receiver's volume. "I guess CDs aren't perfect after all. Let's try it again."

The mellow deejay's apology was replaced by the song's beginning, and Martin turned it off, strumming an off-key chord. The electric guitar's notes were barely audible when it wasn't hooked up, but the sound was loud enough to prove how much the instrument needed to be tuned.

Wanna take a bath?

Martin sighed. The kids were in bed, Leigh was gone for four more days, and there he sat. *Alone.*

The house was locked up, the kids were in bed, and visions of sugarplums danced in his head. Sugarplums from the past he had let slip away, even as his command over this guitar.

Sugarplums—not watermelons like Lisa Murrow. When he picked up the kids she had offered to come by tonight and keep him company, rubbing against him as she did. He could smell her raw onion breath and see her irritation as he told her he would be busy all weekend with some volunteer work.

He laid the white and black stringed instrument on the floor, picking up the slick copy of *Penthouse* he'd bought on his way home from the sitter's. A timeless half-hour passed in fervent study of the naked pictures before he turned to the Forum pages and began reading the descriptive letters about sexual activity there. After the visual feast those blatant passages made his heart pound, though he was suspicious of their veracity, and they reminded him of *back then.* Even so, he *wished* they were true. He wanted to believe the lurid narratives of how these men and women, beyond the giddy explorations of teenagers, found their perfect one-night stands in the most everyday situations.

Martin unbuttoned his shirt's second button and stood up from the padded chair to look around the living room, passing from the drapes to the picture window, then to the stone fireplace. Though he and Cissy and Will were still there, it seemed terribly empty without Leigh, without a *woman.*

He let his glance rest on the TV screen that had stayed dark tonight, put the magazine under his arm, turned out the lights, and sighed. Leigh was gone for the rest of the week, and if he had ever had an opportunity, this was it.

Was that why he hadn't wanted her to leave? Not because he didn't trust her, but because he didn't trust himself? Ten years were behind them now. The first three, when they struggled the hardest to make ends meet, seemed very long ago. Money caused the arguments in those days, but it had been a better time. The pressure of living kept him from his regrets. Now, close to financial soundness, they still argued, even if about other things, and he had time to regret.

But tonight Leigh was gone, and he could do what he wanted.

Except that Cissy and Will were still there.

Glancing at the dishes resting on the counter beside the kitchen sink, he walked past the children's doors, shuffling toward his own.

He wanted a woman besides Leigh. He wanted a woman with whom he could be himself, or at least the way he used to be. He wanted a woman who would center herself around him more than Leigh did now. He wanted the freedom he'd had before her.

The master bedroom door was open, and Martin went in, closing it behind him. He swallowed, seeing the unwrinkled blue quilt folded neatly on the empty bed Leigh had carefully made. He walked to the closet and opened it, looking at her dresses and skirts.

He wanted to escape, to play his guitar like he used to, late into the night, without worrying about getting up the next morning. That guitar had been his magic wand, a key to the gates of sex. When he and his friends had formed a band, women had suddenly wanted him. The mirror still showed the reflection of his unimpressive face, a small nose and high forehead, big ears; but with longer hair and the sounds of his guitar, women had looked at him differently.

Martin backed up to the bed and sat down, laying the magazine open beside him to the Pet of the Month . . . Miss September.

Leigh was gone.

He swallowed, tracing the woman's outline in the photograph with a finger, remembering his mother-in-law's plaintive offer to have Cissy and Will spend a couple of nights. He remembered that time before Leigh, back at the university, those lazy, unstructured days of cutting classes and playing with his band at the noisy bars. It made him think of the night he and Darrell shared a bottle while Jim talked to a coed after their set. They finished it off with McCartney's

"Helen Wheels," Martin's own practiced finger control at its best.

That girl named Sally sat down next to him admiringly and bought him a beer. She said he was handsome. They drank and touched, barely speaking, and he brought her to his room to finish the night. She was as tall as he, almost six feet, her model's body sleek inside the Oklahoma State T-shirt and tight jeans she dropped beside his bed. She rolled two joints, and they smoked wordlessly. Then their bodies came together, and they made impulsive love until they were both wet with saliva, sweat, and their own juices. He lay back as she rested against his chest, sharing more of her grass. He closed his eyes as she told him something spaced-out about dreams. And they fucked again.

Sally smiled as he lay on top of her hot, slippery flesh, tensing each time he poked into her, the spit from their open kisses drooling down her cheek in the window's moonlight. "This is my dream," she'd breathed, "and I've made it real. That's what I mean about our dreams, Martin. You have to want them to be real and believe them into being. You have to believe it so hard that you make them real."

You are your dreams.

They climaxed, and she breathlessly laid her head against his chest.

"*It's real.* You can make anything real if you want it bad enough, but you have to really *want* it. Then, if you send out the vibes hard enough and really believe in them, they'll go out and come back to you. It's kind of a law of the universe. A cosmic law. A guy told me about it a long time ago: that you've got to connect your thoughts of what you want into a kind of big universal reservoir, you know? Like the place you get to when you're really high. Or maybe it's where you get your music." Her slim face brightened. "I didn't believe it either at first. But I thought about it and started to believe a little, and now I've tried it, and it works."

Martin remembered laughing so hard he choked.

"Oh, yeah?" Sally rebuffed him, scooting away and staring defiantly into his eyes. "Well, look at this: I wanted you tonight, and here I am, huh?"

He pulled her on top of him. They made it again and fell asleep in each other's arms.

Sally was gone when he woke. He went to the bathroom and came back to sleep some more, ignoring his morning psychology class. He woke again in the afternoon and met Jim for lunch. They exchanged their nighttime stories, then Martin forgot Sally for a long time. He never saw her again.

Wanna take a bath?

He closed his eyes, imagining how it would be if he had never made love to Leigh on that night, weeks after Sally. It made an interesting fantasy, and he fell into a blissful sleep, dreaming of Sally . . . and Miss September, and making love to them both.

4

"Hi, Marty." Cara Barnes walked—swaggered—into his office munching a crumbling powdered-sugar doughnut in her right hand and holding a coffee mug in her left. She smiled and posed like that: "Coffee, doughnut, or me?"

Rising from the proposal he was outlining in pen, Martin leaned his head past the back of the swivel chair and stretched his neck. His office was small. The door was behind Cara, and a plastic chair stood empty in front of his metal and wood-grain desk. He yawned, stretching his arms out until the left was an inch from a white wall and his right brushed the gray two-drawer file cabinet.

"Well?"

Martin looked at her directly, stifling a yawn in mid-gape. Cara Barnes was younger than he, twenty-six years of age. Seven years younger. Her eleven months' employment as the secretary of Dex Sales hadn't changed her a bit. Most conversations she began with her own life story, starting with how her youthful marriage had fallen apart, leaving her either to stay a waitress for life or to go back to school. She always emphasized how hard it had been to work and finish junior college, but she apparently refused to let that exhaustion interfere with the heavy social life she claimed. Once, when he had lunch there in the office, she told him the story of how she had once managed five dates in a single evening. He had hung on her every word. She wasn't slender, but she wasn't chubby either. Nor was she beautiful in that same respect, or unattractive.

"Martin?" she huffed, still posing, her smile fading.

He chuckled. "What?"

A quick irritation creased her forehead, and a blush as red as her hair followed. She lowered her left hand and slid the dribbling coffee cup toward him on the desk, then took another nibble of the doughnut. "Coffee, doughnut, or *me?*"

Leigh was gone. That knowledge burned him as he reached for the mug.

"You're choosing coffee over this tasty doughnut?"

His hands stopped. "I . . . you've already eaten half of it."

"That's not your only choice." She batted her lashes.

Martin swallowed hard. "Okay . . . *you,*" he said.

"No coffee, then?" She touched the rim of the steamy cup and raked that finger over her lips.

"Can't I have both?"

With another dainty nibble she shook her head. "You know better than that, Marty. Didn't your mother ever teach you that you can never have your cake and eat it, too?" She waved the steam to him as if for greater temptation. "Now choose. Do you want what you can see now or what you can't?"

He imagined her body under the lavender mid-length skirt and matching top, closing his teeth together unconsciously. "What . . . I can't."

"Oh, yeah? And what would Leigh say to that?" She took a bigger bite of the disappearing doughnut, dropping a crumb on his hand.

Confidence suddenly bolstered his weak smile. "Leigh's out of town."

"Oh yeah?" She raised the mug to red lips. "So you'd trade your coffee and doughnut for what's behind the curtain?"

He nodded, denying a brief tremor of guilt.

"Yeah? Well, that's your lesson, Marty. You can't ever get anything without giving something else up." She slurped loudly, then giggled. "And you just gave up your morning snack to talk to me and learn that lesson."

He shifted with discomfort.

"Lesson number two is that I'm not that cheap, Marty. Nothing is. I mean, you're not exactly Mr. America, are you?" She laughed, her face filled with her bright joke. "But dear God, I had you going, didn't I?" She set the mug back down, still snickering. "I really had you going!"

"Real funny," he muttered, his disappointment welling larger as he understood her joke. She always seemed to know his thoughts and always knew how he would react.

"Want another cup?" She picked up the mug again.

Martin looked back at his unfinished sales proposal, picking up the ballpoint. "I'll get some later," he mumbled, trying to let go of the fantasy she had begun inside his head, only to squash it with her own brand of cold, hard reality.

Like Leigh.

He sat still for a long minute, put the pen back down, and looked at his Rolodex. When he found his mother-in-law's number Martin reached for the phone.

"Do we have to go to Grandma's, Daddy?"

Martin felt a moment of guilt and forced it away. "You'll enjoy it, Cissy. You always enjoy Grandma, don't you?"

"I . . . *we* . . . wanted . . . to play a game . . . with *you."* Her little lips curled up, and she nudged Will.

He nodded with her, twirling a finger through his tousled hair. "Please?"

Martin frowned, eyeing the dark TV, remembering the way his father had never had time to play games with him. He had decided to play his own fatherhood differently. He had taught a lot of games to Cissy, but the kid rules bored him all too quickly, even though he enjoyed the grin of joy his attention put on her slender face.

Will's childhood was suffering like his own had. Marty was grateful for those times he sometimes helped Will "make movies" by adding to the pretend stories Will built for his Star Wars action figures.

Martin looked down at their despondent faces, swallowing hard.

Leigh was *gone.*

"One game of Sorry, okay?" he offered.

"Yay!" cheered Cissy, echoed by Will's lesser grin.

Martin went to the closet to get down the box, refusing a glance at the guitar. He began setting up the pieces on the big dining table while Will went back to get his favorite toys, lining them up hopefully on the shiny wood.

Martin fought a grin at the child's insistent nature.

Cissy chose the yellow pieces. "I get the blue!" Will finally shouted, sticking out his tongue.

"Cool it, you guys," muttered Martin.

"Blue is cool!" Will yapped. "Better than yellow!"

The smile tugged at Martin's lips, and he gave in to it at last. *"Everything's* cool," he soothed them. "Come on. No bickering, okay? We'll pretend that the champion Sorry player of all time is here with us. If we fight, he'll bump us right out of our chairs, right back to the start."

They both looked at him, then Cissy glanced around and snickered. "Okay."

"O . . . kay," Will answered less certainly, moving his eyes around the room as if he really expected some great Sorry god to be present.

Strangely, a few minutes into the game, Martin begin to enjoy the feeling of being there with his two children. They met his eyes with looks of adoration even when he bumped their pieces right back to the start. The whole thing made him angrier at Leigh for deserting them all, though. As the childish giggles filled the room with sarcastic blurts of "Sorry!" Martin relaxed a little. They played *two* games, and then Martin and Cissy watched as Will "showed" them a "movie" with his action figures.

It was fun, but it didn't take away Martin's gnawing desire.

5

Your dreams are you. You are your dreams. You can't lose your dreams because they are yourself. You are your dreams. You can make anything real if you want it bad enough, but you have to really want it. Then, if you send out the vibes hard enough and really believe, it'll go out and come back to you. It's kind of a law of the universe. . . .

"Far out, Sally," Martin whispered to himself.

"Last dance, boys and girls. Choose your partners carefully, 'cause you may wake up next to 'em!" The deejay shook his long black hair with a merry laugh that was cool and rang of professional falsehood. His empty gaiety boomed and faded in the exploding guitar strains that followed, played through tinny speakers mounted on the ceiling. Most of the remaining crowd slipped onto the dance floor. They groped and strutted to Elton John's "Rocket Man." Not at all like the days when Martin had played the nightclubs with Jim and Darrell. They had stood up there in person, unable to do more than grin and try to cover for the occasional mistakes.

> Mars ain't the kind of place to raise your kid.
> In fact, it's cold as hell. . . .

Martin strummed his fingers across the air, watching the patrons and wanting to be out there, dancing with a mushy-eyed partner. He put down his half-finished cigarette, sipping his tepid beer and glancing at the hands of his watch. It was nearly two a.m., and his back hurt from working on the '58 T-bird's engine all afternoon.

Two a.m., and all's not well. Two a.m., the night's shot to hell.

After taking Cissy and Will to Leigh's mother last night he'd steeled himself with the *Penthouse* and read through one of Leigh's self-confidence books. It said, "Anything you want, you can make happen, if you take the initiative."

"I want," he whispered.

Nothing happened.

"I want."

But the words were just bullshit in a self-help book Leigh had bought, just words with no power behind them.

Sometimes you must sacrifice to achieve your wants. Cara's words.

Martin watched a tubby woman in jeans far too tight skipping across the dance floor. He had sacrificed two nights now, coming to these bars, sitting and watching, neglecting the opportunity to watch Sean Connery as 007 again on the VHS tapes he collected.

Your dreams are you. You are your dreams. You can't ever lose your dreams because they are yourself. You are your dreams. Sally again. Sally, whom he had mastered just days before he had been mastered by Leigh.

The high quantity and low quality of the booze he downed made him tired on top of those hot hours tuning the T-bird's engine. He had drunk more as the night wore on, hoping to build up the guts to sit down with one of the very few women who were by themselves. He only succeeded in making himself tipsy. His college quips and self-confidence were casualties of the years. After last night, when that young blonde in the slinky pink pantsuit had laughed at him and made such a scene, it was a wonder he even tried coming to a place like this again.

It still hurt pretty bad. He'd sidled up to her as he would

have when he was ten years younger, but he had to labor hard for that appearance now. He told her of his guitar and how he could sound a lick that rivaled Jimi Hendrix, chuckling to himself when she accepted his initial invitation for a drink, and his next, and then the next. He talked to her freely, gushing over the color of her eyes, pumping her with admiration, smiling at her flirting replies, confident he had it made. His one-liners were coming out as impressively as Connery's ever had, and he almost felt like the person he had once been. He drank and she drank. He anticipated. He had, as Cara said was necessary, sacrificed. He spent close to forty dollars on their drinks and hours softening her up for the right moment.

And when he came out of the bathroom to ask her to go home with him, she was sitting at another table with another man.

He moved beside her and looked at her, but she met his eyes only once. She laughed at him loudly when he tried to take her hand. He could do nothing but turn and walk quickly to the other side of the bar. He ordered three whiskey sours in the space of the next fifteen minutes and finally left drunk, hurt, nothing to show for it, vowing never to do anything like it again.

But here he was only eighteen hours later.

He had sat alone for the last six hours. First at another bar, then here.

Yeah, and here, in this semi-cowboy saloon decorated with sweat-streaked saddles and wagon wheels on the walls, almost all the women had escorts. The wallflowers were fat, ugly, or so old that even caked makeup couldn't hide their spreading wrinkles.

Elton's piano-banging grew louder, splashing him like a tide coming in. He sighed and slurped his beer disinterestedly. He pushed his glass to the table's center before standing. He took a leisurely puff on his cigarette before stubbing it out. Leigh would be home the day after tomorrow—Monday. She had called earlier tonight and affirmed that reunion, her pleasant voice as distant as she was, aggravating with the tone of a woman enjoying herself, pleased by the changes in their lives that were slowly making him more and more dependent. She was giving him a final taste of what could have been in this brief separation. She would crush it anew when she came back, making him partake again of the bitter reality she brought him. The time was so short his unrealized fantasies were already beginning to fade.

Though he dreamed and hoped, nothing happened, making it all worse. He had taken the initiative, but the words in Leigh's book were just words. Sally's drugged-out meanderings were only the warped psuedo-profundities of a generation lost in the panic of survival he knew too well. Tonight was his last chance, and it was passing him by.

It had passed him by.

Just as well, he thought. Perhaps it *was* just as well.

Martin dropped two quarters beside the ashtray, steadied himself, and walked carefully between the tables, trying to watch the floor and the bodies weaving back and forth at the same time. A scarred Hercules wriggled a potbelly that was a ludicrous Frankenstein addition to the biceps stretching his T-shirt and darted within inches of Martin. His chewing-tobacco/Coors breath stabbed the air, then he was gone, leaving the mark of his existence in Martin's wrinkled nose.

Martin staggered back, just missing an unshined cowboy boot tapping the concrete floor. He took a gulp of fresher air. He wasn't drunk yet tonight, but close enough. Thank God Leigh's mother had offered to watch the kids until after church tomorrow. He could look forward to sleeping past noon.

But he would wake up by himself, lost in quicksand he knew he would never escape.

He wanted!

"Leaving alone?"

The gentle contralto voice startled him and made him blush as he stopped dead. Shivers iced his back, and he tried to resist looking around, but couldn't stop the reaction. He turned his head and jerked a nod at the auburn-haired woman seated lazily at the table he'd just passed. Her chestnut eyes were relaxed and hazy, underlined by dusky circles sunk in high cheekbones. Her perfect row of teeth shone between lightly reddened lips, and he swallowed, unable to think of anything to say. He shifted his eyes quickly, considering how much she looked like a hundred girls he had wanted over the years, several that he'd had. But she was *better,* like a compilation of them all, but drawn from their best features. Her body was sleek and curved just right in the right places, with breasts that begged to be fondled. Most of all, the voice and eyes reminded him of Sally. It made his chest tight and his knees weaker. "I . . . yeah. I . . . gotta work tomorrow." He tried to dismiss his wishful contemplation.

She leaned over the table. "On Sunday?"

"I—" But he nodded, already into the lie and tormented by a confusing guilt and the memories of being laughed at before. "Yeah. Catch-up stuff."

"Early?"

Martin shrugged, more confused. "Uh . . . well . . . I—"

"If you didn't have to go, I'd ask you to sit with me and have a drink." She smiled, pursing her lips until the lower one hung out and she was nearly pouting. "It's the last dance, but they won't close for another fifteen minutes." She patted the chair beside her.

Hope finally replaced the caution and made him hot. The dream words she spoke spread the flush into his cheeks, and he just stared into her luscious eyes . . . found himself taking the hard chair clumsily. "M-my name's Martin."

"Jeanette," she replied. "Call me Jan."

Martin grinned, wanting to fall into the 007 character that he once was and now remade for himself in those daydreams that sometimes slipped into the nights. He tried to become that suave persona for real, though last night's failure made it harder. "What, uh, is a pretty . . . girl like you doing by yourself in a . . ." His words tapered off as he realized that his physical clumsiness was more than mirrored by his mind.

"Place like this?" she finished for him with a smirk. "That's so old it's almost original. No one's asked me to dance or even offered to buy me a drink." She sipped from the glass smeared with her lipstick but kept her eyes steady. "I've been watching you forever, Martin, and you were looking at me, but you never came over." Jan put down the glass, slipping her fingers toward him. "Playing hard to get?"

He gulped, unable to recall her in his tireless studies of the women in the bar. "I . . . I just came in for a drink."

Jan nodded, tilting her head so that her hair spread over the bare tan of her shoulders. She sucked in her cheeks and crossed her legs so that they included him and almost claimed him. "Are you married, Martin?"

Hot blood tingled into his cheeks, and he looked down, afraid she would see his embarrassment even in the shadows that followed the gyrating patrons. "Naw." His wedding ring seared his finger, and he felt her looking at it. "Just . . . just got divorced." He displayed the ring with brazen carelessness. "Th-this is my first try . . . to get over it."

Jan—Jeanette smiled, touching his hand with hers to feel the rough gold band. "Most men take their rings off, even if they're just making the story up, Martin."

"I . . ." His throat was tight.

"Not that it makes any difference to me." She put her other hand on the table, spreading her fingers and letting him see the shiny circle on her own finger. Its single embedded diamond twinkled as brightly as her eyes.

He sighed loudly, knowing that he was too drunk to think quickly and hold up a good lie. "Well, I guess I am married," he admitted. "I just—"

"Didn't want to go home alone again?" She stroked his palm softly with a red nail. "Your wife's not there?"

The words were like a physician's examining stick, probing his thoughts and emotions so deftly it seemed she could gaze into his mind and his heart. Swallowing, Martin nodded again. "She . . . she had to go out of town. Business. She . . . she works in advertising."

Jeanette raised his palm, and her forenail traced its lines as though she were a fortune teller. Her eyelashes dropped, and she touched her lips to his fingers, raking first her teeth along his thumb, then her tongue.

Burying the guilt before it had a chance to regain its

foothold and shutting his life out with the lust she was so quickly reviving, Martin made a cautious smile. "Want to take . . . a ride . . . with me?"

She chuckled. "To your place?"

"Uh—" He looked at the dance floor hesitantly, considering the chance he could be taking.

But could his life be any worse? Didn't he want to escape it? Leigh? But he shook his head, his brain fogged by the drinks.

"Do you make a good Tom Collins?"

He nodded, not daring to open his mouth.

Long seconds.

Jeanette licked her lips. "What if I said that made me yours for the night, Martin?" She scooted closer, then closer, touching those slick lips gently to his, then again, more surely.

Her touch swept him with the promise of everything he had ever lost. He opened his lips in desperate uncertainty at her invitation, not listening to Leigh's screams somewhere inside him. He reached to rest his fingers on her side, brushing the material over her breast with his thumb. Her smell was a bedroom muskiness inviting him under satin sheets. Her smile drove everything else from his mind, filling his insides as those beginning seconds stretched to a full minute. His fingers instinctively pressed her rounded nipple.

She pulled away.

He gulped and released her, blushing, very aware of the beads of sweat tracking down his forehead. "Excuse m—"

"Not in here," she whispered, licking her lips and smoothing the silken white blouse. She glanced at the exit and traced his palm again. "Do you want that drink, or are you ready to go, Martin?"

He caught his breath, staring at her body and its lithe perfection. He forgot about dreams and looked into a promise of reality. He chuckled at his good luck. At the very last minute he'd found a woman who was just what he was looking for. It was like Sally had said, but this was *real.*

"I can get a drink when we get ho—to my place."

Jeanette picked up her black leather handbag and touched his hand. "Then let's go, huh? Like they say, the night is waning." Her face posed seductively, and she waited.

Martin stood slowly, not wanting to fumble this moment like the footballs of his youth. He held out a jittery hand. "Uh, yeah. Let's go."

She rose gracefully, letting him see the full effect of her slit skirt when it exposed a milky leg, flashing up to her hip. She nuzzled against him. "Lead the way, Sir Lancelot," she purred.

In a blur he took her hand and tried not to hurry. He could scarcely believe he was there and not sound asleep, but the pain he felt when a big boot flattened his toes assured him he was awake.

Martin frowned at the big cowboy as he walked on, wincing but saying nothing. He was wide awake.

They made their way past dancing, faceless bodies to the slate-gray metal door that was flanked by a cowboy and the lanky, big-breasted calf he was trying to rope. They ducked between them and went to the dark parking lot. He glanced at Jeanette twice, still disbelieving she was with him. He saw several of the people back at the door with perplexed expressions. He smiled back, then took her to his gray Lynx.

"Interesting car," she mused as he fumbled in his pocket for keys and opened the passenger door. He stood back for her and again sniffed her perfume as she sat down, her every movement a meticulous work of art.

"Uh, thanks. I . . . I've got a nicer one at home. A '58 T-bird."

"Really?"

The heat came back into his cheeks. "Yeah. I, uh, I'm rebuilding it."

"I love classic cars," she said.

Gulping, he closed the door solidly and marched with heavy, drunken steps to the driver's side, opening that door as she reached across to unlock it. He stared into the cool night with unblinking anxiousness and desire, then got in beside her, shutting out the night sounds of the world. He misaimed the key twice, then got it into the ignition. The car started.

Her perfume grew stronger: brash but sweet. Powerful, soft. Invigorating. Captivating.

"Are . . . you sure . . ." He stopped, a queasiness assailing his nearly realized ambition. "I . . . what I mean—"

"Sure?" Her thin eyebrows arched, and she sat back with aloof confidence. "Yes, Martin. I've been watching you, remember?" Her nails reached through the air to graze his cheek. "Are *you* sure? I made my decision when I spoke to you."

He gulped. "I . . ." He frowned. "But why did you . . . why do you want to go with me? I—you don't even know me."

Jeanette's legs moved an inch, opening the slit in her skirt wide again and showing the edge of her red panties. "But you want me with you, don't you? That's why you were there, wasn't it, Martin?"

The truth made him gulp, and he shivered. "I . . ."

The tip of her tongue slid over her lips. "I told you that I was in there for the same reason." She leaned forward in slow motion, kissing him again, her eyelashes brushing his cheeks.

A tenseness gripped him, and he considered Leigh and his children. This passed with her touch, and he reached for her. Leigh would be back Monday afternoon, and Cissy and Will were safely at her mother's. An exultation bathed him. *No one would ever know!* She was beautiful, miles beyond any other woman he'd pinpointed the past two nights . . . his entire life. She was far more beautiful than Leigh.

"I'm actually glad you're married," Jan whispered, pulling away but leaving her warm hand on his thigh. Her fingers rubbed his slacks knowledgeably. "I don't think I'd want to mess around with an old pro too much these days, you know?" She settled back in the seat.

Martin's laugh was nervous. "Yeah? Don't worry about that . . . Jan. I'm, uh, clean. I haven't—"

She squeezed his leg and moved her hand across his crotch. Her fingertips measured him with a casual pause. "Let's get to your place, Marty. I think I like you."

His throat was full and tight as he looked behind and shifted into reverse. "I . . . like you . . . Jan."

Her voice was moist. "I know." She watched through the windshield as he waited for another backing car, then he followed it to the exit and into the late quiet of the street. "I'm glad I waited. I'm glad you found me."

"M-more like *you* found *me,"* he said, watching the speedometer and picking a path toward home. "I was just leaving. Giving up. I'd been hoping . . . to meet someone . . . like you." He frowned, not liking the cheap sound of the words. "I mean, my wife and I have been married ten years, and . . . I was curious. I—" He broke off, unable to unravel what he was saying and hoping she would overlook it. The drinks had gotten to him more than he thought.

"Don't be shy, Marty." She chuckled deeply. "That's why I was in there, remember? I was waiting."

"For what?"

The street light made sultry shadows on her face but didn't mar it. The heat of his lust was burning away his alcoholic impairment. He stopped at the light confidently, waiting for it to turn green.

"For *you."*

Her ready nearness made him feel good, and he grinned, reaching to touch her. He slid his palm over her leg. Her left hand brushed his and moved it under her black skirt. "You've got beautiful hands," she whispered. "A musician's hands."

"I . . . I used to play the guitar." Martin took a heavy breath, incensed by the moist warmth soaking her panties, taken completely by the intensity of his bulging desire. He closed his eyes.

"I love the guitar." Long seconds passed. "The light's turned, Marty." She nudged him gently. "Let's get to your place." She licked his fingertips provocatively, letting him see her glistening lips. "Hurry, okay?"

Opening his eyes and feeling a secretive triumph he would never have believed, he brought his hand back to the wheel and turned onto the expressway, pushing the pedal past the speed limit. He lost Leigh and the children in the cloud of odors filling the front seat, rushing madly to the dream of ecstasy ahead.

I *want.*

6

The Lynx turned off the expressway fifteen minutes and six miles from where it had begun. It moved west, passing the shadows of the silent cemetery and the darkened stores. The Lynx slid forward. The houses were dark, nestled in the cricket chirps and humidity. The only sound of life was the hum of heat pumps and central air-conditioning units. The Lynx slowed halfway down the block.

Martin looked at his own dark home, the T-bird just visible beside the driveway in the porch light. He had made sure to leave that bulb burning after five minutes spent trying to find the right key last night.

"Nice place," said Jeanette.

"Yeah." Martin's voice was strained, and he knew it, so he smiled as widely as he could, turning the wheel, steering into the empty drive.

A vacation . . . time away from each other . . . Leigh's words.

Sacrifice. Leigh's book.

Dreams. Sally.

You can't have your cake and eat it, too. Cara.

But I can, he told himself. He peered at the woman he didn't know, gulping, aware of her foreignness here in his neighborhood's haven of familiarity. It made him more like

James Bond than ever, an agent on a secret mission to have his cake and eat it, too.

"Is that the T-bird?" asked Jan, looking at the raised hood through the windshield.

"Yeah." He pulled up on his handle and pushed out, stretching his legs to get out on the pavement. Martin spent a moment trying to steady himself and went around to her door. He pulled it open and held out his hand.

"What a gentleman," she cooed, letting him assist her as their eyes melded together and the warm air traced them gently.

"I—" He stopped himself.

Jan took his palm in her delicate fingers and squeezed.

Vacation.

Martin picked out the house key and led her up the stone walkway to the porch. He breathed deeply as he opened the front screen and the scrolled door. He let her pass, then shut out the world. His heart pounded. The life he had lived now surrounded him with crushing potency. The lingering smells were of his children, the wispy scent of Leigh. He was back home, creeping in behind their backs.

He felt almost as though he were a burglar rather than 007, breaking into a dwelling that was not his own, coming in to steal the relative peace of *home.*

But wasn't this what he wanted?

Martin turned. Jeanette was already into the living room, turning on lights to examine the pictures of Cissy and Will on the coffee table. "Nice-looking children, Marty." Her eyes twinkled, and she rubbed her forefinger along her lower lip.

"They—they're good kids," he stammered, walking past her to the kitchen. He did not even glance at the large framed portraits she gazed at, and refused the memories of his children even more than those of Leigh. He didn't want to think about them. He wished he hadn't brought Jan back here.

The house frowned at him through the shadows.

This fantasy was his and had nothing to do with *them.* He

was betraying them by bringing the object of his lust here. He had brought in an intruder.

He was an intruder.

"Do you have a picture of your wife?"

He swallowed hard, then stopped beside the stereo and flipped it on. He nodded slowly. "On . . . on the mantel."

Jeanette walked to the fireplace and cocked her head back. "She's pretty."

Again Martin didn't look. He found an easy-listening channel whispering "I honestly love you" in Olivia Newton-John's velvet tone, and felt a tingle. "Tom Collins?"

Her dark eyes turned to him, and she laid her purse on the couch. "Just an excuse," she murmured. "I'd rather spend our time in other ways."

His heart pounded harder, and his hand trembled.

"What's in there?" She pointed at the dark hallway.

He made an exaggerated invitation toward it. His breath was coming faster and faster to feed the blood quickening in his veins, pulsing for the anticipation that tugged his stomach down into the edgy tightness of his slacks. "Uh, let me show you the house, Jan."

She unbuttoned her white blouse to her navel, exposing a silky red bra stretched by firm moons. "How about just the bedroom, Marty? Especially if you have to work tomorrow . . ."

A shudder of both terror and success shook him. He stared at the barely tanned skin that began the curve of her breasts, gulping, hesitating.

This was it.

He had been too long in a steadily declining relationship. Though he often accused Leigh of infidelity, he knew better. She was faithful to him, and until this night he'd stayed faithful to her. He'd only dreamed and wished, remembering girls like Sally, associating the freedom of his past with them.

"Let me see your body," she said. "I want it for as long as I can have it."

"I don't really, uh, really have to work . . . tomorrow. I really . . . don't have to work. I don't *have* to."

She fastened both eyes on him and stepped to him casually, her feet making soft pads on the carpet. "Then I can look at the rest of the house later, right?" She giggled and was beside him, bringing his arms around her slender body, moving his palms to a pliable but firm ass.

He lowered his face to hers, overcome by the magic. Sensations shook his lips and arms. He wanted to say something but stopped the tender words that grew out of the hot breathlessness, unable to forget Leigh in spite of it. They kissed wetly, the pulse of their wrestling tongues driving hot fire into his brain, and he allowed that, even knowing it was making that invisible tie to the past in him disintegrate. Wordlessly, their hips crushed together, he led Jeanette down the unlit hall to the bed.

"Aren't you going to turn on a light, Marty?"

"Uh . . . yeah." His tongue was thick at the roof of his mouth as they went through the doorway. He reached the nightstand and twisted the small lamp's switch. Sixty-watt brightness shone through its yellow striped shade, spilling onto the unmade king-size waterbed that filled the room. Jan brushed her hand over the blue sheet with her invitation and intent and held that hand out to him.

Goosebumps crawled up his arm as he took it. "You—you're very beautiful . . . Jan."

Her face brightened, and she touched her hair, pulling it over a shoulder. She tugged him nearer, raising an eyebrow at his resistance. "What's wrong?

Shifting his weight, he rested a hand on the sideboard and tried to look surprised. "Nothing. I . . . I don't know. This is just—" So unbelievable. So unexpected, though he had sought it. So . . . *scary*. "—so unusual, Jan. I mean, we hardly know each other, but here we are. I never really thought—" He broke off, his mouth dry, not daring to look at the closet where Leigh's clothes hung, not daring to look at the bra she had discarded on the floor the night before she left, the night she'd intended to make love to him before he ruined it with his angry accusation.

Jan's voice was quiet and certain. "In a way, I feel like we've known each other a long time. I was waiting for you."

"Or someone like me."

She shook her head. "For you, Martin. I know it was for you. I knew it when you turned around in the bar and spoke. If we want something bad enough . . ."

Sally's words surprised him coming from her lips. She closed the space he was allowing to grow between them. She leaned close, her cool fingers on his shoulders. "I need someone. Marty. That's what I mean. I don't talk to anyone most of the time. No one listens. But look at me now. You—it's so different with you. Just being with you makes me feel *real.*"

Her voice in his ears and her calming fingers made him relax. A fling. He had always hoped to meet someone like her just for a fling. It was a hope and desire that had consumed him but that he never expected to actually attain. It was just a grand quest, like the story of gold at the rainbow's end, or of King Arthur and the Grail. A wish upon a star.

Hopping onto the bed, she lay on the rippling sheets. Her body quivered for him, but he didn't move. "Hey, I don't want to do a solo act, Marty." She held out her hand and pulled his hesitant fingers to the remaining button of her blouse.

She wanted him, needed him. One look in her eyes told him that. And even if he didn't really want her, wasn't it too late to say so now? He had told her he *was* sure, and he wouldn't hurt her or anyone with the frustrated embarrassment that had blasted him in his own rejection only twenty-four hours ago. Leigh will never know, he thought, his clumsy fingers obeying Jan's insistence and opening his shirt. Holding his breath, he released her final button and helped her take off that barrier between their flesh, tugging it past her elbows and burying his qualms under the impulses stirring him. No one would ever know. He had endured the things he didn't want for too long and would have to endure them the rest of his life. This evening was like a belated birthday present. He would have his cake—happy birthday cake!—and eat it, too. Leigh had wanted them to be apart for a few days, hadn't she? It had been her idea.

That determination made him steadier, and he unfastened Jan's bra by its front clasp, gasping at the unsagging quality of her perfect breasts.

Jan sighed, pressing his fingers deep into her flesh, making white imprints with the coerced pressure. He bent his head to lick the brown circles of her nipples, tasting their mysterious sweetness. His face drifted to her navel.

"Oh, yes," she sighed. "Please . . ."

The words drove him, and he rose a little, investigating her skirt to find its zipper, then unfastening the hook and sliding the teeth apart to the red silk of her bikini panties. Black tufts of hair peeked from the edges, and he touched those nearest him with his tongue. He brought the skirt carefully down over her knees, past her feet, dropping it from his hands. It rustled as it fell to the floor.

Her thighs flexed, and Martin tugged her panties down her hips, down her legs to follow the skirt. He dropped his mouth onto the sweet mound of hair dripping with Jan's excitement. Her breaths were loud in his ears.

"Oh, Marty—" She grabbed his face and struggled to pull him against her. "Please fuck me."

Wrapped into his drive, he hardly heard her. He shoved his underwear down, moving back up to taste her breasts again, and at last, her mouth. He filled her as slowly as he could to savor the moment, pushing deep into the damp folds that swallowed him passionately.

He did not pull away, and lost himself in the world they created for each other.

7

Leigh looked in the dresser mirror and brushed her lanky hair one more time for good measure, then swept her eyes over the nondescript motel room that had been her home the last four days. She would sleep on the foreign, ungiving mattress once more tonight and be back on her own tomorrow.

Zipping the plastic-handled hairbrush back into her leather handbag, she swallowed, ignoring the loud, hungry moans of her stomach. The "vacation" was almost over, and she was glad. She had killed two birds with one stone: furthering her own importance with Zelasco Advertising, thus ensuring the promotion she needed, and using the time as a trial separation from Martin.

She hadn't liked it.

"Want to cap the night with a drink?" Tom had asked her as they left the final official meeting with Don Reavis, the client they'd come to sell their abilities to and succeeded in capturing. "A kind of private victory celebration for a job well done?"

Leigh nodded slowly, her nerves sapped by her on-the-job training in following and memorizing Tom's pressured pitch. He used his words well to convince Don Reavis and the Big Wipe Tissue board that Zelasco Advertising could best serve their company. She had been, as she knew she was intended to be, pleasant window dressing to gaze on, holding the clients off guard as Tom measured them and coaxed them into agreement. Businessmen were generally polite and still found it difficult to deny a well-dressed, attractive lady, or even the man she was with.

She was fluff this time, decorative icing on the corporate cake, but she had learned Tom's methods as she played that part and even used them to help him toward the end.

"You did real good." Tom had smiled, getting out as the cab stopped in front of the hotel and helping her slide out his door. "Damn good. It almost scared me when you started up on your own because I didn't think he'd made up his mind yet. But if he hadn't, you certainly did the job to convince him." Tom had laughed. "This is going to be a real nice account."

She'd nodded, and they went in through the revolving glass door. He took her arm and led her to the lobby bar. It was late, and most of the tables were empty, the few remaining inhabitants clustered at the front watching TV. He took her to a booth, and they sat as she tried to gaze at the rerunning exploits of Steed and Emma Peel. While she drank her single glass of wine he suggested she stay the night with him.

She refused.

Not entirely due to her upbringing and increasing religious faith, either. She'd almost agreed, in fact. Her marriage had been bad for quite a long time, and Martin seemed more abusive each day. He accused her and sulked. He'd even accused her of taking this trip to do just what Tom had suggested.

That was what stopped her. Martin stopped her. Though the giddy rush of pride at their business success grew with the wine's warmth and urged her towards Tom's handsome embrace, she could not go through with it. Her desire for him was strengthened by the trouble back home, but that same trouble stopped her because she loved Martin. She *did* love Martin.

She said no.

Leigh came back to the present in the hotel room and put down her handbag to smile at her reflection. She knew she loved Martin enough to make it work, and though it was worse than ever before, she wanted it to work.

"Knock, knock," said Tom's muffled voice outside her door. The knob rattled gently.

She turned toward it and swung the bag against her hip, opening the door to go to breakfast with the man she'd refused. Tomorrow she would be back with the man she had chosen.

8

A sweetness hung in the air. Martin woke slowly, his lips turned up at the lingering memory of his sleep. He breathed it in. His yawn was groggy, and he tasted the beer he hadn't bothered to brush and wash away on returning home.

God, he couldn't even remember coming home.

He had dreamed of his greatest desire becoming truth . . . and—

He had dreamed of Leigh.

Shuddering, he closed his eyes tighter. That part of the memory made him frown, and he fought the blush of his nightmare: Leigh had walked into this very bedroom as he lay atop Jan, the beautiful dream-woman he had brought into their home. Leigh's eyes were wide and panicked, her lips white and stretched with terror. She screamed his name in blood-curdling despair.

He'd cringed, crying out himself in the crumbling pleasure of an interrupted orgasm, shackled anew by his marital chains.

Martin swallowed hard. In the midst of the greatest moment of freedom Leigh had unexpectedly returned and caught him between another woman's shapely thighs. But none of it was real.

He managed to smile at the fantasy now, erasing Leigh's

intrusion as he tried to regain the powerful satisfaction of his dream-climax. He rolled onto his back.

"Good morning, Marty."

"Wh-what?" His eyes widened at the features of the woman in his fancies. He knew suddenly the fiction of his dream was limited only to the appearance of his wife. The woman he believed a nocturnal figment was only inches away. She scooted closer, pumping his heart hard when she touched her bare legs to his, sending an electric tingle through him. He opened his mouth, hearing his quick intake of air, staring with momentary disbelief. He dove through the inebriated sensations of last night and felt that potent pleasure anew.

Her eyes twinkled. "Glad to see me?"

"Very glad . . . Jan." He breathed more slowly and pushed aside the pillow to buss her full lips tenderly, his fears disintegrating into the lust of his sleep.

"Again?" She laughed.

He laughed with her, not understanding why. "I . . . I think I love you," he told her, using the words he'd been unable to express last night.

She laid her head back into the pillow, closing her long lashes over dreamy eyes. "No, you don't." But her voice was thankful and happy. "You love your wife. You told me so last night, Marty. You said that you loved her and that you only wanted to escape for a while . . . to nibble the forbidden apple."

He rose on an elbow and watched her beauty, afraid she would disappear. His hand held a yielding breast. "I love *you,* Jan."

The dainty smile she gave was doubtful. "What about your wife, then?"

Pausing, he thought of her, how she had even invaded his dreams to force him back into the everyday world. Time was passing. The kids would be home in a few hours, and *she* would be back tomorrow afternoon. "Yeah," he said sullenly.

"See. You do love her, Marty. I was there when she wasn't,

and you wanted to be with someone." She shook her head sadly. "But you love your wife."

He started to shake his head, but something stopped him. Leigh would be back tomorrow. He thought of her while gazing at Jan. He shook his head. "It's not like that. I love you, too."

Her ready humor disarmed him. "Both of us? You can't love two people at once, Martin."

"I do."

Jeanette's smile tapered off.

"I love her because of the things she and I have been through, Jan. But"—he lay back on the pillow with her—"but I love *you*. I feel things for you I've never felt with her." He enjoyed the way he had regained a breath of his past in their coupling, returning him to an independence he'd almost forgotten. "I've never felt that way with anyone else," he told her.

The frown inside him took his face slowly, and he forced the memory of Leigh far from his mind, dragging back the words he and Jan said to one another. "It's like you said. I feel like I've known you a long time."

Her eyes went over him cautiously. "Do you really feel that way?"

"Kind of." He shrugged. "Yes."

A hopeful pleasure played on her face, marking her forehead and cheeks. "Then do you want to make me breakfast, good-looking?"

He kissed her neck. "Would you like that?"

Her tongue slithered over her lower lip.

His fingers felt her perfect breasts with a new longing. "What would you like, perfect lady?"

"Surprise me," she countered.

He started to move on top of her.

"After breakfast, Martin." She pulled back. "I just can't believe you're not worn out. You have so much life in you!"

"I'll show you life," he murmured, pulling the sheet down to expose her curly jungle, overcome by the raw scent of their encounters last night. He tried to separate her rigid legs.

"You need to eat something first, doll." She kept her legs together.

"Yeah, we both do." With her promise burning inside him, he sat up and scooted to the edge of the bed, unembarrassed by his nakedness, as though he'd lived with her for years. Not like it had been with Leigh in the beginning. "After breakfast?"

"Sure." Her lashes batted together. "But we have to eat to sustain our strength, don't we?"

He nodded, backing out of the room slowly. In the hall he hurried to the kitchen. He wanted to hurry back and see Jan again.

Even so, out of her presence, he began to feel curious, uncomfortable. The confines he'd lived within these past years with his family seemed unfamiliar and changed. Martin stopped and touched a wall, recalling how he had painted it with Leigh just last year. It was as though he had been someone else.

He scratched the paint with a fingernail, sniffed it, then snorted off the memory of paint fumes and the way those splatters had been all over Leigh's T-shirt, how he had merrily lined circles of the paint around her boobs to their wild laughter.

"That was then, this is now," he whispered, walking with forced purpose to the stove and taking a skillet out of the cabinet.

The memory of Leigh and their past fun surrounded him. Martin looked over his shoulder uneasily, half expecting to see her. His teeth chattered as he opened the refrigerator door and took out the margarine and five eggs. He closed the door, shrinking from the chill that had swept out, then took a loaf of bread from the countertop.

The two slices he chose fit into the toaster noiselessly, and he stirred the melting butter at the bottom of the skillet, smelling the rich scent of the breakfasts Leigh made for him. Peering behind himself once more, he saw only the shaft of light that shone through the window there.

Leigh.

Last night's near-defeat in the bar had introduced him to

Jan. He had been prepared to give himself up to Leigh and the life she planned for him forever, and the weight of his guilt grew lighter in that knowledge: He had actually been mentally giving up his halfhearted act of being a swinging single to come home, innocent of adultery and unspoiled for his wife, when Jan spoke to him.

It had been like magic.

She had spoken to *him.* He'd been pleasantly buzzed, feeling no real regrets, and had only responded to her rather blatant invitation. He had even changed his mind at that last instant, but couldn't make himself hurt her by telling her that.

The nervous tingling he wanted to be rid of eased.

Jan had seduced him. Though maybe he had wanted her and what she gave him, she had, after all, seduced *him.*

Pouring coffee grounds into the maker and filling it with water, he flipped it on and broke the eggs, scrambling them impatiently until they were moist yellow and white shapes, then scooped equal portions onto two large plates. The toaster popped, and he buttered the browned bread and got out two clean glasses, filling them with milk.

He had only responded to her advances, right?

A wanton sigh surged in him as he picked up her plate and drink, carrying them back to the bedroom. She did something to him inside, releasing those desires he had hidden away for so long. They were desires he downplayed so relentlessly that they were nearly those of another man, except in the dark of night.

He hadn't even needed to lie to her.

At the bedroom door he held out what he'd made. "Compliments of the chef." He grinned.

"Thanks, lover."

He set the plate on her lap, gave her a fork, and set the glass on the stand beside her.

"Where's yours?"

Martin shrugged. "I'll go back for it. I've only got two hands, you know."

A giggle broke out of her. "Last night it seemed like you had four or five."

"Oh? Wait until you see all the things I can do with my tongue."

She put a fork laden with egg into her mouth, managing an intense sexuality even in that. "After we're done I'll expect you to show me, Marty."

He let his tongue hang from his mouth with a lewd motion.

"Damn, you get me horny. You and these eggs. I love eggs." She chewed with a smile and giggled.

He ignored her personal joke. "I've never had dessert after breakfast before."

She swallowed and smiled.

Time passed meaninglessly. Martin was lost in another incredible union with Jan. She tasted fine, and he lapped up her never-ending juices like nectar. They'd discarded their plates and crumbs on the floor and begun making love with their mouths still half full. Afterward they smoked and talked, and then they were at it again twice in succession. And now again. Close . . . very close—

The loud whine of the phone's ring crescendoed against their panting moans and the slaps of their sweat-slippery skin moving together. The intrusion was as shocking and jarring as spilling hot coffee on a sleeping person.

"I'm coming, Marty—I'm coming!"

Her rapture drove out the violence of reality, and the phone rang on, forgotten and unheard now as he drove hard to catch up, pushing himself into her slippery hole mindlessly, feeling his insides bursting into flame. He collapsed with exhaustion onto her as she made a high-pitched whistle in her throat, like a bird. He breathed heavily, his damp, slick hair cool on the heat of his forehead.

The phone was ringing.

Jan pulled a lock of hair out of her face and relaxed, her breaths still fast and deep. She stroked his red face. "Marty . . . the phone."

"Fuck it." It jingled as he spoke, harsh and more insistent.

What if it was Leigh, interrupting reality like in his dream?

That jolted him sourly, and he weighed the thought of her against Jan again. He had loved Leigh once, but she had changed. As the woman she'd been to him had disappeared, so had his love.

The phone jingled.

"Better get it, Marty," Jan sighed under him. "Whoever it is isn't going to quit." She raised her mouth to his and lay back again.

"Yeah," he mumbled, rolling off her with a grimace at severing this latest union. He sighed with irritation, reaching to the side of the bed and knocking over an empty glass. His fingers wrapped around the receiver and brought it to his ear.

"Martin?"

The excited tone was loud, and he held the phone back, frowned, and recognized his mother-in-law. "Yeah?"

"What's wrong, Martin? Are you all right?"

Reaching to Jan beside him, he ran his fingers through her sex hair, smearing its wetness up her stomach, then brought the fingers to his lips, savoring the taste and smell. "I . . . I'm fine," he replied after a moment. "I'm fine," he repeated.

"It took you a long time to get to the phone. Are you sure you're okay? You sound funny."

His eyes lingered on Jeanette's slick body, and he scooted back to lay his head on her breasts. Her delicate thumb wiped and caressed his cheek. "I feel really good," he said, blushing. Cissy and Will. His stomach jerked. "How are the kids?"

"Ready to come home, Martin. I thought you'd call or come by to get them before now. Do you want me to bring them home? I have to go to a meeting at the church."

Jan's finger slid down his chest, fondling the sparse hair, moving lower.

"Do . . . do you mind?" He held his breath as the fingers dropped, tugged, and pulled. "I—I'm having problems . . . with the car."

"One more time," Jan whispered in his ear.

He arched his back and smiled. "For the . . . road?"

"'Why don't we do it in the road?'" she giggled, quoting one of his favorite Beatles tunes.

"Martin? Do you have company?"

The voice on the phone startled him, and he coughed. "Uh . . . it's the TV."

Long silence, then: "I'll be over in a few minutes, Martin." Her voice was nippy as a winter wind. "Has Leigh called?"

The teasing fingers worked him faster, bringing another erection. He gasped in disbelief.

"Martin. Has Leigh called?"

"N-not since yesterday . . . afternoon."

"Are you sure you're okay, Martin?"

He shut his eyes as Jan slid her body on top of his, tangling the phone cord. "I . . . yeah . . . I'm okay. I got to . . . hang up."

"We're on our way," she promised in words that sounded more like a warning, as though she knew who was with him and exactly what he was doing with her. "Good-bye, Martin."

The line clicked, and he dropped the phone, moaning, forgetting the call in the disbelief of his own virility, amazed at what was happening to him, at how Jan made him feel. "Jan . . ."

Their lips pressed together vibrantly.

9

"Mind if I take a shower, lover?"

Martin was buttoning his shirt and looked up, dazed and exhausted by the past few hours. He didn't want them to end, but Will and Cissy were on their way home. It made him remember that Jeanette's car was miles away—a good half-hour drive in Sunday afternoon traffic.

"I was going to take you to get your car—I thought you wanted to get back."

"Not really." She was behind the bathroom door, and she posed for him, taunting him by moving from side to side. As she disappeared and reappeared her poses were lewder each time.

Now you see me, now you don't.

She didn't say it, but he actually thought he could hear it in her thoughts. He stared at the parts of her that most enticed him.

She reappeared. "My husband won't be back until tomorrow afternoon." Disappeared. "I thought we might clean up and go out to dinner." Reappeared. Her lips parted, closed, and parted again. "We have to keep our strength, don't we? For tonight, I mean." She stayed put this time, mashing her breasts together with her arms and squeezing each nipple between thumb and finger.

"You mean you stay here again tonight?" The torn security of his home was like a knife twisting in his gut. Though he'd given up so much because of it, he had worked hard for this house and the furniture and playthings within it. He thought of the James Bond tapes he'd planned to watch this weekend. No time for that now, even if there was nothing else planned. Everything he'd given up had been for those luxuries, right? Could he give them up, too? And if so, could he do it this easily?

She swayed back and forth in his full view now, rubbing the inside of her thigh with a wet finger, moving it back inside her.

"Jan, don't. My—my kids are on their way home. Leigh's mother is bringing them. Now."

Licking her fingertips with a slow tongue, she lost her smile. "I knew you didn't love me, Marty."

"I . . . do. I just—" He shook his head as opposing walls seemed to draw together, crushing it between them. "I've got to have some time to think, Jan."

"How about tomorrow afternoon? Plenty of time to think then." She walked to him and pressed against him until his arms were around her, sliding her tight, smooth flesh against him. "Or I'll just hide back here in the shower. The children won't even notice me."

"Hey—they're not stupid, you know."

"I didn't mean that, Marty. You know I didn't mean that. But kids don't notice things like adults do, do they? You can tell them I'm a friend of Leigh's who came over to help you clean up the house. How's that for an excuse?"

"Esther's bringing the kids over, Jan. She'll come in, and if she sees you, she'll think—"

"I told you I'll stay back here, Marty. I'm going to take a shower."

"Well, the kids aren't stupid. They might say something to Leigh, and—"

"Then I could be your cousin from up north," she drawled. "Your kissing cousin." She pushed away from him and raised her hands above her head, making her breasts stand out as firmly as a detailed, sexy mannequin's. "I just got into town for a stopover on the way to California and dropped by to see my dear, sweet, loving, and very satisfying cousin on the way. And rather than make me spend the night in a hotel, you offered to let me stay here and shower . . . and share your bed."

Sweating, Martin tried to recall what he had told Leigh of his family. She had met most of them over the years, but with all his relatives, he knew there were some he hadn't mentioned. He had plenty of uncles, aunts, and cousins. The excuse could work. Leigh would never see Jan, and Cissy and Will were kids, after all. Their descriptions of Jan would hardly count, and his own account to Leigh would be far from the truth.

"Sound feasible?"

He nodded, knowing his acceptance of her idea would let him anticipate another night's pleasure with her. "Good idea," he replied, unable to stop a grin.

"See how a little deceit can keep things moving smoothly, Martin?" She blew him a kiss and returned to the bathroom. "Now finish dressing while I shower so Momma-in-law won't think you spent the whole day in bed."

He frowned, his eyes moving from the sheets rumpled on the mattress to himself in the dresser mirror.

She giggled.

As he fumbled with the buttons she closed the door, and her muffled voice spoke again. "And tonight, after dinner, I'll be the one having dessert, okay? I'll give you your just desserts."

He wanted to follow, but a moment later the shower was running, and he began to recapture the control he could feel only when she wasn't so near.

What the hell was he doing? What was happening to him? The consequences of the risks he was taking made his stomach quiver.

He'd wanted only to escape. He'd wanted almost any escape, and her promise was stronger than any of the threats he could imagine. He had gone out to taste the freedom he once knew well, knowing he might never have the opportunity to enjoy it again. Not even divorce promised a permanent escape, because a new woman would become as familiar and restraining as Leigh, and he would be fighting to escape once more.

But luck had paired him with a woman unlike any other he had ever met. Luck. He felt a cold tingle.

In some ways meeting Jan made it even worse, but he didn't dare believe it would be any different with her in the long run. He wanted to believe in her, but he was afraid to jeopardize his life with Leigh, bad though it was, for something that might be even more hellish.

But she tempted him.

As he went to the closet to find a pair of slacks he knew the temptation was hot. "Get hold of yourself," he growled, imagining himself as 007 being offered Pussy Galore or Plenty O'Toole. He took down a brown pair of slacks and slid them up his legs. Almost as soon as they were on, the doorbell rang.

"God." His stomach turned to Jell-O all over again and quivered like in the TV commercials, that tremble moving into his hands while he closed the pants and zipped them up. Water ran loudly in the shower, and he glimpsed the mess of the bedroom, seeing the plates still lying on the floor. The glasses and coffee mugs sat on the chest of drawers and nightstand accusingly. Most telling, Jan's clothes lay among his own all around the bed where he'd stripped them off her. The fear of being caught even though Esther would never come into the bedroom prompted him into action. He gathered the clothes up in a bunch, his and hers, and stuffed them under the sewing machine, draping his robe over them. He straightened the bedsheets as fast as he could and picked up the plates and milk glasses, leaving the mugs, trotting to the kitchen as the doorbell rang again.

"God damn," he muttered, feeling the blood drain from his face. He dropped the plates into the sink and hurried back to the living room, glancing at himself again in the entry mirror and smoothing his hair as best he could. It was plastered solidly against his drawn face, greasy with dried sweat.

But there was no time left.

He touched the doorknob, cringing with the newest ring of the bell. "God damn," he whispered, knowing he was forgetting something and that Esther would suspect.

But, twisting the doorknob, he opened the door.

"Daddy!" cried Cissy, running to him and grabbing him around the waist. Her slender face was pink with excitement, and her hair's blond length sprayed behind her, then fell back on her pink Sunday dress.

"My daddy!" Will shrieked, his mouth wide under his undeveloped nose while he followed suit with Martin's leg.

Brooding pain stabbed through him at their delight, and he put a hand on each head, rubbing Will's light brown locks and smiling guiltily. "How're my monsters?"

Esther stepped inside, pushing past him carelessly, and put a full satchel down on the floor. "You look awful, Martin," she informed him with a sniff. "You need a shower."

For an instant his tongue lolled uselessly in his mouth, and he was frightened that his romp with Jeanette showed. He cleared his throat. "I was working on the car. I was just getting ready to take one."

"Working on the car?" The older woman lifted bushy eyebrows and fiddled with the gray roots of her Revlon-black hair. "In your slacks?"

"My jeans were filthy," he lied quickly, and more easily than he expected. "I changed when I came in—didn't have time for a shower yet." It seemed he could hear the shower's splashing, though, clear at the other end of the house. "I . . . I just turned it on and was getting ready to—" He broke off, watching for signs of doubt on her chubby face that was still colored in winter's pallor. It made him wonder if Leigh would be so flabby and unattractive when she grew older. He sniffed her heavy church perfume and shuddered.

"You need a shower," she said again, as though she wasn't listening.

Cissy and Will released him and ran noisily back to their rooms. He watched them disappear into the hall and shrugged. "I was getting ready to take one."

"What's wrong with it?"

"What?" he asked blankly.

Looking out the door, she nodded at the gray Lynx. "Your car. Did you fix it?"

Thinking, trying to make something up, he shook his head slowly. "I . . . think it's the plug wires. I . . . I'll need to change them to be sure."

She sniffed again. "I knew that car was a mistake when you bought it. You should have bought Chevrolet. Leigh knew that. Don and I have always bought Chevrolet."

Martin shrugged.

"Marty?"

Heart nearly stopping dead, he turned at the clear sound of Jan's voice, saw her in the hallway, her hair dripping and her body wrapped too revealingly in a towel. He gasped and turned back to Esther, but she was still looking at the car and didn't seem to have heard. With a bare relief that didn't quite stop his chattering teeth he turned back to motion Jan into hiding.

"You should have bought Chevrolet," repeated Esther.

Jan had already turned around and was nearly back to the bedroom. He held his breath, entranced by the smooth lines of her buttocks that invited him to be with her. Damp terror grew in his armpits, and he exhaled loudly when she shut the door behind her.

Esther turned around.

The lump in his throat was unbearable, and he tried to gulp it down.

"I thought you would call or come after them," Esther said. She stood with an aloofness, one leg forward as she nodded at the squeals from Cissy's room. "You should have called me to tell me you were having problems. It was inconsiderate, Martin. Now I'll have to drive like you do to get to my church meeting on time."

"I . . . I'm sorry." He kept an eye on the bedroom door. What would she do if Jan came out again and—

"You've really got to take your responsibilities more seriously, Martin. I know it's not my place to say, but it's terrible the way that Leigh has to wear the pants in this family. In my day she would have been here at home, and you would be gallivanting off to God knows where for these job assignments. If you would just find a proper job that paid more money, she wouldn't even have to work, but you spent your college time taking worthless courses and playing that guitar you never even touch now."

Her carefully chosen words brought anger, though he was afraid to express that emotion to her—but not because he was afraid of her. He'd sparred in this ring before, and always well, reminding her that Leigh's job was her own choice. It was a fact that always brought blood, and he had to force himself not to use that weapon this time.

He didn't dare with Jan here. Fighting words punched at Esther always brought the quick retaliation of her machine-gun reply. The argument would stretch out into minutes that would quickly become longer and longer, and Jan might come back out, and Esther would see her.

He wanted to spend this time with Jan.

"Don and I didn't want Leigh to marry you anyway, Martin. She told us you'd change, but you still don't even go to church with her and your own children. A proper family man—"

Change. He wanted to hit her in the face as fear was replaced by fury, but for the first time in his life he held on to his control. "I'm sorry," he cut in quickly, hating himself for it. "I know. You're right. I'm trying."

Her close eyes were suspicious.

"I'm sorry I didn't call you. I should have." He swallowed the rebuttal that wanted out so bad. "I just lost track of time." He'd lost track of *everything.*

"You should have been wearing your watch, Martin. I don't mind helping you and Leigh out, but you must have more consideration." She licked her curled lips and seemed to relax. "You really need a shower."

"Yeah." How many times had he agreed with her on that one already? "Yeah, I need to get cleaned up so we can think about getting some dinner. I don't want to keep the kids up too late."

She looked him up and down uncertainly. Her face became watchful once more. "Well, it's nice to hear you finally talking more sensibly, Martin. You keep those children up far too late. They're hard to get out of bed at a proper hour, and that's why they're always so cranky and tired." She turned, as if waiting for him to give his usual argumentive reply at last, then crooked a smile when it didn't come. "You shouldn't let them watch those awful horror films," she tried again. "Cissy was telling me a terrible story about one of your sick movies where dead people came back to life and ate living people!"

He couldn't hold back the grin, imagining Cissy's excited descriptions inciting Esther's horror, but again he made himself stop.

"It's not funny, Martin. Things like that warp a child. They don't do you any good, either." She tossed her head higher. "Still, they're your children. I can't tell you how to raise them, even though I'd like to. That job is yours and Leigh's. But I must say that I thought I raised Leigh better than to allow that sort of thing with my grandchildren. If you want my advice, you ought to be more selective about what they watch, and what you fill your own mind up with, too. That kind of thing is pure garbage, and you know it. Seeing anything like that would give me nightmares. It would give any *normal* person nightmares."

"Leigh and I will talk about it," he murmured passively, again avoiding the argument she expected. He wanted to get rid of Esther, go eat, put the kids to bed, then spend these hours as he might never have the chance to do again.

"You shouldn't let them watch those violent James Bond films either." Esther made her last jab deep.

Martin's mouth quivered, but he held it shut. He thought of himself inside Jan.

Reaching into her black purse for her keys, Esther saw this last ploy fail. She shrugged dejectedly. Her features sagged and became as near to apology as he'd ever seen. "Well, I've got to hurry to my meeting. Tell Leigh to call me as soon as she gets in tomorrow," Esther commanded, walking out to her car.

"I will," he promised, standing and watching her open the car door. She drew the harness seat belt around herself with showmanship and started the car in her old lady's slow fashion. It seemed an eternity passed, and he sighed in relief as she finally backed out and drove away.

He jerked as soft hands stroked his hips from behind.

"Jumpy, aren't we?"

Wheeling around, he saw Jan loosely wrapped in the towel, her breasts barely covered, and he slammed the door quickly. "God damn, she didn't see you, did she?"

"I waited until I heard the car moving, but she wouldn't have seen me anyway, Martin. People don't see what they don't want to see."

"She would have *loved* to have seen you—"

She pressed against him and kissed his lips with her wet ones. He opened his mouth, and their tongues stroked. He let his eyes shut, and his hands slipped under her towel.

"I'm gonna tell!"

Martin jumped back with pale fear, gasping as Will's scream burst from Cissy's room like a banshee's. Then he slowly let the air out of his lungs as he knew his two children were battling it out again. He pulled Jan's towel higher to hide more of her breasts. "N-not now," he warned.

She followed his eyes to the children's room with disappointment. "Okay, but where are my clothes?"

"I put them under the sewing machine with mine." He sighed, the tension of Esther's presence disappearing again as Cissy and Will grew quiet. He gazed at Jan's near-nakedness. "Why? Is that why you came out earlier? Good God, I almost had a cardiac. Esther was right here."

"She didn't see me, did she?" Jan reached down to tweak the growth hidden by his slacks. "You just worry too much, Marty. I bet you weren't like that *before* you got married."

He winced. The world that had captured and trapped him had done its part to change him, too. He forced a faint chuckle. But he didn't feel it. He hated what had been done to him.

She laughed with him, but more merrily. "Come on." She took his hand, pulling him to the hall. "I want to give you a bath."

He let himself walk with her, and listened to Cissy and

Will playing cheerfully now, then slipped his hand over her bare bottom, groping the cheeks that were his for yet a while longer. "I'd like that." He followed her into the room where they'd spent most of their time and closed its door, pushing in the lock button.

Jan unbuttoned his slacks.

She stopped and put her arms around his neck. "Lying—even silent lying—makes the world go round, Marty. Do you see what I mean now? It's easy, and it avoids problems—right?"

He swallowed with a new discomfort, wanting action and not talk. "Uh, right."

She continued to strip off his clothes.

Her slow attention made him hard again, and they made it once more before she got him into the shower.

10

Cissy and Will sat quietly on the couch, still in their Sunday-school clothes. Martin stood beside the fireplace and yawned, exhausted by the activity with Jan. He smiled as she came into the room, dressed once more in her clothes. They didn't look rumpled at all.

Neither did she.

"I'm ready," Jan sighed, patting her handbag and curtsying immodestly.

Martin gulped as the slit in her skirt showed she wasn't wearing her panties. A glance at his wristwatch told him that two more hours had slithered by since Esther had left the house. He remembered their shower, the warm spray on his back as he slipped and slid on the wet tile, trying to stay inside her before finally exploding into her once more.

The water had turned cold, and she slowly dried him off after. Amazingly, she stirred him so erect that they coupled once more and might have again if he hadn't been so exhausted he felt ready to black out. He barely managed to make her stop teasing by promising her whatever she wanted after dinner. She relented with a pout and helped him dress.

He could not understand the amazing virility she brought out in him. He had not even fucked Sally this many times.

A tiny smile wrinkled his cheeks. Maybe, he mused without real seriousness, it was all the sex Leigh had refused him at last finding an outlet. Maybe it was really what Sally had told him so long ago: Dreams could come true if you wanted them badly enough. Ridiculous as that explanation might seem, it certainly appeared a bizarre truth after these past hours.

Jan had raised him out of bleak resignation to the heights of his lost expectations. This was more real than any of his previous thirty-three years.

You are your dreams, Sally had said.

He held his hand out to Jan, and she took it.

Right on, Sally.

"Can we get up?" asked Cissy with a child's boredom.

"In a minute," Martin said. "Don't you want me to introduce you to your Aunt Jeanette?"

Will looked up quickly, wiping unruly hair from his eyes and anticipating an acquaintance that might result in another gift for his birthday next week. "Is she coming over tonight?"

His eyebrows met on his forehead. "Who do you think this is?"

Will stared curiously. Cissy watched Martin, too. "Where is she?"

"Boy," giggled Jan in Martin's ear. "Aren't the games children play cute?"

"Real cute." He worked his jaw, then held out a hand to his daughter. "This is your Aunt Jan."

Cissy's eyes went wide, then narrowed. Her smile was hesitant, a missing front tooth making her curiosity into a warped stupidity. She crossed to hold out her hand timidly. "Is she . . . the invisible lady?"

"What?"

"I—"

Staring into Cissy's blue-green eyes, he saw the blankness between laughter and caution. He opened his mouth, then looked back at Jan, feeling her fingers leave his shoulder, and for a brief moment it seemed as though her face and entire body wobbled out of existence, just like a picture fading in and out on a television, except that the surroundings remained. He blinked, caught by momentary shock, then knew he was exhausted as her sultry form appeared once more. She bent closer, as much there as Cissy or Will. He was exhausted, so much so that even the playful suggestion of a child was making his tired brain and eyes accept and further Cissy's youthful tricks. His heart pounded out of rhythm, and he swallowed the rapidly surging nausea of the past hours' exertion.

Jan's fingers were tight around his wrist. "Martin . . . are you okay? Are you *okay?*"

"Daddy?" whined Cissy.

He shook his head and felt it pounding, stared at the stricken face of his daughter, and saw Will jump up off the couch. Their animated concern made him struggle between fear and laughter. "Give . . . me . . . a second," he gasped. "G-go to your rooms . . . until . . . I'm ready."

Cissy's small fingers curled around his thumb, "But Daddy—"

The sound of her little game becoming overt fright made him wave her away without reassurance. Her little mischief of make-believe had caught him at the wrong instant. He was just so fucking tired.

Jan's grip slid up to his armpit, and he felt her dragging him. He tried to walk in her direction, breathing the air his lungs gasped for. The very room wobbled as she had a moment before, and he croaked, feeling a gray pressure in his eyes as they fogged.

"Martin?" She helped him lie down on the lifeless cushions and put her cool fingers on his hot forehead. "Martin?" She moved near until her sweet breath was in his face. "Are you okay?"

He swallowed, but his mouth was dry. He tried to nod. He couldn't talk.

"Do you want me to leave?"

The tone was sad and hurt, pricking his heart against the memory of Leigh and the knowledge of the few remaining hours until her return. Jan would have to leave then, and he would be back to the mundane existence he'd come to hate.

Those hours were short, but not yet over. He wanted her and this paradise he'd found with her for at least a few more hours!

He looked at Jan through his half-closed lids, reaching up to her. Even if she was only a dream of cosmic law, she was more real to him than anything had ever been!

You have to make them real. . . .

The memories of Sally had bugged him in his thoughts all through the night, and he fought them hard now. He looked into Jan's full lips, her pink rouge worn by their kisses, and he knew she was as real as he. If she was the gift from the cosmos Sally had spoken of in her stoned soliloquy, then he was, too, and as much a dream.

Jan tenderly wiped his brow, licking his cheek. "You're all sweaty, Marty. I'll get you a drink and some aspirin, okay?"

Nodding made his head throb, but he did it, wanting and needing to get over this and feel better. He was just tired from the whole incredible experience. It was something beyond what the pages of *Penthouse* or any other such magazine had ever led him to suspect. He had to clear his head, clogged by the excitement of finally gaining these precious moments of the freedom he'd craved for years. He had to rebuild his strength, and eating would help him do that.

Jan slid her hand from his face and stood up, and he heard her steps go into the kitchen, then listened to the water in the sink as she filled a glass for him.

"I don't care, Sally," he whispered. "This is as real as I am, and more real than *you* ever were." He felt the lead weights stacked on his head slipping off as the perspective was reinforced. At least Jan was still there when he woke up.

11

Will was crying.

"Stop it!" warned Cissy, trying to sound like Daddy and empower her voice with his firm command. "Stop it, William!"

The use of his full name drew a gasp, and Will shook his head back and forth as he did when Daddy and Mommy used it. It was his *bad* name. The only time it was used was when he was in trouble or when Gramma was with them. They were always in trouble with her.

He coughed and sniffled, once again shaking his hair back and forth but without the prior nervous twitch, as if realizing that it was only his sister using the magic incantation against him.

He tried another sob.

"William Paarman!"

That made him jerk upright, and he bit his lip. "You," he sniffled, "you can't call me that!" He picked up a movable plastic Luke Skywalker and fit a tiny accessory pole in its hand from the toys he'd brought into her room earlier. *"Za-zow,"* he gurgled, facing Luke off against the black Darth Vader figure he took in his other hand. *"Za-zow! Za-zow!"*

"He's a Jedi knight, Will. He's a Jedi, remember? Jedis

don't kill people, especially not their own fathers, and Darth Vader's his father, remember?" Cissy huffed as he continued, not listening, and watched the tiny Luke kill his nemesis, rewriting the Star Wars saga to Will's own liking. She shook her head and walked past the big stuffed shaggy dog in the corner, picking up a Barbie doll. "You're too little to understand."

He dropped the black figure and picked up a grizzly creature. "Am not." Then he stared at the ugly facsimile he'd grabbed and choked, dropping it again. He sniffled. "I'm scared," he mumbled. "Daddy was w-weird."

Untangling the Barbie's jet-black hair with her fingers, Cissy nodded. She was kind of scared, too. She recognized that feeling because she knew about fear, more than most ten-year-olds did, anyway. Cissy shuffled to her white enamel desk and twisted its lamp switch, blinking in the brightness when it flashed on. She often met fear in the horrortapes Daddy brought home. She watched them because Daddy watched them, and maybe because Gramma didn't like them. Maybe because Gramma hated to hear her tell her about them. The remembrance made her smile a little. And they didn't scare her so much anymore, either. It was like getting spanked, kind of. After so many of them, they didn't bother her so much.

Daddy told Mommy she was getting hardened to fear.

The smile grew bigger, then began to slip away. She knew how Will felt: Daddy *was* acting weird. Really weird. He'd pretended to introduce them to an Aunt Jan she'd never heard of, and no one had been there.

Daddy had crooked his finger, and Cissy had stepped forward expectantly. "This is your Aunt Jan," he said. But no one was there! Except for maybe just a second Cissy thought she saw something, maybe *someone,* standing right beside Daddy, almost like a part of Daddy.

But the air was so wobbly—fuzzy, and she was hot. It was like when she was sick and had what Mommy called the high temperature. "D-did you see anyone, Will?" she asked.

He looked up from the violent combat between Luke and

his supposed comrade, Han Solo, then tossed his head again. "Huh-uh."

Cissy dropped Barbie on the light blue carpet, pushing her right thumb into her lower lip. "I thought I saw *someone.*" She swallowed, then spoke in her imitation grown-up voice. "I thought—"

"Huh-uh." Will stopped her, then dropped the little men and stared down at a mock monster's figure. He covered his eyes, drawing back. "I . . . I didn't see it—didn't see *nothing!"* He scooted back, his polyester slacks making a fart sound on the carpet, then sat close to the bed, his hands still in front of his eyes. "I . . . don't want to see . . . I . . . I don't wanna talk . . ."

Cissy closed her mouth, now knowing he *had* seen, and feeling more scared because of that. She backed to him with her eyes hard on the door. It hadn't looked like an aunt named Jan or an aunt by any other name.

"C-Cissy," Will moaned, clutching her hand, "I'm *scared."*

She bent her knees and sat down by his trembling body, shivering herself, and thinking about that horrortape where the living dead came back to life eating people.

"Cissy?"

"It . . . it's okay," she told him bravely, remembering all those monster movies where the good guys saw things that weren't really there. "If . . . if you see something again . . . don't look at it, Will. Pretend it's not there." She reached out to his toys and picked up the Obiwan Kenobi doll. "Just remember that the Force"—she paused, listening to footsteps at the front of the house—"is with us."

12

Unplanned parenthood, right?

Martin glared at Cissy and Will on the other side of the black vinyl booth as they picked at their food, remembering how they'd hardly spoken or looked at him or Jan. Jan's remark had followed Will's announcement that he was not going to see Jan because she wasn't there. It pissed Martin off, but he had felt a lot better after the aspirin and relaxation on the couch, resting his head on Jan's lap. When he'd begun to feel horny again he forced the sensation away with the knowledge that he had to eat first, to keep up his strength like Jan said.

He'd stood up and called the kids back into the room. He'd hoped eating would make him stronger.

"This is your Aunt Jan," he'd said, as he had half an hour before.

Cissy and Will had stood still. They didn't look at her but kept their eyes on him.

"Huh-uh," Will shook his head, grabbing and squeezing Cissy's hand. "She . . . she's not there."

Cissy had said nothing, and Martin frowned, opening his mouth.

"That's okay, Marty." Jan had smiled. "Childish games, remember?" She bent down but did not step toward either child. "I'm Marty's cousin from New York," she had told them with smooth confidence. "I'm on my way to California and thought I'd stop in and see him and his family." She'd then created a grimace of disappointment. "I didn't know your mother would be gone."

Cissy had still said nothing, and Will stared down at his shoes.

"Will you please stop your nonsense and say hi to Aunt Jan?"

"I"—Cissy glanced at her, then quickly back to Martin—"h-hi . . . Aunt Jan."

"Will?" he'd snapped.

The boy would not look up. "H-h-hi," he'd finally managed. Cissy took a breath. "I didn't know . . . we had an Aunt . . . Jan."

"Oh, I've got family everywhere." Martin smiled in the smooth lie that was also the truth. "Mommy's never even met half of them." He'd turned to Jan, feeling his passion for her quicken. "I . . . I haven't seen Jan since we were teenagers, and I'll have to take her back to the airport for her flight in the morning." He frowned at the way Cissy's face seemed to pale. "Jan's going to sleep in the guest room. There's no reason for her to stay at a motel."

Jeanette had giggled, her eyes on him. "We'll stay up all night together, anyway. I probably won't get any sleep until I get on the plane."

"Right," he'd agreed. "We're all going out to dinner first, though. Are you two hungry?"

Will nodded. "Is it pizza?" he'd asked hopefully.

Martin shook his head. "Not tonight, Willy. Real food tonight."

"Aww." But he still didn't look up.

"Is she married?" Cissy asked, darting her eyes at Jan less furtively, gulping, and settling them on Martin again.

"Yes. Her husband couldn't come with her."

"She's leaving tomorrow?" Cissy took a deep breath.

"In the morning."

Cissy had sighed and wiped her fingers along the pink ruffled dress thoughtfully. "Mommy will miss her, then."

"Yes." Her eyes seemed to be tight, like a balloon about to burst, full of an uneasy despair, as though she had seen the guilt still under his skin. But he chuckled and blew it off, knowing she couldn't. "Come on, I'm hungry."

And so they had left in unusual reservation. Cissy and Will continued their silence, getting into the back seat of the car as he directed, not even arguing about whose side was whose. He drove to Emily's Steak Haven in that unheard-of quiet, leaving his thoughts free to enjoy the fingers Jan kneaded into his crotch at every stoplight.

Yes. He enjoyed accompanying Jan in this higher atmosphere amongst the well-suited and silken-dressed patrons. Martin couldn't keep his mind or eyes off of her as he chewed his rare, barely cooked meat; steak the way he liked it. He was unable to ignore the enticing way she opened her mouth, and especially the way she chewed the side plate of carrots. She slipped each one in and out of her mouth like a Popsicle, sucking on it as she moved her jaws slightly.

The past eighteen hours had been amazing. Everything Jan did was something he had always wanted to happen. She was as perfect as the dreams Sally had spoken of almost a decade ago. She took away the bitterness that had darkened his sight for so long and made him laugh, feeling pleasure with himself and his life for the first time in longer than he wanted to remember.

Best of all, her attention was riveted solely on him. So much so that he practically forgot his previous life. He might have forgotten it altogether but for the dogged reminder of the silent, uncertain eyes that caught his from across the table.

"Do I have to eat it all, Daddy?"

The peas on Cissy's plate were hardly touched, and he glared at her. "Cissy," he began.

Sitting next to him in the booth, Jan nudged him and leaned forward, picking up her fork. "They're hard to corner, hon, aren't they?"

Cissy's mouth fell open, and her eyes were wide. "I—"

"Jan's going to help you, Cissy," warned Martin, eyeing her closely.

Cissy backed up in the booth seat, and Will backed up with her, his teeth gritted. "They're j-just hard to pick up," the ten-year-old told him. "I . . . I can do it."

"Watch this." Jan reached to the girl's plate and pressed her fork down over several of the peas, squishing them and impaling them through the prongs of the utensil. She brought them back to her mouth and dragged the fork back out through closed lips.

Cissy stared, her pupils tiny and caught in the action. Will's eyes were enormous.

"Isn't that easy?" asked Jan.

"They—they're squashed!" Will shrieked.

Martin shook his head, misunderstanding their young panic. He patted Jan's thigh. "They like to eat them whole," he told her.

She shrugged, putting down her fork and letting her hand drop into Martin's lap. Her fingers found his shape and rubbed until it was growing quickly.

"Eat two more bites and we'll go," Martin ordered Cissy breathlessly. "You, too, William."

The four-year-old was trembling and looked at Cissy. "Obiwan," she whispered. "The Force."

He gulped with a squeaky noise, then made a face. "T-two?"

"Two."

"Awright," answered Cissy for them both. "Then can we go home? And . . . and you'll take her . . . uh, Aunt Jan, home?"

"I'll take her to the airport in the morning." Martin glared, surprised at Cissy's rude manners. But he tried not to dwell on that irritation or their slow eating habits. He waited sternly, unsuccessfully ignoring Jan's manipulation through his pants.

"Do we . . . get dessert, Daddy?" Cissy asked uneasily, finishing.

"If you're good," Martin sighed, his face hot. He didn't dare look around and felt that everyone else in the restaurant must be staring at him as his pants bulged. "If you're good, you can have a cookie when we get home, and then straight to bed, okay?"

Cissy looked at Will, and he stared back earnestly. "Oh . . . kay," she said, speaking for him again.

This unusual obedience made him look at her closely, and then at Will. It made him angry all over. He felt the hatred of having children fill him. Unplanned parenthood, Jan had said. He gulped, knowing she had shown him that truth, even though it made him blush with guilt. Unplanned and unwanted. Both of them.

Unwanted! Part of the great trap that had snagged him and forced him deeper inside itself. Leigh had been the lure, and Cissy and Will were the flypaper that held him fast while he decayed, feeling the agony as his self and his dreams disintegrated inside a healthy body. Angry, he scooted out of the seat and stood up, then quickly reached to help Jan, bending down to hide his erect lust. Impatience boiled in him as Cissy and Will slowly followed, and he prodded and ushered the children to the miniskirted cashier behind the counter, close to Jan to hide his needs.

The teenage girl behind the register smiled vacantly. Her Clearasil had caked into her makeup, making her look like a burn victim. Martin gave her fifty dollars, impatient as he waited for her to count out his change.

"Do I get dessert, Daddy?" Jeanette asked as she walked out with him a minute later, following the whispering children to the car. "I'll be a good girl, I promise."

He remembered her promises. "Wait till we get them to bed."

"Yes, sir." He walked her through the crowded lot to the passenger side of his Lynx and opened the door, gently scraping the BMW beside it. A glance at the tiny mark he made in its sky-blue paint job brought him hateful satisfaction. He didn't need things like that car to make his life perfect. He had worked and scraped like the owner of the car too long, finding only fleeting moments of pleasure in the possessions money paid for.

"I want in the front!" hollered Will, forgetting their silent game. "Mommy's not here, so I get in front!"

"My turn," Cissy countered forgetfully. She shook her long blond tresses. "You sat in the front with Gramma!"

Jan leaned back and closed her eyes. Martin felt embarrassed, frustrated because his time with her was growing so short. "Aunt Jan's sitting in the front," he told them. "Stop it! Get in the back!"

His shout shocked them, and both children stared up with dumbfounded expressions. Will's face screwed up as he neared tears.

Martin flushed at his own violence.

"The back door's locked, Daddy!" whined Cissy.

"I . . . sorry." He walked around to his side of the car and opened his door, pushing the button to unlock the car, then pulled on the door behind him. "Get in."

Fussing as though to make up for earlier, the two children climbed into the back seat. "Let go me!" griped Cissy.

"You hit me!"

"You poked me!"

"Shut up!" Martin growled, trying to slide under the shame that he was ignoring them with his fervent attention to Jan.

But she would be gone tomorrow, and everything would go back to the way it had been. Jan would be a pleasant memory locked inside him.

"Daddy . . ."

"Hush!" he warned, his tone harsh as he turned in the chair. Cissy and Will shrank back in their seats as though he'd slapped them. Hurt grimaces tore their young features. Cissy bent across the seat and whispered to Will once more, and they sat back. Again they were silent and pale.

He felt and knew they were scared.

"That's why I never wanted children," Jan whispered as he finally turned back to shut his door and start the engine.

He'd seen their frightened eyes, filled with fear as if they no longer knew him.

And he could not help but think of their hateful game of pretending Jan wasn't there, a game they were still playing. Martin gritted his teeth noisily, scraping the plaque. "Yeah. Yeah, I feel that way sometimes."

"I know."

He pulled out onto the black street with a short sideways stare at her and turned in the direction of his house. It was almost eight o'clock, and the precious time was slipping away too quickly. After the intensity they'd shared, he felt closer to Jan than he'd ever felt to anyone. It was a companionship that rivaled the camaraderie he'd shared with both Darrell and Jim in the band—more potent than the hours with Leigh those first years.

Guiltily he peered in the rearview mirror at his daughter.

Jan had miraculously entered his life. He wanted to know more about her. His intention of a quiet one-night stand was fading as their time together continued.

He didn't want to let her go, did he? After all they had done, to separate himself from her and the wonders she created in him, to never see her again or even know her last name was too much to consider.

"I know what we can do tonight, Marty."

"Oh?" His voice was low as he peered back at Cissy, leaning on Will as she yawned. He hoped Jan understood the hint.

"Your fondest fantasy, Marty, come to life."

"You think so?" He smirked. The dread of losing her slipped away fast as her fingers stroked him to a new hardness, returning him to life.

He had lost count of their encounters today and knew the total must be close to physiologically impossible. But she was bringing him to life as Jesus had brought back Lazarus.

He stifled the chortle that brought, thinking of the shocked stare Leigh would deliver at that simple blasphemy.

Jan giggled. "I know your wildest desires, Marty."

He tried to forget impossibilities, overcome with her possibilities. "Think so, huh?" He swallowed, his curiosity at her words making him quiet. He drove as quickly as he could, thinking of the pleasure her tone implied, wondering again what he might have said to her last night.

But he couldn't remember. Drunk as he must've been, it wasn't surprising. He might have said *anything*.

"You're going to love it even more than you thought, Marty," she whispered, moving to the middle of the seat.

Again he glanced back at Cissy and Will. They were slumped in their seats, their eyes fluttering closed.

Did he care if they told Leigh and caused her to suspect? She had arranged for all this to happen, after all. She had wanted him to have a vacation, too.

"Okay." Martin grinned. "Okay, then. We'll see if you're as good at reading minds as you are at . . . other things."

"I just hope you cut the grass," she murmured, turning and licking his earlobe, her hand back to its sure labors.

"What?" The shiver struck him, and his eyes jerked off the road to her. He opened his mouth, unable to reply.

"Of course, if you did, I hoped you raked up after."

"What . . . what do you mean?" he demanded, not daring to believe the way she had stolen so steathily into his thoughts. He must have said something last night.

Right?

"Your fantasy, Marty," she continued, her understanding fingers just the way he wanted them.

He tried to keep his attention on the swaying road. "I can get into it," she said. "I've never done it in the yard either, and the weather is lovely. It'll be fun."

Continuing to drive, he gulped and said nothing. He remembered again that far-off day when he and Leigh had nearly made it in the country grass. He'd told her he loved her, and she told him how much she loved him. That was back before the pressures became such a heavy weight. He seemed to feel her body right now, slick with summer sweat. They had dreamed a future that had never come to be. He saw her, lovely then, the hair light and breezy on her shoulders.

But she had chickened out. She had pulled him into that deserted, vacant shack rather than accidentally expose their love to a passerby. It had been almost as if she were ashamed to be seen making love to him. He swallowed hard. "I—I must have said a lot last night, huh?"

Her hand fell away from his crotch. "No, Marty . . . all

we did last night was fuck." She giggled and gave him a playful squeeze.

"D-don't," he whined uneasily. The children were in the back seat.

She stopped. "All we did last night is exactly what we'll be doing tonight, Marty."

He wanted her to go on. Wanted to stop the car right now and tear off her clothes and just have her now, right in the middle of the road.

But he kept driving. "I mean, I must have said a lot . . . while we were . . . fucking," he whispered.

"No." Her smooth lips stretched tight as the smile grew into her pink cheeks. She let her tongue slip out, sucked it back in, then poked it out again and wriggled it with invitation. "I just know about you, Marty. We didn't have time to talk last night." She squeezed him playfully. "We were busy—like we're going to be tonight."

The denial coaxed him and squeezed his stomach at the same instant. "I—but I must have told you, Jan. How could you guess at something like that?"

Her fingers traced lazily along the inside of his thigh. "I didn't guess, darling. I told you, I just *know.*"

Turning at the green light onto the street that led home, he wound through the blocks and clucked his tongue. He did his best to hide the nervous taint coloring his voice. "Are we, uh, *psychic?*"

"You bastard," Jan whispered, but with glee instead of anger. "Don't act like that to me—I'm not Leigh, you know."

He swerved tightly to miss a car parked in the road. "What? You *what?*" He slowed, barely cruising down the dark street, the beginning snores of his children behind them.

She shrugged.

"What did you mean by that?"

She scooted back to her door and folded her arms, and he imagined her flashing her unprotected bush through the slit of her skirt. "Boy, you're in a mood, Marty. Are you on the rag or something?"

"I'm fine. I just—what the hell do you mean? Why did you say that?"

A moment passed as they looked at each other, and she touched her long finger to his mouth, then waved her other hand at the windshield. "Shh. The kiddos, remember? Just drive, Rochester. Unless you want to fuck me now." Her eyes glittered in a street light. "I could just lie on the hood, and you could stick yourself inside me."

Martin gulped, seeing it happening, wanting it to happen.

"On second thought, someone might come along and interrupt us." She laughed. "You'd probably lose that hard-on, trooper. I know something that will be just as fun—what you really want—and if we don't get back, you'll never get the little monsters to bed on time."

Curiosity warred with his annoying responsibility. He opened his mouth and closed it, then turned back to the wheel and went on. She knew things and denied that he had told her of them. Fingers clutched his throat from the inside, and he choked, jogging the car dangerously before he could regain control. She knew things the way Sally had. But as he looked at her sideways he knew she was not Sally.

"How? What do you know about me, Jan? *Do* you know me? Have we met before?" His tone was more panicked than he wanted it to be, and he tried to relax. But he was suddenly suspicious, forgetting how perfect he'd found their time together.

"I'm not psychic, Marty. Don't spoil it by asking so many questions. Don't spoil it by wondering so much and trying to figure everything out. You always used to say that people aren't only a mathematical equation, and now you're trying to make me one." Those chocolate eyes dripped hurt from his prodding.

But she had done it again. She had said—

"What we have is what's important, Marty. What you have in *me.* What you have in *yourself.* Isn't that what's important?"

"Y-yes," he replied. "But then how—"

"How is only an explanation, and explanations never justify the pain or increase our joy." Jeanette's expression twitched. She seemed to enjoy his consternation. Her superior expression disappeared. Her tongue slithered between her lips once more. She raised her knee, shifting her skirt higher. He smelled her desire and saw the glistening wet spot on the upholstery as her juices spread out. "Maybe I'm just attuned to you, Marty. Like two peas in a pod. Can't that be enough? Can't it be enough that there's a definite attraction between us?" Her pupils gleamed, black pools. "I knew it as soon as I laid eyes on you, Marty, just like you knew it when you saw me. We didn't need to say much, and we haven't said much until now. We don't need to speak through words and questions. We should just be with each other and accept it. It's just like we're made for each other, Marty. I do what you need, and you do what I need."

His house appeared in the night, and he turned in the driveway, thinking of what she was saying. Were the explanations necessary? Weren't they only part of the world he didn't want?

It was true. Although they had not talked much, at least as far as he could remember—and why should she lie?—she knew exactly what he enjoyed most. Their union was perfect.

It was what he wanted. And if that was so, why should he care? Maybe Jan was a dream. Maybe Sally had been a dream. Maybe Leigh and the kids were a dream.

A nightmare.

Shifting the car to park, he turned off the engine.

"Sometimes people just think alike, Marty. It doesn't have to be mysterious or psychic or anything like that. I just know you, and you know me. If you dare to believe it."

Martin bit his lip. While he watched she did exactly what he was thinking of her doing. Her long fingers touched her skirt and unbuttoned the fastenings to open its slit wider, showing him all the perfection of her nylon-wrapped legs. She ran a long nail up one of them and onto bare skin . . . to her damp, naked crotch, rubbing in small circles. "Take the kids to bed, Marty. We've got things to do."

Shifting so that his pants weren't so tight, he held his breath as she opened her blouse buttons one by one.

"Carry the little ones inside and put them to bed, Marty. Then come back for me, okay?" She pulled the shirt off as though she were a dancer from the Showplace bar and dropped it on the car's floor. Her thumb slipped under a bra strap. "I'll be waiting right here."

"You—you're taking your clothes off."

"Brilliant deduction, Holmes—know what comes next?"

He gulped, feeling the skin close around his Adam's apple, feeling the excitement renewing, though laced with a new fright. It was all too real. He could see her, hear her, and touch her. The neighbors—

"Know what comes next?" she purred again.

His throat was dry, and all he could do was shake his head, contemplating the dangerous fantasy taking shape in her actions.

"You do." She licked her lips. "And don't worry . . . it's too dark to see anything even if someone does look out his window."

He was sweating. Martin opened his door with damp hands, his legs quivering as the dome light came on. He swallowed again, got out reluctantly, and opened the back door to pick up Will. His physical weakness made it difficult, but he held his slumbering son dazedly. Lights exploded in his brain with Jan's heady temptation, and he clutched Will tight with one arm and found the door key, then reached in to take Cissy with his other arm. Fitting both their bottoms in the crooks of his elbows, he carried them as noiselessly as he could to the porch, panting hard from the exertions of the day.

He strained to put the children down there and go back to Jan.

He might never have another chance.

But responsibility—what was left of it—made him unlock the house door and struggle inside. Though Cissy was heavier, Will was slipping out of his hold, and he went to that farther room first, stepping on something beside the bed and hearing a plastic snap. Huffing, he laid Will down on the bed hurriedly and saw the Darth Vader doll he had crushed in the faint light from the window. He then went to Cissy's room and laid her on her bed. His thoughts were filled with Jan's undressing as he pulled down the spread and brought the sheet up to Cissy's neck, not even taking off her shoes or doing more than shutting out the idea that he should get her into her gown. Rushing back to Will's room, he draped a sheet over him as well, crunching his shoes on Darth Vader loudly.

Then he was running to the front door, clipping his shin blindly on the credenza. He jarred to a breathless stop when he heard a crash and saw that one of Leigh's treasures, a glass goblet, had fallen and exploded into a hundred tiny shapes.

"God damn!" Leigh would explode like it had when she saw it.

Jan was waiting in the car.

Then the lawn.

He pushed through the open door.

Jan. Gasping, he caught his breath and closed the door gently, rushing to the gray Lynx that became black in the night.

Jan's slender white body lay in the center of the yard, her shirt, skirt, shoes, stockings and bra a hopscotch trail to the car's open door. She was naked, her legs spread apart with promise.

He thought of Leigh's broken treasure and laughed.

"What took you?" Her head rose. She was still licking her lips, hungry for him.

He felt his heart stammer.

"How's this for a fantasy, Marty?"

Here? His fingers tingled and jumped. "I . . . I was thinking more of the back . . . yard."

"With all those bushes around the fence?" Her eyebrows turned down with exaggeration, and she put an elbow under her, offering a dark nipple between a thumb and forefinger. "Come on, Jungle Jim. Where's your spirit of adventure? I've got a jungle just waiting for you. I'll stay here, and you can come scout around."

Spirit of adventure. It was the exact question he had asked Leigh when he tried to talk her into doing this a long time ago.

But in the back yard.

"Come here," she commanded him.

"I . . ."

"No one will see," she whispered. "Come on . . . please? *Please,* Marty?" She reached out with that pleading, licking her lips and panting. His feet moved as if guided by those breaths until he stood over her. She raised her hands to touch his.

"Pull me up, Marty."

He took her hand and tried to lift her, but she just slid on the grass toward him, between his legs.

"The grass is slippery," she murmured. She got up on her knees fluidly, like an acrobat. Her head tilted up, and their eyes met in the dim light. Her lips shimmered with wet anticipation, and she reached out to touch his zipper, her sure fingers lowering it with leisurely deftness.

The combination of excitement and the dread that this was actually happening in the front yard froze him. The house across the street seemed an ominous witness, and he felt goosebumps as he saw its lit windows. He thought of the nosy older woman and her husband inside, peeking out.

Without raising his watch Marty knew it was well before ten. Everyone was still awake. Cars would still be going by with fair frequency, catching them in their lights, exposing his secret desire to everyone.

Someone would see, and Leigh would find out.

Did he care? Unsure, he didn't say anything, letting Jan pull his slacks and undershorts down to his feet. He moaned when the moist confines of her mouth slid around his hardness that was tender with the incredible use he'd put it to.

Weaker than ever, even in his frightened anticipation, he could do nothing but stand there, dreading and desiring all at once. Her teeth raked his flesh until he neared pain and gasped, then her tongue caressed the tingling skin in apology, driving all his thoughts away.

Except for the desire. Except for the captivating need billowing inside him. His fingers dug into her hair while he built to the climax already so near, building hard because he wanted this so bad.

Jan had not done this last night, and he was afraid to ask because Leigh hated it. It was what she would never do. Not since the beginning. Not since he had been trapped by her.

And Jan was doing it. Without his even asking, much less begging, Jan was driving him wild with the knowing probe of her tongue.

A door slammed somewhere down the street, and he heard distant voices, and then the sound of a starting car engine. For an instant terror tried to wheedle its way in, but it was too late. Far too late as the energy built inside him with Jan's careful motions. Even the car's lights far down the street, coming closer, didn't affect him.

This was it. This was the meaning. This was the meaning, wasn't it?

He groaned. He screamed, not caring that his exuberant cry broke loud into the silent night.

Silent night, holy night.

He laughed at the new blasphemy, wishing Leigh could see this sight of his purest orgasm ever into his new lover's mouth. He wanted to sing that little jingle to her while continuing to push harder and harder into Jan's mouth. He exploded endlessly.

Jan swallowed him and licked wildly for more.

Then it was over, and he was collapsing onto the cool grass as her sticky tongue licked his hot face and her mouth covered his, giving back to him what he'd given her.

Out of the corner of an eye he saw the white car drive slowly past. He held his breath, then exhaled with a tremble as it continued and disappeared from sight.

"How was that?" she asked breathlessly.

Martin couldn't say anything, barely managing to nod.

"My turn now."

The car. His neighbors. Reality buzzed up around him. "Jan, I . . . don't you think—"

She pushed him down to the damp grass so that he was

staring at the blinking stars. She sank, sliding her bare ass up his chest until it was hanging over his mouth, tickling his nostrils with her heavy, ready scent. "Fair's fair, Marty. My turn—then together."

Another car went past, and though his heart was pounding he began to obey. He wanted this, too. He wanted to taste her like he had this afternoon, to run his lips over her dribbling cunt and make her shriek. To smother her with his own power that brought him as much pleasure as it would her.

To smother her body with the power Leigh had once craved and now refused.

He pushed his face up between her drooling thighs, felt their tremble, knew she wanted him.

And though he was growing more exhausted, he wanted her, needed her.

13

Maggie Petrie yawned as the dawn slowly crept into the house. She liked the morning: waking up before Dirk, her husband of the last thirty years. She enjoyed a few moments to herself.

She sighed, pouring a cup of hot tea and sipping its lemony taste, feeling approval of her long life in its sweet tanginess.

Another day of watching TV, or the dull confines of this neighborhood. Still, after all the hard years behind, the placid sameness of day-to-day life was kind of luxurious.

Expecting the usual sight of an empty street, she habitually opened the kitchen curtain anyway, gazing into darkness as the night's gloom slunk away.

She did a double take at the sight of someone else slinking—or trying to slink—away. The dim light and the shadows made it difficult to see.

Maggie dropped her jaw. She nearly dropped her cup, too. A low hiss came from deep in her throat, and she barely heard the shuffle of Dirk's feet and the yawn as he came down the hall.

"What's wrong with you?" he grunted.

She couldn't take her eyes from the scene in that not-so-distant yard. The naked man stared blankly at the sun, then at the clothing strewn all around him. And although it was still too hazy for her to be certain, it looked like something —someone else, almost a shadow—was right at his feet. A woman?

Maggie caught her breath, remembering that the woman named Leigh lived there with her husband and two children. "Good Lord Almighty," she blurted.

Dirk glanced out the window, searching. After a long second he chuckled.

"Did you see?" she asked, feeling the heat of embarrassment on her face.

"Better than *Playboy,"* he smiled.

"Was . . . was that a woman with him?"

Dirk nodded, staring back out. "And you said nothing ever happens around here."

A chill started through her, and she wondered what the world was coming to. "I want to move if it's come to this, Dirk. If street people are going to come into our neighborhood and sleep naked—"

Dirk shook his head. "Goddamn, woman, nothing satisfies you. Just last night you wanted to move because it was so dull around here, and now—"

She shivered. "We ought to call the police!"

Watching intently, Dirk put a reassuring hand on her shoulder. "If they don't move on, we will. Don't get so flustered, Maggie. Everyone needs a place to sleep."

"They could do it with their clothes on! Now get away from that window, Dirk. You shouldn't be staring at a sight like that!"

With a final gaze out, he sighed and followed her to the table.

Ragged coughs ripped Martin's chest in growing discomfort as he awoke. His muscles and joints were stiff and sore. He was cold and damp.

"Son of a bitch," he grunted, reaching groggily for the blanket and touching wet grass instead.

"Son of a bitch!" He opened his eyes and jerked up.

For another stunned moment he had no idea of where he was, then he recognized his night-shrouded front lawn.

Martin exhaled, and he chuckled when he saw Jan lying a foot away, curled up.

But it was growing lighter.

His breath quickened, and he turned back to see a sky tinged with the first streaks of dawn's red glow, exposing him and Jan in their pink nakedness on the front lawn.

Jan's clothing was spread across the yard, and they lay at one end of that scattered fabric path, only ten or twelve feet from the curb.

"Good God," he wheezed in a frigid panic. *"Good damn God!"* People would be awakening, getting up, and coming out to their cars, and he was naked out here. With *her!*

He crouched back on hands and knees like a dog, furtive eyes sweeping the empty street. He crawled, scraping his knees, retrieving the line of her clothes and his own as fast as possible. *"Jan?"* he called softly, his arms full as he shinnied back for her through the dew-slick grass like a snake.

Like James Bond?

He shook it out of his head. "Jan! C-come on! Get up!"

"Hmm?" She turned over, showing him temptations that stirred him only briefly now. She stretched, bending her knees and opening her thighs as she yawned. "Hmm? It's not even light yet, Marty. Go back t'sleep."

He looked away, fearing the sight of her that made him want to ignore their exposure and fuck her again. He was frightfully awake now. A frenzied caution overtook him, and he berated himself that they'd fallen asleep out here. "Jan, *we're in the front yard!"* He had a sudden vision of neighbors heading out to their cars and smiling at him, waving, wishing him a grand good morning.

"Get up, girl! The sun's coming up!"

"Shit, Marty," she sniggered against a deep yawn, "you sound like a vampire."

"Jan!" he whined.

"Oh, hush!" she mumbled, trying to keep her eyes shut. "Let me sleep, will you?"

Sleep. He wanted to, yes. He was weak with what they'd done over and over, and weak with shock at where they were. It was as though he hadn't rested at all. He wanted to sleep, but not here!

"Jan," he pleaded, *"God damn it!"*

"God damn it is right, Marty," she muttered, lifting her head. Unwillingly she pushed herself up, then stood and stretched upright in the red morning glow.

"Jan, *come on!"*

"Haven't you come enough?"

He hit his palm with a fist, unable to speak.

"Oh, all right." She walked to him as he got back up to his knees and then his feet. She laughed as he covered his nudity with their rumpled clothing. He backed to the front door, sweating at her unhurried gait until she stopped on the first porch step. His heart battered his chest like a fuel pump gone berserk.

But Jan turned back around. "Let's watch the sun come up, Marty."

"Like this?" His only relief was that they hadn't yet been caught. He reached back to open the front door and choked when the knob didn't turn. "Shit!"

He tried again.

The door was locked.

"Oh, shit." He dropped the clothes and found his slacks, searching for keys that weren't there.

"Locked out?" She grinned.

"It's not funny!"

She sat down on the porch steps, bathed in the early rays of light. "Let's watch the sun come up, Marty."

His nerves rat-a-tatted a warning, and he stepped into the pant legs, pulling the waist up to his stomach and zipping up. "Okay . . . o . . . kay." He tried to calm himself, taking shallow breaths. "But put on your clothes first, okay?"

She shook her head. "I feel like greeting the day and nature in the natural state. Get with it, Marty. Don't you think it's more fun like this? Fuck the world, right? Just the way you fucked me last night. Hmm?" She raised her right hand and slipped it in his slacks to stroke his bare buttocks underneath.

Marty gritted his teeth, began gnashing them. Life jumped into his worn penis against his will, and he pictured them both on the porch, him pushing up inside her as they started the day off right.

He was becoming scared again. Of what?

"Please, Marty?" Her eyes filled with that longing, warning of the sorrow his refusal would bring. *"Please?"*

She wanted him again. The crazy understanding formed a proud smile against the insanity and the consumption of his strength. "I . . . can't we do it in the back?"

"The back?" Her face twitched disbelievingly. "In the back? You mean like *this?"* She got to her feet, and her fingers circled him through the slacks. She pushed against him and rubbed her ass against his firming flesh. "Like *this?"*

"I . . . I . . ." A regular squeak came from the street, and Martin jumped back with a hot blush, trying to drag her into a shadow as he saw the paper boy riding his bicycle. The teenager tossed papers lazily, landing one in Martin's yard. He stopped with a wry smile as he glanced up and Jan posed for him. He waved.

"Get back here!" Martin breathed, crouching down behind a lawn chair.

"I'll get your paper," she chuckled.

Before he could protest she was running out into the yard, the dew glistening on her skin. She picked the rolled package up as the boy shrugged and rode on, not seeming to care. As though he saw such sights every day.

Martin felt anger at the newsboy's nonchalance. After all, Jan was beautiful!

She stood in the yard's center, watching the boy continue down the street. She waved at his back and faced Martin, holding the newspaper between her legs like a mammoth dildo. She began to mimick a masturbatory act with it, and he gasped in his panic at the way the light caught her, making her into a wretched-looking caricature of herself for that moment. His lungs sighed out every previous desire as her skin suddenly seemed to be a covering of dry, brown leather, her hair ragged sprouts of weeds on a bald head.

He blinked, drawing a deep breath of relief as his eyes cleared and she became as beautiful as ever, snickering to herself lewdly as she fucked his newspaper.

"Jan!" Martin hissed.

She squealed and jumped up and down as if she were coming with the paper locked between her thighs, then cocked her head and came back, dropping the rolled paper beside Martin's bare feet. She hauled him back up from behind the chair. "He didn't see a thing, and even if he did, he's just a kid. If he says something, who do you think will believe him, huh? All pimply-faced, teeny-boppin' guys make up stories."

Although his legs were still unsteady, Martin allowed the vague truth in her words to pacify him, and he stood. She pressed against him, the warmth of her soft skin like an electric blanket while he opened his mouth for her kiss. The fear of discovery was drifting away.

Seconds passed. She rested her head on his shoulder. "Want to give the neighborhood a *real* show?"

The crazy suggestion went through his head, and he trembled. "Are you *nuts,* Jan? We could be arrested!" He backed away, his hands diving into his pockets once more. Was she *crazy?*

"Huh-uh. Everyone would be enjoying our show too much to bother, Marty." Her lips puckered, and she darted the tongue in and out of her mouth. "Everyone would love it. You'd be the most popular guy in the neighborhood, Marty. I'd love it. You'd love it, too."

"I've got to find my damn keys!"

"You'd really love it, Marty."

"I'd really *love* to find my keys!"

Her eyebrows twittered. "How establishment of you." She rested her hands on her hips and sighed as he searched the porch.

"I must have dropped them."

"I thought you were different, Marty. I thought you

wanted to give up all this pretend world and just be yourself."

She was still quite naked. Very real and very naked. "Get your clothes on, Jan. People can see us."

"We can see them, too. Who's right and who's wrong? We're just being ourselves. I am, anyway. They dress up in their hot-shit duds to impress the world and hide the flab underneath. Even you. If you're embarrassed by your body, why did you show it to me? Do you think so little of me?"

"No," he whimpered. "You don't understand. None of these people know you from Adam—"

"Eve."

He drew a deep breath. "None of these people know who the hell you are! But I have to face them every day! They'll tell—"

"Leigh." Her eyes narrowed. "I knew you loved her. I told you you did."

He passed her and strained his vision, studying the grass for a telltale glint of metal. "I've got to think of the kids . . . of my job."

"You love them, too, huh?" She dropped her eyelashes, making her expression sad.

It turned him to a confused mass of nervous jelly. He hated his job. Sometimes he hated Leigh, even the kids, but . . . "No. I love you, Jan."

Their eyes consumed each other's for a long moment of truth, then she dropped a lithe hand between her legs and held it out. His keys lay in her palm.

"You had them—"

She held them back. "You have to love me to keep me, Marty."

Snatching them fast, he ignored their wetness, took her arm, and pulled her back, then unlocked the door and moved with her into the entryway. He shut the door. "I love you," he whispered. "But even if I hate the way things work, we have to live in this world—"

"Do we?"

"Good God," he stammered, stepping back from her with a shiver. He was unable to believe the way he'd gone along with her, even if what they'd done was something he'd always wanted to do. "Ow!" he screamed abruptly, a sharp pinch shooting up his heel. "Ohhh!" He wheeled with his arms outstretched and leaned against the wall, gasping hard, then wiped a hand on the bottom of his foot, standing like a stork on the other. His fingers slid over oozing warmth, and he stared at the gooey red stream coating them. It dripped over his thumb and down to the hall's linoleum floor. He grimaced, feeling the every wrinkle that expression made. "Sh-shit!" he croaked, and reached to his foot to pull out the piece of glass. He remembered breaking Leigh's ornament last night. He had not cleaned it up.

"Watch your step!" he warned Jan as she passed him.

"I'll get a washcloth," she said, and walked right into the pile of broken glass. Martin winced, expecting her to cry out painfully.

But she didn't. Her bare feet passed over the jagged shards unhurt. She stepped on them without a flinch and went swiftly on to the hall.

Blinking and unable to stand any longer, he allowed himself to drop to the floor, banging his tailbone. It was nothing compared to his throbbing foot. He squeezed it tight to close the hole in his skin while the shock and exhaustion turned him faint. He gulped and stared at a piece of the glass Jan's foot had come down on, expecting to see her blood but it wasn't there. He reached out weakly and touched it, drawing in a hiss when it sliced his finger. "God . . . God damn!" He put the new wound into his mouth with a grunt. How?

How?

"God, you look silly, Marty," Jan reproved, appearing from the hallway with a dripping rag. She shook her head, and her firm breasts swayed and jiggled.

But they didn't arouse him at all now. The sting still jolted him. He dropped his jaw and stared at her as she bent down, sponging the blood from his toes gently.

"When you stepped on the glass, Jan, didn't you hurt yourself?" He took the washcloth with dizzy hands, motioning her to him, cringing when she stepped in the middle of the glass again.

"I'm okay," she told him.

"Let me see." He patted the floor beside him, and as soon as she was sitting he reached to hold her foot, examining it carefully.

"That tickles, Martin!"

The skin of her foot was smooth and perfect, like the rest of her body, without even a callus. No cut or abrasion showed—not even a slight break of the skin. It was soft and sleek like a baby's foot. He peered in awe, then looked back at the angry glass that had cut him when he'd barely snagged it.

"Let me clean your wound for you, Martin." She pulled her toes out of his grasp and dabbed the cool cotton fabric on the bottom of his foot, tenderly swabbing. "That's a pretty bad gash." She wiped away the red drops and handed back the stained cloth, then stood. "Hold it tight on your foot while I get something for a bandage and to sterilize it."

Seeing the red molasses oozing from his flesh, Martin felt a lightness in his skull and forced back the sickness in his throat. "In the bathroom," he groaned, holding his foot in the vise of his fists to slow the sticky flow.

"Back in a sec."

He grunted, his forehead hot. The room became dimmer and hazy, and he hacked a cough, shaking with that force as dry heaves began to throttle his gut. The room began to swim and vibrate with lunatic glee. Colors faded and exploded within his brain. He stared, trying to focus, his hands reaching out to stop the motions racking him.

A mental photograph of Leigh magnified and leapt out to him, and he felt her familiarity, remembering how she pampered him and looked after him when he was ill. She always watched over him as though she were his mother, caring for him, answering his calls for comfort and refreshment, even when she was ill herself. Suddenly he wanted her.

"Leigh," he rasped, hearing his own thin voice.

14

Daddy!"

The pitched cry from half an eternity away washed over Martin, and he recognized it at last, dragging open his eyes to see Cissy standing in her wrinkled pink Sunday dress two feet away.

He coughed, wanting to vomit the queasy discomfort filling him. The floor was cold under his bare limbs. When Martin inhaled deeply he rose to full consciousness with a shock, staring stupidly at his naked body and the tiny pieces of scattered glass and the blood on the floor surrounding him.

How in the hell—

"D-Daddy!" Cissy was shrieking, and Will cowered behind her, keeping his distance.

Martin swallowed. He put the flat of his hand on the floor and pushed up too quickly, sliding on the sticky blood puddled around his foot and just catching himself by clawing the credenza. He managed to pull himself up, avoiding the glass splinters and breathing deeply when pricks of lightning shot up his ankle. New sweat dripped on his greasy face, and he wobbled awkwardly, favoring his right foot and wincing at the shrieking fire that burned it. "I . . . I'm okay." He sucked in more air to fight the nausea.

"Are . . . are you *living dead?*" Will asked cautiously, edging back.

"He's our daddy!" reprimanded Cissy, holding her small hand out to Martin as if to help.

"He . . . he *could* b-be living dead," Will insisted, his heart-shaped face contorting as he took another step back and made ready to run.

"I—I wish," Martin moaned, trying to right his thoughts in the whirl of dreamlike memories struggling inside him.

His eyes squeezed shut with the continued pangs, adding a wild stagger to his limp as he grappled the heavy air to reach the bathroom. Here he was, in agony, and Leigh was gone. It reminded him of the children, and he turned back. Will huddled in a ball on the living room floor. "St-stay away from the glass," he said with the last of his strength, letting his daughter guide his stumbling feet. It was all a bad dream.

Martin stopped. Dreams again, catching his thoughts, bringing a haunting, wispy vision of a woman named Jan to assail his mind, combining all the foggy images into one. He remembered her the way he remembered the parties where he got drunk too early.

He had craved someone in the loneliness of the bar. He must've come home alone in a drunken stupor and languished in that mindlessness for hours, truly living inside his head.

Jan was his figment. She didn't really exist. The children had said they could not see her, that she was invisible.

He sighed.

"Here, Daddy," Will said, running up to him and holding something up.

Martin took the blood-soaked washcloth from his son's hand, and his heart skipped. He squeezed it, hot sweat coating his forehead because of its telltale existence.

How could he have gotten it? Why would he have gotten it out of the bathroom and come back to lie naked in the entry hall?

He looked at the floor, bare of all but the smallest broken fragments. There was nowhere near enough wreckage on that floor to account for the goblet that had broken. And how could *he* have cleaned that mess up as much as *someone* had? Most of the blood was wiped up, too, except for the single spot where his foot had rested.

The big pieces of the glass were gone.

"Where's the invisible lady?" asked Will, tagging after Cissy as they reached the inner hall. "Did she leave?"

He almost froze in the loud memories that came rushing vividly back, doubling over with the vertigo blasting his belly when he tried to shut them out and reach the bathroom door. Biting his tongue, he pulled himself inside, holding himself up by the countertop. "Stay . . . away from . . . the glass," he whispered to the fuzzy shapes of the children, and he closed the door behind himself solidly, then limped to the toilet seat and dropped onto the closed lid so hard it hurt his buttocks.

A chill enveloped him. If she wasn't a dream, where did she go? How did she step into the glass without a mark?

The textured bathroom walls seemed to close in and move away. Martin shuddered, stared at his throbbing foot, and saw the bandage in place there. His lips shivered, and he reached down to touch the stained gauze timidly, examining the expert wrapping that was far more careful than what he was capable of.

He trembled and felt relief at the same time. Dreams could not manipulate physical matter that way.

Suddenly he floated out of the dense clouds in his brain and noticed the sunlight bathing him from the window. Martin checked his watch. It was nearly nine.

"Holy shit." He forgot Jan for the moment and grabbed the tile cabinet top to get to his feet, biting his lip harder and bringing salty warmth as he did. He was late for work, and he was lost. He felt worn out.

"Jesus," he breathed, twisting on the sink faucet and watching the rapid, clear stream flow down the drain. He closed that hole with the plug, lowering his face clumsily into the basin as it filled, then repeated the ritual five or six times before turning off the water and limping back to the toilet. He sat more carefully this time and held his wet face in his hands. "Jan?" he whimpered.

She was real. She had left him without even saying good-bye or telling him her last name. It squeezed his heart cruelly. He didn't know who she was or where to find her. She was gone. Leigh was coming home.

His perfect one-night stand was over, and Leigh was coming home today.

A light tapping came hesitantly from the door. "Daddy? Daddy? Will and me are hungry. Aren't you going to go to work, Daddy?"

"Aren't you going to feed us?" whined Will's voice, joining Cissy's. "Daddy!"

Their insistence gnawed him, and he wiped his torn lip, then drove his palms into his cheeks, forcing out the gulp of air he'd taken. He choked a sob.

"Daddy!"

"Just a minute, damn it!"

A hushed murmur came through the hollow wood, and feet scurried away. Living dead, Will had called him, and he felt every bit of that description as he forced back the tears. Agony flooded through his body and into his soul—the agony of losing Jan, not of his wounded foot. And maybe the agony of what he'd done to Leigh. She went away on a job, to *work,* giving him the time he wanted for a "vacation," and he had tried to find his own past. To find himself, as they used to say.

And he had, though it made him feel guilty, because when he'd felt that wrenching stab rip into his body from the glass, he had wanted Leigh. It confused him because of the ways he didn't even want her, yet had screamed out for her in his pain.

Uncertain, he did his best to block those complexities from his scattered thoughts and rested his throbbing brain. After a few minutes he managed to stand again and took a towel hanging from the rack on the wall, wrapping it around his waist. He wanted to eat. The damn kids wanted to eat. It brought the shame again, and he shrank from it, not accepting it. He was trapped. The unwanted responsibility stalled his actions, and he was torn between it and his desires. Between what he did not want and what he wanted.

"Daddy . . . please? I'm sorry you're hurt . . ."

Cissy's remorseful tone made it worse. It was the sticky flypaper that held him while he disintegrated piece by piece. "God damn," he said to himself, reaching for the doorknob and glancing back at the watch face on his wrist. "Who the hell are you, Jan?" The fuzzy images of the recent hours hung inside him like a lure, and only the cold reality of his own growling stomach caused him to refuse it.

Jan had left him. She was probably unable to rouse him from the shocked faint that had combined with his physical exhaustion, and she had called a cab.

"Right," he murmured. He put those considerations far back in his mind for later recollection, then opened the door to Cissy's face. Her anxious stare made the screws tighten over his heart until he ached all over in his neglect. Martin put his hands behind her and brought her close, inhaling her child's mustiness. "Daddy's going to feed you now, baby girl."

"I can feed myself." She smiled. "But you get mad when we pour the cereal. Will's the one who spills."

"Am not!"

He held Will near, too. "I'll get your breakfast, and I'm going to call in sick to work. After we eat I'll play a game with you guys, how's that?"

Will clapped his hands, then frowned. "A real game, okay? Not like that Lady Ghost."

"A real one." He ignored the emptiness of his pleading stomach. As they walked to the kitchen he snatched a hope and searched the countertop for a note from Jan, then felt disappointment at not finding one. After all they had shared he could hardly believe it was so easily finished.

He'd look in the bedroom after he fed the children. He found himself praying that if there wasn't a note, she would call. He didn't want those amazing hours to end like this.

"Are we gonna have cereal?" asked Will as they moved into the kitchen and Martin opened the cabinets.

"I want lunch," said Cissy. But he reached for the cereal and brought it down to Will's excited squeals.

Even if Jan didn't call, he would try to find her. He had met her at a bar, and might do so again.

"Is Mommy coming back today?"

He frowned and nodded, thinking with more clarity. Life went on and on, didn't it? Perhaps Jan's disappearance was for the best. Though their ending was abrupt, it managed a mischievious comfort. Leigh would be back home in five or six hours, so perhaps it was all working itself out perfectly. Knowing who and where Jan was could lead to complications in his life and maybe make it even worse than it already was. Having her to go to would not remove Leigh from his life except in the ways they were already separate. He'd had the proverbial perfect affair, pleasure with no strings attached. It was better like this.

Martin could still feel her sleek body and swallowed hard, trying to deny that he wanted to see her again to feel her hands on him, and her mouth . . . and her tongue.

Martin grinned darkly.

Maybe it was best to just leave it that way.

15

If you were going to stay home all day, you could've at least cleaned house, Martin," Leigh said with lighthearted exasperation. She sat, her hair mussed and body slumped, beside him on the divan. A golden lock hid an eye. She studied the bandaged foot he lifted to rest on her lap. "Does it still hurt?"

Holding inside the nervous anticipation that had been building since her return that afternoon, Martin shrugged. He worked to a tone of nonchalance. "A little. Not like this morning. I took a nap."

"Well, I don't blame you for missing work. Probably did you good to spend some time with the kids anyhow. Mother said you were working all weekend and that she had to keep them." Leigh touched the foot carefully. "Pretty good job wrapping it up, too. Did you do that?"

His jaw froze tight. He cleared his throat. "Ah—"

Leigh chuckled. "It looks professional. Maybe you should have been a doctor."

"Yeah. Maybe." He let it slide.

"Martin?" She gazed at him more seriously, an eyebrow arched on her high forehead.

"Yeah?" He relaxed into the cheeriness she brought home. She had listened in horror to his falsification of how he broke her goblet and cut himself in an effort to clean the mess up. She surprised him by showing little remorse over the treasured object, concerned instead with his injury.

"This may not be the time," she sighed. "But Will . . . and Cissy, too, I—" She lifted her shoulders and met his eyes. "You scared them both pretty bad with that ghost story last night."

"What?" His mouth twisted, and he wondered if there was yet more he couldn't remember about the past hours. Jan. He hardly dared believe what they had done. But he stopped that train of thought as suddenly as if someone had jerked an emergency brake, refocusing his attention. Ghost story?

"I know they don't seem to get scared when you let them watch those bloody movies, Martin, but it frightens them all the same. I just think you're pushing things a little too far."

"What are you talking about?" This confrontation was far from anything he'd expected. Martin felt his face stretch as it displayed his baffled thoughts. He watched Leigh's blue eyes and tried to put everything into a new order. "You sound like your mother, you know that?"

"You don't even remember, do you?" She reached out and combed the hair out of his face.

"I—"

Some of her earnestness faded out. Her lips sagged. "Well, I guess it's no big deal, but they were afraid to talk to you about it. That's my point. If you scare them, then you make them afraid to come to you with those fears . . . and maybe other ones, too." Her giggle was limp. "I guess it was kind of funny, even though cruel."

He flinched.

Her tiny chuckle trickled down to a smile. "They really thought you had let some kind of a ghost into the house last night, Martin. They said you told them that their Aunt Jan had come to see them, and that they had to sit in the car's back seat when you went out. They said you even bought 'her' dinner at the restaurant."

Martin gulped.

Leigh scooted down in the chair. The robe she'd replaced

her dress with wrinkled around her middle. She repositioned his foot on her legs and massaged it tenderly. "They thought you were putting them on because they said they couldn't see anyone, Marty. Not at first. But then they thought they did see something. Cissy said it was a monster ghost, and that sometimes she could see it eating the dinner. Will wouldn't talk about it at all. When I asked him what he saw, he gave me this." She held out one of Will's Star Wars alien dolls. It was green and scaly.

Martin blushed and felt words catch in his throat. This was not what he'd expected at all. He anticipated Will or Cissy mentioning Jan and had constructed the story for which she laid the groundwork. They had not seen her? He stopped a moan, his chest tight.

"It's no big deal, Martin, but I thought you might want to go easier on that kind of thing until they're older." She put her elbow on his knee.

Again he flinched, but this time the pain was more direct as ribbons of flame shot up into his worn groin.

"Oh, I'm sorry!" She sat back up with apology. "Are you okay?"

He bit the air as though it were solid. "Uh . . . yeah." The children's game last night had continued even to this point, and rather than relieving him of having to give the explanations he had worked up, it made him angry. He tossed his head back and forth, knowing he ought to just drop it and let it go. "But really, Jan's cute, Leigh. She—she's not—" He stopped himself. What in the hell was he doing? It was better this way, wasn't it? Didn't this make the short liaison more perfect? No strings attached and no one the wiser?

"There really is an Aunt Jan?"

Martin blustered a quick laugh. "I could get you going, too, couldn't I?"

"You ornery cuss." But her smile was pure now, and her cheeks tinted pink.

He smiled, falling into the yarn that was part truth. Hadn't Jan said that lying makes the world go round? "You probably wouldn't like her, Leigh. It's just as well you didn't have to meet her." Martin licked his lips and avoided direct contact with her eyes.

Leigh leaned toward him and touched his hand. "Well, I do think it's kind of funny. I wish I'd been here."

"It was just as well you weren't."

Leigh nodded. "Probably. Promise me not to do it again until they're older?"

Martin nodded.

"I think it's for the best." She yawned. "Lord, it was a long day. Ready for bed?"

The clock read nine o'clock, and her voice made a promise he would have jumped at before, but Martin shook his head. The recent events and their increasing mystery came back to life as curiosity replaced the driving longing that changed to exhaustion. The children proved beyond any doubt that it all must have happened. That it was not merely one of long-lost Sally's dreams. "Not really. Are you?"

"Definitely." She smoothed her blond locks with a small hand and yawned again. "About four hours ago, in fact. But I wanted to sleep with you tonight." Her fingers tracked up to his belt, and she tapped it provocatively.

He was exhausted that way especially. Beyond provocation. Her blatant invitation was futile.

"Marty?"

A bad thought came into his brain at the sound of her budding disappointment. She had refused him so many times, and at last, without remorse, he could do the same to her. He could refuse her without second thoughts of how he was cheating himself, too.

"I don't think I'm ready to sleep yet," he told her. "My foot still hurts."

"It . . . must," she whispered, but she still tried to smile. "This must be a first, Marty."

"Why don't you go on to bed? I'll just watch TV for a while." The ability to refuse her made him stronger, and he liked that power, knowing it had been given to him by Jan. It hurt in that realization, too, though. It reminded him of her virtual disappearance without even a sad final kiss or mushy parting words.

He fought a tear and shut his eyes. Jan had been his vacation, bringing him back to his reality and out of the gloomy trap he had struggled in for so long. She had brought back his past. She had brought back his self! "I, uh, might even go for a drive."

"You fixed the car, then?"

He recalled the blatant lie he'd told her mother, and Leigh had called her after getting back. He nodded cautiously. "Yeah. It . . . was the plug wires. I replaced them. I kind of wanted to try the thing out."

"You took the kids and your ghost out to eat last night. Did you use the car then, or the broomstick express?"

He laughed with her, then shrugged, thinking of Jan, seeing her luscious body superimposed over Leigh's. He wished he could thank Jan for this power she gave him over Leigh.

He wanted to see her just once more.

The thought stirred him in the way Leigh hadn't been able to. "Well," Martin went on, "we didn't go far, and it was hard to listen to the engine with the kids there. Besides, being cooped up all day with this foot has made me feel like a POW."

"In a special torture chamber with the kids as your jailers, no doubt. I know the feeling." She agreed softly, a little sadly. She got up and out from under his foot with attentive caution. "You're sure it won't hurt you to push down on the gas pedal?"

"I'll be okay. I'll watch TV first. I may not even go." Sliding off the cushions to put his weight on the left foot, Martin stood beside her, steadying himself and grinning sheepishly while he thought of the things Jan would do for him if he ever saw her again, of the satisfactions she would make him feel.

"Well, come put me to bed first."

Keeping his mental distance from her, Martin let her take his hand as they went to the bedroom. He glanced in at the sleeping children when they passed their doors. He looked at the waterbed sheets he had barely managed to change, gaining Leigh's unsuspecting appreciation. He remembered Jan on that spot and on the floor. In the shower, where he had not had to remove any evidence of his infidelity.

Leigh stripped off her clothing without Jan's sexy showmanship, though he believed she made an earnest try to unknowingly emulate it. She slipped between the sheets naked, something she hadn't done in months. "Come to bed soon, okay?"

Leaning over her, he met her lips without passion, smelling her familiar scent. "I won't wake you."

"I won't mind," she told him.

Power. He felt it all over, like he had in the early days. It made him feel good. It gave him a mastery again.

Jan had given it to him.

"Wake me if you need me, Marty. Call me and I'll wake up, okay?" She pursed her lips, nearly creating a pout. The bulges her breasts made under the bedspread heaved a sigh. "Wake me if you want to, okay?"

He shook his head, repeating the words she had stopped him with so many times before. "You need your rest for work tomorrow."

"I . . . I missed you, honey."

"Maybe"—he pretended to waver, enjoying the sense of being her temptation—"maybe I'll feel better tomorrow night."

"I'll *make* you better," she teased, then reached up to turn out the lamp on the nightstand. Her elbow bumped something, and Marty's heart leapt with a sudden jolting speed, erratically.

He flipped around in the dark.

She had knocked something over. He heard it rattle on the nightstand.

"What was that?" Leigh yawned.

Marty's power began to disappear as a loud thud came from the floor. He knew what had happened and what had fallen. He had seen the mug when they entered but had given it no more thought than she apparently had.

Now he did. He hurried blindly across the room. Awkwardly, pushing his foot faster despite its complaint. As Leigh twisted the lamp back on he picked up the mug before she could see it. He saw its rim smeared with Jan's lipstick, wanting to touch it to his own lips even though he knew he should wipe off the telltale sign. He exhaled sharply, his legs jittery at its forgotten proof. His hands shook.

Leigh was frowning and tilting her head. "What's that?"

"An . . . an empty mug. I put it down yesterday. . . ."

She reached out a hand. "I thought I saw lipstick on it—"

The hot blush covered him, and he knew he was caught, then showed her the damning rim with that guilt. "It . . . it—"

"Oh, God, Martin"—she giggled suddenly—"you didn't let your ghost-cousin see our bedroom, did you?"

Her innocence of him formed a slow sigh, and he sagged back against a wall. "Well, your mom was drinking from this cup, and we were talking." He examined the mug and cackled stupidly. "We were back here. She . . . she wanted to look at . . . at your clothes—"

"God," Leigh groaned, "I hope it was cleaner when she was here."

Frowning, Martin swept his gaze over the room he had spent a painful hour sweeping and straightening this morning. Bitter, self-righteous anger at her judgment pumped him, and he sniffed. He was right, indeed. Nothing had changed. She was so pleasant and sweet only because *she* was horny, just as he was to her when he got that way. "I thought it was clean," he muttered, very glad he had refused her, dragging the delicious disappointment she'd shown back into his thoughts.

Tired laughter bubbled from Leigh.

The sound stung him. He wanted Jan back. Without any guilt now, he wanted out of the trap. "I tried to keep the place clean."

Lying back on the pillow, she blew him a kiss. "Men just don't know what clean is."

Despite his victory, the barb stung, but he knew it was only her anger at his rejection of her. Exactly the same as when he lashed out at her in his frustration. It proved how deeply he'd managed to plant his knife. He limped back to the door without another word.

"Hey!" called Leigh. "I'm just kidding! I love you, Marty. I—" She stopped when he reached the doorway, passing through it. "Marty! I love you! I'll be waiting for you."

He stopped and turned, blinking in the hall light, knowing the illumination would show her the smile she couldn't comprehend, and it grew as he posed sullenly for her misunderstanding.

"I do love you, Marty. I mean that. I love and want you." She hesitated. "Be careful if you do go out, okay?"

He touched the doorknob. "If I go, I won't be gone long." He didn't know or care if it was a lie. Then the door closed, and he closed Leigh out of his mind with it. He moved as best he could to the front closet, then took out the electric guitar, using it as a cane to go to the TV and switch it on. He sat on the couch, holding the instrument the way Jan had cradled his head, barely seeing the television screen's flashes. He raked his fingers across the strings, waiting until the news came on.

He needed to find Jan. The feel of the old guitar showed him that clearly. Only Jan could take away the old hurt and humiliation Leigh's backlash of laughter had brought surging home. Only Jan could close those old wounds that had reopened and replace them with the feelings of glory he knew only with her. He staggered back and returned the guitar to the closet, behind the upright sweeper. His past was affirmed in the sting those strings had given his bare fingers. He limped ahead to his keys and wallet on the credenza, and hoped he could find Jan tonight.

Martin pocketed the wallet, limped into the living room, and fit on his shoes. He'd awakened from the long nightmare Leigh had seduced him into. Jan had been like a splash of frigid water on his sleeping mind, but far more pleasurable.

Letting his desire boil up, Martin opened the door and stepped outside. He went to the car, got in, and started the engine.

"Jan," he whispered, and he put the car into gear, driving through the night to the expressway.

16

The images of the last few hours whirled inside Martin as he drove, and he braked at a stoplight. He couldn't recall the miles behind him. He blinked, turned, and stopped at the next light, then went left. Heart pounding forcefully, legs tingling, he saw the sign of the bar where they'd met.

Grimly, he pulled into the parking lot, driving out the thought of Leigh on her side of the bed, and of Cissy and Will. "Jan," he whispered, and pulled up on the door handle. He got out and stood there against the car, seeing it all and feeling the finality his next decisions could bring.

That emptiness put him into a hot sweat as he closed the door, but Martin bit his lip and walked to the front door of the bar building, passing a man in a cowboy shirt and jeans. He passed another man in a dark wrinkled suit and the plump woman he held tight. He heard the cowboy spit on the asphalt lot and pushed open the door. Loud country rock splattered against him, followed by the voices that rose above it as he entered.

He stared with searching eyes.

The dance floor was empty but for three couples, and he turned to the tables and booths. His eyes searched each face with a sinking sensation.

Jan wasn't there. He gulped, almost turning back to go home.

But the place was still relatively empty.

Setting his jaw and standing back as a young T-shirted man brushed past, he walked to the empty table where he had sat with Jan Saturday night. Tears struggled for control, and he kept them back, finding a seat and dropping down heavily. He watched each woman who passed, hoping it might be her, that he'd somehow overlooked her.

"Can I get you something?"

Martin saw the gum-smacking brunette coming toward him and twisted his lips with an effort. "How . . . how about a beer? *Two* beers."

She put a hand on her hip and chuckled brightly. "How about one, big guy, and I'll watch for when you need another."

"Okay." He shrugged.

"Draft?"

Martin shook his head. "Bottle."

"Bud or Coors?"

"Bud."

"Gotcha covered."

The waitress moved away with a practiced gait. He watched her tight ass cheeks move up and down, and sagged in the chair. He licked his lips, but didn't want her. He wanted only Jan. Time itself seemed to stand still as the thoughts of her—of her and him—repeated themselves endlessly. He barely looked up when the glass and bottle were set in front of him.

"Anything else?" the waitress asked.

Martin met her dark eyes for an instant as she touched his shoulder. He dropped his gaze to her ample tits, then back up to her face. "How about you?" he asked. But then he knew he didn't really mean it.

She winked. "Stick around until we close, and I'll think about it."

His face burned with a new feeling of infidelity, and he shook his head, reaching for the cold bottle and touching it to his lips. "Maybe another night."

Her clipped eyebrows fluttered. The waitress was puzzled. He took a deep drink as she backed away. The brash liquid bubbled down his throat.

A light touch brushed the back of his neck with gentleness. "You starting without me, Marty?"

The unexpected, familiar voice jarred him, catching him in mid-swallow. He choked, spitting some of the beer out his mouth and just managed to keep down the rest. Drops ran down his chin, but he ignored them and swiveled in the seat as fast as he could. He saw the long reddish hair and chestnut eyes as they were in his mind, the full, red lips.

"You're early," Jan said.

He put down the bottle so slowly it was as though time *had* stopped. He shuddered, weak as his eyes took her in.

But he reveled in her fresh proximity. She sat next to him and scooted the chair close, reaching both her hands forward to meet his, grabbing him tight with her precious fingers.

Martin could barely speak: "I . . . I was afraid you wouldn't be . . . here. I didn't know how—where . . . to find you—"

Jan looked over her shoulder at the waitress. She was with a group of men at another table, but her gaze was on Martin.

Martin shook his head. "I don't want her."

Jan sniffed. "That's not the way it sounded."

He swallowed. "But you—you just left. I didn't know—"

She dropped her lashes briefly and released his hand. "I couldn't stay, Marty. I was worried, but I couldn't stay. You didn't want *me.*" She sniffed. "You didn't even see me, Marty. You kept calling for Leigh." The pain of her disappointment marred her. "I wanted you, Marty. The time we spent is such a treasure, but I couldn't stay unless you wanted me."

His hand wrapped hers. "I do. I . . . I was—"

A frantic guitar riff burst from the speakers and blasted the air, drowning her words out. Its flair was not nearly as sure as his own once was. Martin winced, then leaned closer to Jan: "I did want you. I *do* want you," he repeated. His awkward fingers crushed hers with his emotion.

The guitar solo went on, the wrong notes wrenching as the room darkened and spotlights danced through the new shadows. "What about your wife?" Jan whispered.

He squinted, having to read her lips in the bright flashes to know what she was saying, though he felt her words in his heart.

"What about *Leigh?*"

Martin shook his head, taking a breath as the loud reverberations grated in his ears. "I love you," he nearly shouted. "I . . . I need *you.*"

The incredible near-static of the music finally began to die down, and Martin hoped the player's fingers had been bleeding when he made the recorded sounds.

"You told me you loved Leigh."

Leigh had laughed at him and ridiculed him. She had wanted him tonight, but that was an occasion as rare as his refusal. Nothing had changed. She made fun of him still. Tomorrow things would be as they always were, and when they made love it would be back to her act of masturbatory duty. She would heave and pant for a few obligatory minutes and turn over to fall asleep, the passion they held for one another now a mere biological easing of tension.

"I . . ." He felt beads of sweat on his forehead and rubbed his moist palms, blindly watching the spotlights wheel through the room. Those surroundings began to fog. Martin clutched for his voice, breathing heavily. "Leigh . . . Leigh and I have shared a lot, Jan. I . . . I love what she—" He trembled. In the beginning Leigh had teased him with innuendo and faint glimpses . . . and then the gift of her body.

Martin didn't show the tremor that tingled inside with another memory, forgotten in the years: Leigh on their third anniversary, somehow scraping together the money to buy him a new amplifier for the guitar he was already ignoring, encouraging him to play it, telling him how she admired his ability on the strings. He had meant his thanks so deeply then, feeling such love for her, embarrassed he had only gotten her that cheap twelve-carat gold necklace. The next day he hocked the new amp to buy her a necklace studded with diamonds. In turn she threatened with a laugh to hock it for his amplifier. It had been a strange fun they'd shared.

But Martin tried to forget those moments immediately. Hadn't it all just been part of her trick to tighten her snare?

"I love what she was—what we had together." He got it out briskly, almost harshly, wanting to forget those earlier times that were so far away.

Jan raised an eyebrow.

"I love you . . . now. I love what you *are,* Jan."

She cocked her head to the side, drooping the long lashes and looking into him seriously. "Do you, Marty? You said we barely knew each other, that you barely knew *me.*"

Those words flashed back. "Yeah. But you said we were the *same,* Jan. That we didn't need to talk. That we knew what we wanted." The freedom of this breakthrough was upon him, making him jittery and ecstatic all at once. The sudden gaping hole that swallowed up his hated past was quickly filled with his anticipation and excitement for Jan once more. He'd found her! *He had found her!* "You were right."

"I didn't want to leave you this morning." Her fingers squeezed his tightly.

"I love you, Jan." A moment passed, punctuated only by other murmuring patrons as the song came to its finale and the lights came back up. He blinked but didn't take his eyes away from that so-familiar face that gave him the peace he'd lost since last being with her. His study traced from her high cheekbones to her lips, and he remembered the way her tongue moved in and out of her mouth over them, and then she pulled him into her warm, giving throat.

"And the children?"

Martin shivered and shook his head. "Come on. You know it's not the same."

The gum-chewing waitress walked near and jogged Martin with her skinny elbow. "You're not quite finished with your beer, big eyes. I thought you wanted two."

Lifting her handbag from the floor, Jan nudged Martin's knee under the table. "I think we're just leaving."

The waitress raised her eyebrows, seeming to notice Jan for the first time with a faint surprise. She started to say something, then finally turned away.

Martin took the soft hand Jan held out to him, fighting the tremble her questions brought. For a moment her fingers felt like a bony ice, and he fought a new shudder. His foggy eyes saw again the impossible mirage of her on the lawn so early that morning: brown, flaking skin, withered, sparse hair . . . He felt in the middle of a dream that had turned its dark side to him at last. A *dream*. You make your own, Sally had said. Do-it-yourself dreams, like a kit-car, or the way he was restoring his Thunderbird.

He sighed with relief as the new hallucination ended, knowing it was from the pain in his foot and the aspirin he'd swallowed too much of.

Jan's careful eyes were serious now, and not like before. Not like Saturday, yesterday, or even this morning. They had given to him then. Even when they wanted, they only wanted to *give*. They were different. They wanted him more than before. They wanted him for keeps.

Wasn't that the same, though? Didn't she just want him to keep giving to him? She knew what he liked, what he wanted and needed.

Martin cleared his throat. "Well," he whispered, "what about your husband, Jan—didn't he come home today?"

Bright humor filled her throat. "Oh . . . yes. Yes, he did." Her face relaxed. "But he said he was tired. We went out for dinner because he doesn't like my cooking and came home and watched TV for an hour or so. He was so tired he went to bed so he wouldn't get in my way and I wouldn't disturb him while I cleaned the house." She curled her lip in a pout.

It seemed an overplayed pout to Martin, but the description of her mate's treatment of her reminded him of Leigh even though it hadn't been the case tonight. Wasn't tiredness the usual excuse? And it would go back to that, he was sure. Nothing changed. Nothing but him, and he only changed back, finding the self he'd lost over the difficult years.

"Can we go, Marty?"

She asked. It resurrected the tingling of the power she gave him, leaving him their leadership. She wanted him and wanted to please him, but she left it up to him.

"I need you, Marty," she told him. Her voice was sexy and full. Soft and low. Rich. "I need you, and I want you."

"Yes," he uttered, mesmerized by those full, shining lips and their renewed promise. "I—I want you, too. I came here to find you." He gulped, standing. His legs were empty like the rest of him, shaking for the fullness only she could give, the memory of all she meant to him. He felt the anxiousness Leigh was not able to meet, stood closer, wrapping his arms down around her until she seemed to become a part of him. He lowered his mouth over hers, not caring that the waitress watched them a few feet away.

They kissed, their tongues twisting and licking, making him hard. Jan scooted her chair closer and straddled him. Her legs pressed his hips into her where he wanted to be and where he wanted to stay. She was his meaning. His home, sweet home.

Sweating and red-faced, he forced himself to pull back. He wanted to rip off her yellow button-down top to see the color of what she was wearing underneath it today, to strip away that brown plaid pleated skirt to the bikini panties that hid her vast treasure. "S-so where do you want to go, then?" he gasped.

Letting him help her from her chair, she straightened the wrinkles in her hose, drawing the skirt up her left leg. "With you, Marty."

The skirt crept higher, past the clip-on stockings, up her naked thighs, until he could glimpse the unclad dark bush that called to him.

"I—" He caught his breath and held his hand out, stroking her thigh. "A . . . a motel?" he asked.

"Is that where you're taking me?"

He didn't trust himself to answer that invitation again in here, and he knew they had to get out now. Holding himself back from that tempting mouth, he led Jan quickly through the thin crowd to the front door, bumping a fat man and knocking his cowboy hat to the floor. Uneasy delirium pumped from Martin's brain to his body, bringing him goosebumps. He pulled Jan on, not looking back at slurred curses that followed him.

She put her arm around his waist, filling him with the warmth of her claim. His arm raised to drape itself over her shoulder, and she squeezed gently. They were together again in a world of their own.

It stung him with the thought of Will and Cissy at home with Leigh, who had wanted him tonight. But nothing changed.

No. Everything had changed. Leigh had changed. Cissy and Will had been born.

His life had changed.

But he was the same. Everything and everyone changed around him, leaving him alone, no one to share with.

The front door of the house was locked securely. He'd locked it when he left, leaving his old life safely inside. He'd shut it in and come here.

Marty squeezed Jan back as they went through the exit doors and into the night.

"I want to be with you, Marty." Her head lay on his shoulder as they continued to his car, the noise of the bar disappearing as the doors closed. "My life is such a prison. I had to get out, too, hoping you would be here. I had to get out to be with you."

Unrepentant passion stirred him. "I need you, too, Jan." The fluid summer air bathed him in its night humidity, but it felt good. They stopped at the passenger door, and he unlocked it.

What if Leigh woke up?

So what? The front door was locked tight. She and the kids were safe. That was his real responsibility, right? "I want to be with you," he sighed, meaning it and needing her. Jan had freed the self that Leigh trapped and kept captive in the prison of children and the comforts of material wealth. Trapped and dusty like his guitar in the closet.

Leigh had made him afraid to step off the beaten track,

but he had left that path now, moving into the terror of uncharted wilderness at Jan's side. She was freeing him for what life had stolen away.

He was stealing it back.

Moments passed, and then he opened the car door and stood back to let Jan in. Her secretive smile caressed him as she sank down into the squeaky cushion. He felt his heart thud, then held on to her promise as he shut the door and went around the Lynx, getting in beside her.

"We want the same thing," she breathed, gorging him with the erotic perfume of her touch, brought to life by her hand on his thigh.

He leaned into her, and their lips fused together. His hands renewed desperate acquaintance with the soft, firm build of her body, exploring her anew in a blind haste to return to the world he'd made in her.

Martin's hand slipped under her hemline, edging up her naked thigh as their excited kiss continued. He found her warm, moist hair.

"Oh," she exhaled, gasping hungrily. "Martin—"

She wanted him as much as he wanted her. She was more than ready for him! That intensity clouded each thought, and he forgot all else. He forgot where they were and no longer cared, breathlessly managing his way over the stick shift until they were squashed together in her seat. He didn't care who might be watching them outside the car. He didn't care about anything but this reunion that took him a million miles away from the horrid failure of life, and he squeezed his hips against hers with mounting desire, moving his lips onto her neck, then lower and lower until they nibbled at the soft rise of her breasts.

She squealed as Leigh never did, pinching her fingers into his shoulders and gasping. "I don't think . . . I . . . I can wait for . . . the motel, Marty."

Her voice was lost in his desire as he fumbled with the adjusting lever to lower the chair's back, and her legs spread as wide as they could. She pushed her sleek ass to the edge of the seat, pulling her dress up to meet his growth through the barrier of his slacks. Her hands groped with his belt and unfastened it, and then his pants, lowering the zipper and inching his cotton shorts down far enough to release his strain. Their nakedness met, and he pressed himself against her, feeling the head of his cock brush into her wetness, then deeper, inside her soft cavern. He pushed in and back, in and back, no longer aware of the discomfort of their confines, only wanting her and the release she would give him.

"Marty, *yes!*" She helped his motions. Their bellies met and separated, again and again, him shoving in deep and almost out, deeper.

He moaned, and they moved together as one.

17

The humid night became still hotter in their passion, steaming the windows until they couldn't see out. Then they talked at length for the first time since their meeting. He told her of his rapidly disintegrating marriage, about Leigh's enthusiasm for her job, his dwindling patience and interest in keeping things together.

And then he told her how he was trapped. "I've lost myself," he breathed. "I don't even play my guitar anymore. I've lost all my dreams."

It was why he'd gone out to find some companionship, even if only temporary.

She nodded as he laid his head on her damp lap. He shut his eyes against the headlights of cars entering and leaving the parking lot. "But it's up to us to make our dreams real, Marty. Only you can make them real."

Almost exactly what Sally had said years before.

But this was real. Instead of making his dreams real, he was making reality into his dreams.

"It's up to you, Marty," she said in the car's warm silence.

"But—" He started to tell her about Will and Cissy.

She stopped his words with the gentle strokes of her palms. "You'll never be able to break out of it if you keep going back to them. They're your excuse. That's why

I'm glad I can't have children, Marty. They're a guilt trip."

She was right. Sometimes lately, Leigh and the children even invaded his fantasies, begging him to stay true. They broke into his very slumbering thoughts and tried to keep him theirs. Leigh cried in his dreams.

But Jan allowed him only a moment of thoughtful silence. She tickled him, brought unwilling laughter.

"Don't," he cackled, twisting around to the driver's seat, bruising his thigh on the stick shift. *"Ow!"*

"Did you hurt yourself, Daddy? Poor, poor Daddy . . . See, I can be a much better child than any you dreamed of." She had bent over him casually, sliding her hard nipples through the hair on his legs. "Incest is best, Daddy dear. Your little girl will make it all better." Her tongue massaged him briskly, forcing him back to life. Her hot mouth encircled his renewing vitality. "I can make you feel lots better."

He froze. For an instant she seemed different, and a trick of the lighting and his mind made her appear the way Cissy might look ten years from now.

"Cissy—"

"Yes, Daddy." She laughed, "I'm every girl you ever wanted."

Her tongue covered his tingling flesh with a warm, wet twitch.

Martin blinked, feeling as though it was now.

It was now.

The room wobbled, and he felt her lips rubbing his tight cock flesh once more. He squirmed on the bed, arching himself into her mouth, feeling the steady suction of her cheeks.

Just like last night, when he'd stared at the glare of the bar's lights through the misty windshield and heard footsteps passing the car. He remembered seeing the outline of a couple passing not a foot from what Jan was doing for him.

And what she was doing for him now. Again.

He gasped. The lush burgundy drapes closed out sunlight,

and the room was gray in darkness; a faint ammonia of frequent cleaning drifted through the air. The big double bed Jan shared with him filled its northernmost end, flanked by the varnished nightstand that bore a plain white telephone on one side, and by closet doors at the other. Across the narrow room a scarred chest of drawers stood primly on the wearing gold carpet, waiting for use.

"Hi." Martin grinned sheepishly.

Releasing him and pulling away, she returned the smile.

Then Martin gasped again, his foot suddenly burning with pangs that disrupted every thought. "Oh, *shit!*" He jerked up stiffly. Her naked legs rubbed his, but he shivered under an honest chill as he tried to recall where they were. His dry mouth slid open as his eyes darted over the unfamiliar surroundings of the motel room he'd paid for with plastic. It would show up on his credit card statement. Leigh would see it.

"What's wrong with you, cowboy?" Jan pressed close, rubbing him with her breasts and bringing back the unbelieveable ecstasy she given him only hours before when they'd made it in his car.

It brought back his smile.

It was something he hadn't done since high school. He shifted carefully to ease the pain.

Jan snuggled to him on the plain white sheet, her eyes open and fastened on him with lazy exultation. She rolled on top of him, stroking his chest under the sheet. " 'Oh, shit'? Is that all you can say, stud?"

His eyelids were heavy with the weakness that made him little more than an appreciative corpse. He tried to hold the back of her head and force himself into her as deep as he could go. He felt her throat constrict about him. His balls quivered, and he tried to hold on to their buildup of ecstasy, knowing that when he let go she would swallow gladly.

Leigh would never do this.

Martin panted, then gurgled his pleasure as he exploded into her.

She kept sucking even when he was dry. He winced in the bliss it gave him and bit his lip to keep from crying out.

Then the tip of a sharp blade sheared through his joy, pinching hard.

She was still at him, making him hard yet again. She wanted more.

But this time it hurt.

"I know what you're thinking . . ."

Her voice in his ear startled Martin from his new doze in the motel room, and he choked. Cold sweat still covered his brow, but the piercing sting in his abdomen had finally shrunk to an extracting needle.

He had overdone it. That had to be the explanation. All the years with Leigh after their initial romance, he was lucky to have sex once a week. Usually less often than that. He didn't know the physiological side of it all, but he knew that arms and legs atrophied or became weakened through disuse. He knew it from his own experience of finding his waistline expanding two years ago. It annoyed him beyond having a difficult time fitting into his slacks because he didn't want to become fat like all the other middle-class guys. He didn't want that further proof and reminder of his imprisonment.

But the exercise program he began was just as bad and demeaning. It was a yuppie thing to do, and it was painful. For more than a week his muscles were sore and complained incessantly.

This was the same. He'd become so unused to the sexual experiences Jan was giving him, they *hurt.* He was already dead exhausted despite his sleep. The pain was just another gift from Leigh and her establishment world. They were the lingering chains she tried to draw him back with . . . like the nightmares of her "love."

Jan was lying beside him, and she sniffed when he didn't answer. "You're not paying attention to me, Marty."

He yawned and groaned, sitting up. "I was asleep." He grunted and blinked when she opened the curtains to bright sunlight. The way the shafts of light struck the bed gave him a bad feeling. "What . . . what time is it?"

She yawned and held her face up with a hand. "How

boring, Marty. Why do you care, anyway? You said you weren't going to work today."

The earlier agony of his climax had stirred him out of their bliss, and he had dreamed. Real dreams, not Sally dreams. He had dreamed with the bad guiltiness he still endured. His dark vision was of Leigh awakening to the empty bed he hadn't slept in.

"No," he mumbled, throwing the sheets and bedspread off his legs and scooting to the bed's edge. He moaned with the effort and the discomfort of sleeping on the hard mattress. He punched the mattress angrily, wishing they had gone to a motel with waterbeds, then draped his sleepy legs over the side and dangled them above the floor. "I—I just shouldn't have left Leigh like that with the kids, Jan. She had to go to work."

"Right," Jan replied, her mouth crooked in sarcasm.

Martin shook his head. "Look, Leigh was tired. She just got back from a rough week on a long business trip, and she woke up to find me gone. She's got to be worried. God damn, she's probably out of her mind! She had to go to work, and she had to take the kids to the sitter's!" He rested his elbows on his knees and his head in his hands.

"So?" Jan lay back down and crawled across the big bed toward him, then rested her chin on his thigh. Her fine hair draped over his leg as she scooted closer and pushed her tongue into his curly black sex hair. "So you left her to take care of the children—her children."

"They're mine, too. Damn it. She didn't even know where I was going. She probably thinks I was in an accident, that I'm hurt!"

"So what?" She slipped her fingers over him delicately, rubbing the sticky moistness he dribbled onto her thumb and sticking it into her mouth. "You taste great, tiger. Just great."

"Jan."

"So what, Marty? Didn't you watch those kids and take care of them all week while she was gone? Do you think you ought to be left taking care of them while your foot is hurt, too?" She laughed. "If that's parenthood and marriage, then the whole thing's a crock, Marty."

"But"—her words stayed in his head with soothing justification—"but it's not fair to make her worry like that, Jan."

Her snort was dainty. She licked his raw skin briskly before looking back up. "Worry? You've got that all wrong, Marty. If she was worried, then she wouldn't have ever left you alone last week. It's all in your head, Marty. She was gone for days. You're gone a few hours, and you think she should be worried?"

"It's not the same. At least I knew where she was, Jan. Hell, she has no idea of where I am or what I'm doing."

"A good thing for her, too."

His eyebrow came down, refusing her joke. He wanted to agree with what she was saying, but it didn't seem the same. He had at least known where she—"I knew where she was, though, and what she was doing. God damn, she was working." He felt dismay at the extent of his betrayal.

"Maybe." Jan smiled secretly again, lowering her long lashes. "You knew what city she was in, at least, right? But she wasn't in her motel room all that time, and she wasn't working all the time was she, Marty? She didn't work twenty-four hours a day." Jan turned back over and made a clucking sound in her throat. "And while she enjoyed herself without the strains of responsibility, you took care of the house and family for her, keeping it up for her. Am I right?" Her voice lowered slyly. "Martin, you don't have any idea of everything she was doing, do you?"

His frown grew deeper, and he remembered the doubts he allowed when he called late at night to her hotel. Like on that Friday night, when he'd come home rejected so harshly by the woman at the bar.

"I don't think she'd do what we're doing."

Jan's smile was dark and forbiding. "But you don't know, Marty. Why shouldn't she play around a little? You said things hadn't been going so well between the two of you, and women get their urges from time to time." She reached for him and cupped his palm under her breast, rubbing his thumb over her standing nipple. "I know that very well. Look at me, Marty. I'm married, and you're not exactly my husband."

Jan's insinuations made him see Leigh's unknown co-worker as a suave Romeo, handsome and muscled enough to have popped out of a *Playgirl* magazine. When Martin called and she wasn't there she had been out with Tom and clients. Or maybe just Tom. And maybe not out at all, but in his room and bed as he filled her and slid up and down on top of her, bringing her the fulfillment she refused to let Martin give her, giving Tom the pleasures she wouldn't allow him.

And maybe the clients, too. Maybe a gang-bang with her taking men in every way imaginable, as often as possible.

But he didn't know that she had. It seemed very unlike Leigh.

"I bet that's the reason she was so horny last night, you know it? She was tired, but she was guilty, too, Marty. If she was really so tired, don't you think she just would have wanted to sleep?"

Yes. When she was tired she didn't want to fuck. That was her most frequent excuse, and she'd told him she was very tired last night. He grunted and wondered.

"Hell, Marty, ask me. I'm a woman, and I know how women think. If you believe she withstood all the opportunities that present themselves on a long business trip, you're living in a dream world."

Dreams again. But the dream that Jan suggested was not like Sally's any more than those of his short sleep. They were the nightmares of his gullibility, the nightmares he had never really believed in.

The floor blurred into imagination: Leigh with Tom, with clients who were rich, attractive men and who smiled at her modest figure. He could see her flirting with them, going out to dinner with them, drinking, being escorted to their homes and rooms, to their beds, or maybe just making it in their cars, like he and Jan had done. He could see Leigh slipping off her dress, spreading her legs wide, and welcoming each one. Maybe even three at a time.

She would squeal in ecstasy.

His face wrinkled with hot tears as he guessed at the reason she had refused him all these past years. She was tired, just as he was now. She was tired from her extracurricular fucking, and then she played the part of innocent modesty to him, keeping up her image with church and nightly prayers.

And she probably even fucked that preacher she was so fond of after the sermons, then sucked him dry.

The room was quiet.

"Women get just as horny as men do, Marty. If she wasn't doing it with you, she was doing it with someone else."

He shook his head. "No. Not Leigh." He groaned, hurt by the possibility of her dual life while he languished and disintegrated in his prison. "N-no. She . . . she goes to church—she won't even watch a porn movie or say 'fuck.' She wouldn't—"

Jan just smiled and licked her lips.

He kept his eyes closed tight. Women *did* get just as horny as men did, and Jan proved it. If Leigh never seemed horny, always tired, it had to be because—

"Marty?" Jan's voice slithered to his ear, bringing him out of his thoughts. "You . . . you still want her, don't you? You want her instead of me."

He looked up, the growing doubts making lines on his face. Leigh never wanted him because she was tired from all the other men in her life! "No," he growled, letting the anger out at last. "No. I don't fucking care what she does . . . or *who* she does!"

Jan hugged him, rubbing his tense muscles with tender love. "Easy there." Her nipples pressed into his chest. "I know how it is, love. I've been there. It hurts. It hurts a lot. It's like high school graduation, when you know you're on your own at last, and that all your friends are going away and things will never be the same. It's a lot like that. You and

Leigh have been married a long time and have drifted apart. You've changed."

Martin shook his head vehemently. "No . . . no. She's changed, Jan. That's the whole damn problem." He thought of how she disrupted his life so violently, turning him into the very thing he hated—that she knew he hated! "She's changed, and I'm the same. I want to be the same!"

"That's why I want you, darling," she whispered, pressing him down to lie on his back. She kept her face close. "Because you want what I want. You want what you are, and I want you, too." She let their lips meld.

"I want *you.*"

"Yes," she breathed. "So it isn't all bad, is it? You have me, and you still have yourself. The thing with your wife is over with whether you want to admit it or not. But you're not alone, darling. You'll always have me."

Snorting, he shook his head and swallowed. "And I'll always have myself, right? But will I really always have you, Jan? It could be just like when I married Leigh. Till death do us part, but only if you're ninety years old when you tie that knot."

"Your marriage is dead, though, isn't it, Marty? If it is, then in death you do part, right?"

His jaw worked.

"And you and I aren't married, Marty. We just *are.* We don't need to be married. Like I said before, we're alike, you and me. We were made from the same mold."

Martin tried to smile.

"Like two peas in a pod, Marty."

His feeble grin faded in the memory of what she had done to Cissy's peas in the restaurant, how she had smashed them with her fork.

Jan shifted to the other side of the mattress, only her legs touching him now. "But you'll have to talk to her, Marty. You'll have to be firm. You and I could start over together, but you'll have to be firm with her. Leigh may not understand it like we do. She may not be ready to understand, and you might have to convince her. After all, she's got it pretty good, doesn't she? Keeping you home like her prisoner to watch her kids and take care of things she doesn't want to do?"

The words were the same as the thoughts that warned him so often. Jan's face faded into the appearance of Leigh's and back again. Back and forth. Distorting, fuzzy. He breathed deep.

"Tell her about me, Marty. About us. Tell her you love me. Tell her you just don't feel that way about her anymore. Tell her how I make you feel, and how we're so true and real together. Tell her you love me."

"I . . . I do love you, Jan."

"Yes. And we need each other. We need each other to be who we are. We need each other to feed our dream."

"Yes."

"Then tell her, Marty. Break it off with her."

The words crawled through his mind, furrowing his brow. They threatened the security of the despair he'd lived in and grown accustomed to, even the small pleasure he still sometimes found. "What about your husband?"

"If you go through with it, Marty, I'll be waiting for you. I promise you that. I won't back out." She rose and mashed her body into his, then kissed him. "I promise you."

A sigh arched in the back of his throat. He chuckled.

Jan smiled, letting her moist tongue play on his cheek. "What's so funny, stud?"

"I don't even know your last name."

She shared the barren humor but gave it life with full, boisterous giggles. "Is that important with all that we mean to each other, Marty?" She poked his nose with the tip of her tongue. "Soon I'll be wearing your last name, lover." The mattress creaked under them as she lay on top of him, pinning him down and rubbing her naked shins into his.

"But if I want—need—to call you . . ."

"I'll be there," she promised. "I'll know. We're just alike, remember? I know what you want, and you know what I want."

"Yeah." Her grinding motions were exciting him once

more, and he forgot the pain of the last time, gulping air as he became stiff and she centered herself over him.

"I know what you want now, Marty." She pushed down around him with tight, wet muscles that matched his motions perfectly, pumping him faster and faster.

"It feels so great!"

"I know, darling Marty."

18

You can make your dreams real; just call your Visa number in to the office of cosmic law.

This was no dream, though. Dreams were dreams, and real was real, and he knew the things happening in his life were real because he wasn't waking up. Jan was real. The dread and sorrow he felt at breaking up his family was real, too. It hurt as only real things could.

The greatest reality was that he did not love Leigh anymore. He told himself that whether she had other lovers or not was unimportant. If he really loved her and it was true, he thought he might be able to live with that. But actually, the rejection and anger that had filled him a few hours ago was only bitterness over the fact that he had remained so blind to her certain outside romances all these years, that he had held himself back from his own needs because of her.

The watch on Martin's wrist read two thirty-seven when he parked in the driveway. He closed the car up and looked at the red brick and blue-gray walls with a long, studied stare, knowing Leigh would want the house, just like she'd want to keep Cissy and Will. She'd loved the place the minute she set eyes on it and had tightened her snare over him with the payments it entailed. It was part of her trap, and even if she offered it to him on a silver platter, he wouldn't want it.

"You get the house, Leigh, girl," he sighed, walking past the torn-apart T-bird, "I get the old car." Yes, and he'd get the Lynx, too, while she kept her Town and Country wagon. Under the circumstances, she'd probably get custody of the children as well, though he might get Will if he put up a good fight and got a good attorney.

But was that fair? With everything else the two children would be going through, was it right to separate them?

Reaching out to an unkempt hedge as he came to the porch, he ground his teeth hard, ignoring the stab it brought. It would be better to leave the children together. Despite frequent bickering, they got along well and would each need the other as a stationary point during the coming transition. Besides, he remembered Jan's cool aloofness to kids, feeling certain she wouldn't care too much to have them around every day.

That knowledge was an open sore inside him as he found the right key, opened the door, moved inside, and closed it again. He only hoped she might relax a bit once she got to know them. Though they were the flypaper that held him in the trap so firmly, it was because he loved them both, and they loved him. Leigh was the hunter who had bagged him, and they were only the unsuspecting and innocent by-products of her wiles. Those times when he hated them and wished they would disappear into the womb they'd come out of never lasted long. He understood that his prison was theirs, too, so he tried harder with them and wouldn't write them off as he would Leigh. No matter what else happened, he was their father. He was the one who played games with them and took care of them most of the time, and it angered him to leave them to Leigh.

Martin threw his keys against the screen door with a loud smack. He wanted to kick the damn door in but overcame the bitterness and limped to pick the keys up again. He was shaking as he fit them into the lock and opened the door.

He stumbled inside the empty house, breathing shallowly

against the agonies crushing his heart. He staggered to the divan, half falling onto it.

Will and Cissy.

Cissy and Will.

"You'll probably get to have them every weekend if you want," Jan had sniffed when they'd talked about it. "And you'll get them for half the holidays, at least. It's not like you're abandoning them, Marty." Even so, he could feel her attitude and that she wished he *would* abandon them, and that she only said what she did to make things easier. To ease his mind because she loved him.

"You'll like them once you get to know them," he'd told her.

Jan just smiled coyly, her eyes condescending as they shone near laughter.

Shaking that scene out of his head, he scooted up on the divan and stood up too fast. A searing eruption rocketed out from his arch and into his toes. It was like his entire lower leg was a stick of dynamite whose fuse had run out. He hollered, deafened by those echoes as he tried to fight the surge of wet blackness dropping over him. He fought his senses to take his weight off the damaged foot, grabbing the slick wall. Blood drained from his face, and he tried to stay put, breathing deep in the violence that brought out the hell of emotions that struck his heart with a sledgehammer.

The pictures of Cissy and Will on the coffee table drew near, then swam across the room in his vision, then back, then pulling farther away than before.

He choked.

It wasn't like he was going to divorce them! They were his children as much as Leigh's. He had made them with her, and his blood flowed through them as much as hers did.

He would always be their daddy.

When he caught his breath enough to limp to the hall, Martin looked through the house, already feeling a stranger. The door to his and Leigh's room was partially open, and he stuck his head inside, seeing her robe on the floor and the unmade bed he had refused to share with her last night.

He closed the door swiftly, continuing on to Will's room. He stared inside in the house's oppressive silence.

Toys cluttered the floor as though a cyclone had blown through, and the broken pieces of Darth Vader remained where his foot had crushed the doll. Recollections of sounds of play drifted into his ears, and he half expected Will to appear in the middle of the mess.

Martin shut his eyes hard and bunched his fists. He thought of Jan instead, hearing her words of promise and love.

Pulling the door shut, he started back to Cissy's room and then stopped. Why was he putting himself through this, as though he would never see them again? "Damn," he gasped.

He hadn't even talked to Leigh yet.

A new and harsher guilt pricked him, and he knew he had to call her now. Leigh had awakened alone this morning with no explanation of his absence.

He hadn't even called in to work.

Pressure built in him at his failure to do even that, and he limped back to the living room, dropping into the high-backed cushion chair beside one of the phones. He picked up the receiver as queasy skyrockets took flight in his intestines. His fingers pressed the buttons and stopped, and he shook his head. It would be better to call work first. Hanging up, he fumbled with the buttons once more and waited as the line rang, hoping Leigh hadn't called there looking for him.

"Dex Sales," answered a bright girlish voice.

"Cara?" He cleared his throat. "Cara, this is Martin. Let me talk to Sam—"

"Oh, hi, Marty. Are you okay? Leigh called this morning and said you went out last night in the car and hadn't come back home. She was afraid you might have had a wreck with your foot hurt, and—"

His eyebrows tangled as he thought quickly. "No." He tried to chuckle and made a face at his sound. "I, uh, was checking the car. I did some work on it Sunday and wanted to be sure it would run." What now? "I . . . the damn thing died on me downtown." He tried to make up the words faster. "I was out there with a conked-out car late at night, and my foot was hurting. I . . . I didn't think I could make it to a phone booth. I didn't even know where one was."

"Downtown?" Cara's voice was appalled. "At night? That's not safe, Marty. Winos and creeps hang around there after dark."

"Yeah," he answered readily, groping for a way out. "Yeah, I saw some of them. I didn't want to get out of the car. I just . . . I locked the doors and laid back in my seat watching those guys . . . listening to them talk about Ripple and drugs . . . and . . . I fell asleep."

"You're kidding! You were out there all night and you fell asleep with those creeps right on top of you? Weren't you scared?"

He enjoyed the awe and respect in her tone. It steadied him. "A little bit, sure. But I was exhausted, and it got damn chilly." He stopped and breathed, overjoyed that she had bought his unprepared fib so readily. "A cop woke me up this morning, hammering on the window. He helped me get the car to a garage to get it running. I know I should have called earlier, but my foot was like it was on fire, and I—"

"Are you home now?" Her voice spoke a concern that surprised him.

"Yeah. I just got here. I went to the emergency room, and a doctor looked at my foot and gave me a prescription."

"Which hospital?"

He hesitated, knowing he was making his story too elaborate. "I . . . I guess it was St. John's or Hillcrest. I . . . I don't remember. I came straight home. I should have called from the hospital."

"I wish you had. We've been pretty worried. Leigh is frantic, Marty. She called again a few minutes ago and said she was going to phone the police to look for you. Have you called her yet, Marty?"

"Not yet. I wanted to get in touch with Sam first and—"

"Better hang up and give her a call, Marty. She's worried."

"Well, I wanted to explain to Sam—"

He could tell Cara was shaking her head. "I'll talk to him,

Marty. Don't worry about it. I'm just glad you're okay. I missed you yesterday. You hardly ever *don't* come in, and I really missed teasing you. I really like you, you know that?"

Her admission surprised him. "It's hard to tell sometimes."

"I wouldn't tease you so much if I didn't. In a lot of ways I'm just a kid. But hey, call Leigh right now, and I'll speak to Sam. Don't worry about it. You just get to feeling better."

"Well, I—"

"Jesus, Marty. That must have been so weird for you! I'm sure glad you're okay. Now hang up and call Leigh. Don't worry about us—everything's going great here."

"Thanks, Cara."

"Bye-bye. Call Leigh."

"Bye," he said, sighing, and he heard the click of the line as she disconnected.

Lying keeps everything running smoothly.

Martin sighed, smiling faintly at the memory of Jan's philosophy, and went over his fabrication again, keeping it clear in his thoughts. He could tell it to Leigh.

He didn't have to mention Jan at all.

The choice still awaited him, and he knew it wasn't too late to back down. He thought of Cissy and Will, of Will's room and the toys all over the floor. He could call Leigh with that story.

It might raise her eyebrows, but he knew he could smooth things over and that life would go on as it had.

Never changing. The chance to be what he wanted was now. His opportunity, perhaps his only opportunity, was *now.*

Otherwise nothing would ever change.

"Jan!" he cried out hoarsely, staring into the draw of the familiar furniture and decor all around him, then shutting it out with closed eyes. He didn't even know her last name and would lose her forever.

Forever.

If he smoothed things over with Leigh, how could he face Jan? How could he tell her he didn't love her enough to go through with their plans? How could he do that to himself?

Picking up the receiver again, he held it against his face and choked back a sob, thinking of the promises he'd made to Jan and the promise she was to him. He needed her, and she needed him! She told him so again and again.

Things were so much more real with her. He noticed more, felt more, felt *better!* It was a reality that brought him to his peak, to himself. It was a world they made for each other in which he could be that self.

And did Leigh need him?

Rather than stay away from her job to look for him and try to find out what had happened to him, she had merely made a couple of phone calls. She was at work now, had probably made those calls from her desk instead of this house.

His thoughts became more bitter. If she really loved and needed him, would she have gone to work with him missing?

He punched the phone's buttons forcefully.

"Zelasco Advertising. This is Leigh."

"This is Martin," he replied, his lips dry.

"Martin?" Her voice became hushed. "Martin, are you okay? You sound strange. Where—where are you?"

The whine in her tone slapped him, and he shoved it back. He concentrated on the way she was betraying him. "I'm at the house. I've never . . . never been better."

Her voice blustered a sound of confusion like a car's uncertain ignition, then turned edgy and high. "But . . . where have you been? You n-never even came home last night! I heard you leave, Marty . . . and I tried to stay awake to wait for you, b-but—*where have you been?*"

Her anxiousness approached hostility, but Martin only yawned. For a moment he started to tell her the facts, then shut his mouth and tapped his fingers on the wall loudly. Instead he spoke the words she had said to him countless times in the past when he tried to describe his problems to her during work hours. "We'll talk about it when you get home . . . dear."

"We what?"

"After five o'clock, Leigh. Your boss isn't paying you to deal with personal matters, is he?" An intense outbreak of satisfaction flooded through him at this table-turning. He felt the smile that had already pushed out most of his fearful doubts. "And don't forget to pick up the kids," he added, again using her words in fiendish delight. "Gotta go."

"Martin! Talk to me! Where were you last night—this morning?"

He enjoyed their exchanged roles. "When you get home, Leigh. Please, you're on the job right now. You've got to work for a living, remember?" Before she could answer he dropped the phone into its cradle and chuckled at it.

Martin only wished he could have seen her face.

His smile grew and he leaned back on the cushion, laying his head back and shutting his eyes, relaxing in the strength he felt blossoming on his side. Leigh had come back from a business trip, spending her time doing God knew what, and here she was irritated at him for being gone a matter of hours!

Listening to the reassuring pump of his heart as he waited in the silent house, Martin tried to imagine her reaction to him, satisfying himself with predictions of how her face would twist and turn when he gave her the truth about Jan and what he'd done with Jan this morning, the night before, the day before, and a night beyond that. He would explain his past days in detail so Leigh could compare his new partner to whoever she was fucking around with last week, and maybe for years before that.

He would enjoy the shock on her face then.

19

The chair was uncomfortable now, but Martin stayed in it stiffly. He had set Leigh's photo portrait on the coffee table beside Will's and Cissy's. Their frozen stares met his, and he saw all the fighting and the problems of the past years. He saw Leigh's anger when he had bought the set of James Bond tapes, becoming a virtual ice storm that settled over their waterbed for two months, turning the nights into a hard, frigid hell.

She had slept nude then, too. Every night, taunting him with her body that she wouldn't even let him touch. He refused the nicer memories that had preceded and even surrounded that time. It wasn't the time to weaken himself with those thoughts now.

And Cissy, begging him to take her to the malls and parties with her friends, squalling when he had something else planned.

Will, constantly wanting him to play with stupid GI Joe or one of his kid games.

Martin felt all the heartaches and heard the bitter words, but most of all he felt the pain of pretending to be someone he wasn't. Even when those moments turned to pleasure, especially with the children, they bothered him because they were moments beyond his control. He had suffered with the guilt of his dissatisfaction for years. He had thought there was something wrong with *him.*

Now he felt guilt because he was about to throw off the falsehoods that had trapped him. The full awareness had come, and even if he stayed with his family and rejected Jan, that pain would fester larger and larger as he was forced to work harder and harder to keep everything together.

There would be no end.

Maybe lies did make the world go round, but now that he was wide-eyed with the truth of his life he could lie to himself no longer.

The portraits glared at him, accused him.

Wasn't it better to stop pretending before it fell apart on its own? Wasn't a planned withdrawal better than an all-out rout that would follow the Armageddon he and Leigh had been nearing for years? Wasn't it better doing this the way the United States had retreated from the unending destruction in Vietnam that couldn't be won except at the expense of complete obliteration?

This was the choice he was left with. Martin could get out now that the chance had arisen, with hope for everyone concerned still remaining, or wait until either he or Leigh emerged the bruised but empty-handed victor from the pointless battle they waged, hurting the innocent bystanders, their children, more deeply than the sudden separation he planned.

"Be with me, Jan," he whispered, looking away from Leigh's photograph and thinking of her instead.

It was better this way.

Martin stood up and limped to the wall mirror over the credenza. He studied his worn features, guessing at the lines Leigh and the kids had put into his face.

There were a lot of them. Deep creases in his forehead from endless frowns, circles colored black under his eyes, far more than a man his age should bear.

He gulped at a lumbering icicle that hung in his stomach. It seemed there were far more wrinkles mapping his experiences now than the last time he looked. And more gray hairs.

It even seemed that his hairline had moved further back on his scalp.

Martin blinked, swallowing the sour, gummy spit that wanted to drool from his mouth. He backed away from the reflection, holding out his hands as it seemed to come closer instead of mimicking him and moving father away.

He was tired. Just fucking tired—

Tired from fucking.

The words played in his brain and coerced a chortle. He gave in, trying to drive the ludicrous insanity away. He had been through a lot these past days, too much. He was exhausted, worn down even by the freedom and pleasure he so needed but had lost the stamina for. The exertions showed, but he knew that in Jan's presence they would dissipate and virility would increase. It was already increased beyond what he had ever dreamed possible!

The doorknob rattled as he stood silently. He jerked back but caught himself before his foot screamed again. He backed to the couch, easing onto it when the door squeaked open and crashed hard into the wall.

"I'm first!" Will belted out.

"Cheater!" whined Cissy, entering the house on his heels.

Martin froze, looking into the entryway. Both of them ran into the room, their feet loud on the carpet. Will was still in the lead, Cissy struggling to keep up as she tried to keep the schoolbooks under her arm.

"Daddy!" cried Will, running to him. "Why didn't you come get us? Mommy isn't fun in the car like you are. She griped us out!"

Martin touched Will's reaching hand gently and drew him close, kissing his cheek. "I'm sorry," he said, then he held out his hand to Cissy.

"Yeah," Cissy complained. "She won't let us watch TV tonight 'cause we talked in the car!" She bulged her cheeks ridiculously in a morbid frown. "It's not fair 'cause you let us talk, Daddy!"

It was going to be hard. The turbulent volcano already replacing the ice in Martin's stomach only let him guess how hard. "Your . . . your mother's had a hard day, Cissy." He fought himself and said it charitably, hoping to set the mood for his later revelation. "She's not used to—"

"Yeah. She's blown a fuse 'cause she had to come get us and you weren't here this morning!"

"Cissy, go to your room! I won't have you talk about me that way!" Leigh slammed the door, her hair damp with the sweat on her forehead. "You, too, Will!"

"I'm hungry," Will moaned.

Leigh wiped her face, setting her purse on the credenza where the goblet had rested before. *"Later."*

The children turned to Martin.

"Don't expect Daddy to save you. Now!"

He ignored their sullen eyes as best he could. "You heard your mother," he said, feeling the way their faces puffed and pouted. They shuffled to the hall dejectedly.

"I'm hungry, too," Cissy whimpered.

"We—we'll get your dinner in a little while, kids," Martin cut in.

When the bedroom doors closed, Leigh walked to the divan and collapsed on it. Her eyes moved up and down him uncertainly. A long minute crept around them before she found a weak smile. "Well?"

"Well?" he replied stiffly.

"Don't, Marty. Please. The air conditioner quit in my car on the way to get them, and it's hot out there. That and listening to their constant jabber—"

"Well, what?" He repeated. He thought of the fable he'd told Cara and how he could make things smooth if he told it to Leigh. He could sweep the past hours under the rug as if they had never occurred.

He would never see Jan again.

She made a clicking noise in her throat and put her hands together. "Marty . . . I've been so worried. What happened? You didn't have a wreck, did—"

He shook his head.

"I was so worried. I . . . I didn't know what to do when I found you gone, and—"

"So you went to work, right?"

Leigh reddened. "I didn't know what to do. I called your office, and . . ." She sniffled loudly. "God, Martin, what could I do? I even called the hospitals! I was af-f-fraid. I—I was going to call the *police—"*

"I just went out for a drive," he whispered, trying to stay calm. His thoughts shot to Jan and the aging face he'd seen in the mirror. His face. It was the age Leigh had given him, along with all the other shit in this prison. Just like the guilt she was making him feel now, when all he was doing was trying to be what he was.

"For"—her eyes went huge—"a drive? A drive that long?"

Martin reached into his jacket for his pack of Winstons, took one out, and lit it. He exhaled in silence.

Leigh's face was an acrobat in the contortions that charged the gamut of emotion. "Just a d-drive?" A tear wobbled in her eyes and fell to her cheek. Her hands trembled. "Martin . . . what is wrong with you? A . . . a drive? D-do you know what you've put me through, Martin? Where have you been? *Where were you?"*

He felt nothing. Her hoarse pleas grated in his ears but brought no guilt.

He didn't love her. Jan was right. His marriage had died and only awaited burial. Till death did he part, and now he had to walk away from the spoiling mess of their lives together before he rotted with it. "You mean last night?"

"Of . . . of course I mean last night!"

A tremor jiggled inside him as he took a deep breath. What he said next was the final epitath as this coffin was lowered into the earth. "I was . . . was with Jan."

"Jan?" Leigh's eyes slid wider, her lips twisting into a small circle of confusion. "Jan? Jan *who?"* She sat up and forward. "Who's Jan?"

Martin put his hands together and rubbed them. "Aunt Jan."

"Aunt—" Her features wobbled again, her eyes flitting from him to search the room. "The *ghost?"*

"No ghost. She's real, Leigh."

"This is no time—"

"I don't know why the kids said what they did about her, Leigh. She's real. A real person. You don't know her. I met her Saturday night, at a bar."

"You what?"

Martin dropped his eyelids, satisfied at her puzzled disbelief. He could see Jan's long auburn hair dangling around her breasts. Her perfect tan. He remembered her softness, the giving wet skin that squeezed him more firmly than Leigh ever could. "I met her in a bar. I tried to call you before I left that night, and you weren't in your room. You were never in your room when I called, Leigh."

"Yes I was!"

"The first night," he amended. "But after that I never knew where you were. Just like you didn't know where I was last night."

"Is that what this is all about, Martin?" Leigh asked, dropping her jaw. "Are you trying to get back at me?" The vexation of her features quieted, and she relaxed, beginning a gentle, relieved smile. "I didn't even think about it, Martin. I'm sorry. I really am. It was a business trip, you know? I was so caught up in it and so tired."

Just like when he wanted to fuck her, always so tired. "That's not what this is all about, Leigh."

"God, if I'd known, Martin—I didn't even think—"

"I did meet a woman named Jan, Leigh, and I was with her last night. I slept with her last night and the night before, ever since Saturday. I fucked her, and she sucked me dry."

Leigh's mouth was still open, but she made no sound. She just stared at him.

Martin gulped the saliva filling his mouth with a choke.

Leigh stared.

"I love her."

The silence that followed stretched on. They stared at each other, but she still wouldn't speak. Her eyes shone, and tears were dropping fast now, running beside her small nose to her mouth, to her chin. She looked like an actress in a soap opera.

Anger roared through him in the accusation she would not voice. It battered into his heart, ripping away the cobwebs of confusion, but at the same time it stopped him from saying more. Martin wished that Jan were there with him and clenched his right hand.

"M-Martin?" Her voice was shaking. "Martin, why—what . . . what d-do you mean?"

He kept his distance. "Things have been bad, Leigh. You know that. You told me they were bad, and that's why you were taking your fucking trip. I was alone, more than ever. I couldn't even pretend I wasn't this time. I needed to talk to someone, to be with someone. I want to share my life with someone, and share her life, too. Hell"—he slammed his fist against the arm of a chair—"I couldn't even get you on the phone to *talk* to you. Not even when you're right here in town! And when I could, you didn't want to because you were busy!"

"Marti—"

"I needed somebody!"

"I've always tried to there for you, Marty." Leigh bent over her knees and touched her fingers to her temples. She looked like one of the abandoned dolls in Cissy's closet. "I've made my mistakes, but I—I've tried. I've tried *hard.* I want us to make it!" She covered her face, and her voice crumbled. "But my God, Marty, I—I was gone less than a week. I didn't even know—you could've said something, c-couldn't you?"

His lips pulled back grimly. "I tried to. You were too busy to talk."

She shuddered.

"You were always too fucking busy!"

"But Marty—one week! You can't . . . throw away ten years on a week!"

Her face was red now. Red and blotchy, torn from her safety zone at last. The wrinkles around her eyes and mouth were spreading, giving her back the age she forced on him and that he'd witnessed in the entry mirror. With effort, he stopped the smile it tempted. "It's not just *one* fucking week," he fired back. "It's the whole last year. The years before that! Goddammit, this has been happening ever since Cissy was born! You put the kids first. Then when I started to take care of them more, to give you the time you said you needed, you got that damn job and got all involved in that. And then you leave town, and you weren't even in your goddam motel room when I called!"

"I'm trying to get a promotion! I'm trying to make things easier on us. We'll have more time together in the future! So we'll have more time with Will and Cissy—"

He laughed without humor. "And what about *now?*"

Her red eyes were blank.

It was over. He knew, and now she knew it. It was painful, but he was escaping from her trap as surely as a desperate rabbit chewing off its captured leg. It hurt bad, but somehow dragging this out was making him feel good. He liked throwing it back at her, letting her know why this was happening and that he knew her trap.

"You had me where you wanted me, here at home with all the responsibility, and me not knowing where you were or *who* you were with! But you went too far. I need someone, goddammit, and I need to be myself! I had to get out. I had to talk to someone!"

Leigh got down on her knees, holding her hands up to him and bowing her head as though he were some god revealing himself.

Martin spat. "Jan talked to me, and she listened to me . . . and . . . she wanted me!" He swept his hand over the room and pointed down the hallway, "I brought her *here.*"

Leigh's face crumpled under his admission.

"I fucked her in our bed, Leigh. She couldn't get enough of me. She begged me for more. I gave her what she needed, and she gave me what I need. Not like you. She needs me. She loves *me.* She loves me for who and what I am, not what she wants to make me!" He turned away. "I need her."

"And . . . you're going to throw away ten . . . years of marriage on a woman you've known only three days?" Her voice trembled.

He didn't even know her last name or where she was now.

"Three days." He twisted the knife. "I was resurrected from the dead in three days."

She was already shaking all over. "Why, Martin—*why?*"

"Because I love her. Because she lets me be myself." He tried to load the meaning of his feelings into his tone. "I need to be who I am!"

Her cheeks fluttered, flinging off teardrops. She cringed from him. "What . . . what about *us,* Martin?"

Jan was strong inside him. He could feel her enveloping him like a protective shield. Her smell was deep in his nostrils. It gave him power. She wanted him and what he wanted. He was important to her. She would never go off for even a day and leave him alone like Leigh had. "I don't think . . . I love you, Leigh." He chewed his lower lip, hard enough to hurt. "I *don't* love you."

Her outstretched hands shivered. She sniffed and let the tears roll down her nose, down her cheeks. They dribbled off her chin to her neck. She looked more vulnerable than he'd ever imagined her. The red of her face had disappeared, replaced by a pale shade that made her look like the walking dead. "I . . . I'm going to make dinner, Martin," she gasped, not looking at him. "Cissy and Will . . . are hungry." She cut short a sob, "Are you going . . . to eat with us?"

The sudden formality was the wall he'd just erected, and a part of him instantly regretted it. But it was the regret of uncertainty that binds the pigeon the first time he's set free. Jan was his freedom. He was *free,* and now he could stay a little longer in that liberation, knowing he *could* leave. "If you don't mind."

Their eyes stayed together in that final moment, closing the doors that were half shut already. Then she sniffed, going to the kitchen. "Would . . . would you set the table, Martin?"

The simple request in her tone annoyed him, and he stopped dead. It was a last-ditch snare. He squeezed his fingers together until they hurt. That frown overtook his whole face. "As usual, you mean? Just like nothing has happened and we're still the same old family? I set the table and you cook the fucking meals, except when you go out of town and I have to do both and wash the dishes." He stomped his feet and stopped within an inch of her, hating the smell of her hot breath as more tears stuttered from her throat. "Why don't you just get used to doing it all *yourself?*" He stuck his hands in his pockets, clamping fingers around his keys.

"M-Marty—" Her hands were frantic as she clutched at his shirt. "I—I'm sorry. I will—I *will* do it—"

For that bare instant he seemed to feel her earnest pleading tug him back into her world, felt her promise that they could continue. He wondered if he had made a mistake, recalling each year behind them and what they'd been to each other.

Desperately he pulled his heart back from her misery, then faltered once more, reaching out to her. "Leigh—"

"Marty," she cried, closing her arms around him.

Like a trap.

It was bad, but it was real. If he gave in, it would be bad for Jan too. His decision would crush her, and he would be cheating himself of the promises she made him. The problem was that if he stayed, it would get worse, and if he went to Jan, it would get worse, too.

But only for a while. The wounds would heal under her care. The bad would get better.

"I think I ought to go."

Her mouth worked as though she wanted to say something, many things, but she didn't. She held out a hand cautiously, taking a tiny step to him.

"No. Don't, Leigh. It's *over.*"

She stopped and bowed her head, not moving while he walked to the front door. "Marty? Sa—say goodnight . . . to the kids . . . okay?"

His throat was tighter. Turning back, he saw her as if she were a widow weeping for her husband. He limped back a step. "The kids," he whispered. He twisted to look at their shut doors in the hall, then swallowed heavily past the lump that was expanding in his throat. He couldn't face them now. It would be too much, and he knew he couldn't handle the doubts that would come from breaking this news to them. Their tears would add to the pressure to give this rat race another try, and it was a chance long gone. Leigh had used him and had used them to keep him.

She was trying to do it again.

When Leigh explained to them what had happened it would hurt them, perhaps even more without him there. But he couldn't bear it any more than they. It was all Leigh's fault, and he refused to accept that responsibility. Leigh had made the bed, and despite the cruelty he felt for the way he was forced to do this, it might just help her learn from her mistakes to have to lie in it.

Alone.

"Good-bye, Leigh," he said briskly, and made his way back to the front door. "I'll be back for my things later."

He ground his teeth, waiting for a reply that didn't come. He caught his breath when a jarring shiver ran through his teeth into his jaw. He reached his finger and thumb into his mouth, felt the two front upper teeth wiggle gently.

Shit. How the hell?

He had been gritting them a lot these past weeks, hadn't he? That reaction to his stress had worn and loosened them. The knowledge of an explanation didn't make it any better, but at least it was good to have one. He shut his mouth, careful not to clench, and decided it was time to make a trip to the dentist. True to form, everything happened at once.

But it was worth it. Not daring a smile, he clutched the doorknob and went outside, shutting the door behind him, shutting out the squeals of Will and Cissy from the back of the house. Shutting out the life he'd lived for ten years.

He would enter his new life.

20

The door shut.

"Martin?" whispered Leigh. She hurried past the couch, still feeble from the bludgeon of his confessions. Her heart banged furiously, and she was drifting through the air, but felt the weighty anchor crushing her so flat she knew she should not even be able to move. "Mar . . . tin?" She choked, then saw the empty entry hall and the closed door.

"M . . . m-my God—"

"Daddy?" Cissy called out.

Leigh's hands clutched together and shook. She barely heard Cissy and Will come into the room. She watched their drawn, red faces and knew she did not need to tell them anything. They had heard the shouts and already knew.

Hissing her breaths, she forced her legs to the phone across the room and picked it up, then sat gracelessly and opened her personal directory, locating her mother's number.

Jerry Halverson sat on the other end of the couch, his sports jacket between himself and Leigh. Leigh's mother, Esther, had gone to the children's rooms, moving from one to the other like a guardian angel. She had looked at Leigh smugly when she arrived, and Leigh could hear the "I told you so" on her lips, but Leigh had broken and bawled, cutting those words off.

Jerry arrived a few minutes later. Leigh's mother had called him. Now Jerry kept shifting as though the worn cushions made him uncomfortable. His knit short-sleeve shirt was open at the collar, and his curly black hair sprouted up through it as it did on his thick arms. His face was shaven and mild despite the gruff masculinity, and its broad size was slimmed by dark-rimmed spectacles.

Jerry Halverson was the minister of Riverview Baptist, and easy to talk to. So easy that it was hard to remember he was a minister sometimes, especially since he was Leigh's age and attractive.

But she didn't notice that at all now, and his manner did nothing to emphasize it. Tonight he was a gentle Father Flanagan, and he spoke to Cissy and Will in the tender words of that older, vastly experienced cinematic clergyman. He took their tears and gave them rest.

They slept soundly now, and it was Leigh's turn.

"It's . . . been bad," she blurted.

Jerry nodded, folding his hands over his flat stomach. "Did he ever talk about leaving, Leigh?"

She sniffled, feeling her leaden head jog up and down in a nod. The harsh words of the past echoed in her ears. So many words. Most of them unpleasant, it seemed. Especially recently. It hurt her worse because he was gone and she couldn't apologize. The things she'd spoken and sometimes shouted riddled her as sharply as they must have injured him.

"So this wasn't completely unexpected?"

Now her head was shaking. It felt so heavy on her shoulders. "Yes. I mean *no.* I don't . . . know. I mean I really didn't expect it. Doesn't everyone talk about leaving these days? I know I must've, myself." She gripped the couch fabric with her nails, holding on to it as though it were Marty.

"Unfortunately," he agreed. His brown eyes studied her. "But that's the saddest part of it, Leigh. You both talked of things you shouldn't have, and my experience is that we get what we say we want more often than not. What we say is usually what we believe and think we want. Kind of how the hateful words that come out in hostility are usually those closest to our hearts. In this world it's a terrible truth that bitterness and our own selfish will controls our lives."

"I . . ." Leigh shook her head. Her facial muscles ground and stretched. "I don't need a sermon now, Jer . . . Brother Halverson."

"Jerry is fine by me, and this isn't meant to be a sermon, Leigh. The words that hurt our hearts most are the ones we need to hear."

Her mouth barely opened. "I—I know." She shut her eyes miserably, feeling the pang of tears that would no longer come. She remembered her dedication to a new commitment this past weekend. The choice between Marty and divorce badgered her over and over and had come to a head with Tom's offer to share the night. Sex with another man had been something new to consider, something she hadn't enjoyed since college.

It had made her think, to weigh the choices and consequences.

She still loved Martin. It was a fact she could not deny. She did not even want to. It was difficult with him, but she was not without her faults, and that moment opened her vision wide.

She chose Martin, invigorated by the challenge to make their life together the way it should be. The way that would make them both happy . . .

But before she could share that commitment, he had gone away. He had left before she ever returned.

"Leigh?"

Her wet eyes turned back to him, and her shuddering hand reached to his. "I know." She held back the choking sorrow that saturated her soul. "I know I made mistakes. I made a lot of them, and that's why it's so bad. I went on that trip because I wanted to get out. I wanted to get out so much I could taste it, and I thought . . . I hoped that the time apart would help us both. I thought we could think about our problems, and that maybe it would be better when I came back." She squeezed his fingers with the driving bruise of her emotions and felt the wet tears finally return to spill on her cheeks. "I . . . I thought about it hard, Brother Halverson. I wanted to try harder—to do better, and I came home and *did* try real hard—" She swallowed the memory of how Martin had rejected her last night, and how she'd still tried to wait for him to climb into bed with her.

"But you're trying to say it was too late?"

She pulled on her lip.

He watched her silently, then spoke with mild words. "I wish you had come to me sooner."

The tense of his sentence drew her flinch, and she pulled away. "It *is* too late."

"No." Jerry Halverson stretched his arm after her until his fingers touched hers once more. He held her firmly. "Not too late for you, Leigh."

It was a riddle, and she didn't understand it. All she could see was how she was finally trying to be the woman Martin wanted. And he had slapped her for her trouble. The hurt rumbled in her. "I *love* him! God, despite everything, I love him! I wanted to make up for my mistakes—"

Halverson pressed her palm with his thumb, but gently. "That's the most important thing, though, Leigh. Love is always the most important thing." His lips covered his teeth and moved up in a pleasant smile. "Your love at least gives Martin a choice. I'm very proud of you for that. It gives him the choice of what is best and what he thinks he wants if those two are separate, and it may yet bring those two together. We all dream sometimes, and want the things we don't have."

Leigh wanted to push him away again but didn't. She listened.

"Those dreams capture us sometimes, too. I think you had your own vision, but you tempered it with the understanding of love. Real love, I mean, with a capital L, and you met that dream in reality."

"Yes," she whispered. "I *tried.*"

His expression became even softer, measured in the pressure of his fingers. His own eyes were damp as he sat forward so that his knee rumpled his jacket and nearly touched hers. "With psychology we know the dreams are only our self-repressions, but it is our own will that makes them so. Though the visions of our sleep may be beyond our conscious control, when we make them the fantasies of our waking hours it is through our own will. You, I think, have met your demon and bested him by your defiance of selfishness. You are a better person for it. No matter what happens, you made your choice the right one, and you have become better and stronger."

She concentrated on the cushions he sat on, where Martin had sat so often. Gulping, she took her hand from Jerry's and ran it through her hair, putting a length into her mouth nervously, not liking where the minister was taking her.

"No matter what happens—"

"But . . . I want him. I love Martin."

"That's where I'm proudest of you," Jerry Halverson said, pulling at the knees of his slacks to smooth them. "After what Martin said to you, that's more than most wives I know would say. You're still ready to forgive him no matter what he's done, and that forgiveness is your proof of salvation." He cleared his throat wetly, and his voice was low. "I would like to talk to Martin, but like you, I can't unless he'll let me. No one can ever force anyone to be other than what they are and what they want in their hearts, and that's the only place it really counts, Leigh. A worse Hell than you ever imagined would await you if you could force him to come back to you against his wishes. You might see Heaven in the end, but only in death, and the fire you would go through here on earth might even take away that."

Leigh sucked in a breath, smelling the stale afterscent of Martin's tobacco. But she sniffed it like a flower, loving it. It all hurt.

"Even if you changed Martin on the outside, Leigh," he continued, watching her but no longer attempting to touch her, "you could never alter his inner spirit." Jerry paused. "As with you, Martin's life is his own choice. You had to arrive at your conclusions by yourself, and you must allow him the same privilege. Jesus died for our sins and opened the door of salvation to us all, but the decision to accept that mercy will forever be our own."

"But—" She started to reach out, then stopped and stayed put, wanting the strength of his touch, but at the same time wanting to hate him for each word he spoke; hating their truth.

Halverson sat forward on the edge of his cushion. His eyes were sharp and shiny as though he understood every thought passing through her mind. "If Christ cannot, or will not, force us to accept His Love, then who are we to try to force ours on others?"

Hot tears made a stream down her cheeks. "M-Martin," she groaned.

Halverson's words settled into her ears from a million miles away: "He has a right to his own life and what he will do with it. It's the only right any of us have. You can only wait and pray for his decision. This is the price of Love, and its reward is always the greatest and most lasting. Even if nothing else, that Love will see you through the halls of Hell itself."

No. The denial wanted to usurp her heart. She wanted to make Martin hers! She wanted—

"The dreams are the demons of our desires, Leigh. They can possess us against all else for their own release. We must all do as you have done already and stifle those dreams before they consume us."

The smothering flames of her self burned bright for another instant, then faltered and shrank as the strength of Halverson's authenticity flooded over them and finally washed them to a smolder in her veins.

Jerry Halverson stood tall and dragged her up to stand against him, hugging her. His passion for her made her like jelly, but it was the passion of concern, of *real* love.

"Our self-created demons," he whispered, "are the most horribly real of them all."

21

The white lines centering the Lynx on the expressway were hypnotic under the headlight beams. That sensation, combined with the lush power of Ian Anderson's FM stereo vocals to lull Martin's senses, was pulling down the inflexible walls of hysteria piece by piece:

> . . . and you snatch your rattling last breaths
> with deep-sea diver sounds,
> and the flowers bloom like madness in the spring.

Ahead the flowers bloomed.

He had done it, and he was free. Now he would meet Jan once more, never to be separated again.

The car's tires whumped down the exit ramp, and he twisted the wheel, spying the neon lights of the Cornhusker Saloon up the street. He cocked the wheel further to the right and drove without the crazy speed the moment seemed to beg. Instead he savored this instant between his lives and slurped it deep, snatching his last breath . . .

. . . *with deep-sea diver sounds . . .*

The car zipped ahead past a dark service station and adjoining convenience store, then into the parking lot he remembered like a second driveway. He parked with a nervous awkwardness he hadn't enjoyed since he was sixteen and found a cigarette to light and puff slowly. He fit it between his lips and jumped when his two front teeth wobbled at the push. Biting down on the filter gently, he got out and slammed the door.

He forgot everything but Jan. She'd said she would come. Yes, he snickered, she always *came* for him.

Martin pushed inside to the country rock sounds of "Honky Cat," missing the sound of a guitar in its melody but trusting in its omen. Elton John had played that night he had first met Jan.

That night had started out as a ghastly hell. It had gotten worse, like his whole life. It had been a night just like tonight, but now he knew he would meet her again, and the misery would slide away behind him forever. He was giving up the security of materialism and its empty pleasures for *her,* and she was doing the same for him.

Martin sighed and waited for a woman whose tits flopped on her belly to pass. Then he saw the table where he had sat with Jan. It was empty, and he hurried to it. He sat and leaned back.

"Beer?" asked the nice-assed waitress he'd ordered from last night.

"Bud," he reminded her, "and a margarita."

She flipped up a thin eyebrow. "Hey, I told you last night—"

"It's for the lady who's meeting me." He chuckled and wanted to pinch the ass she shoved against him when she turned, but Jan came in the door right then. He forgot the waitress instantly as he saw in Jan the lover he could now claim totally. He enjoyed her gait as her fluffy hair bounced up and down over the pink of her cheeks, over the flower print dress that wrapped her curves with a promise of future excitement.

She was his.

"How'd it go, Marty?" Jan asked. Her lips slid to his cheek, and she stroked his pants, sitting beside him.

He raised a flat hand and wiggled it back and forth.

"I told you it would be rough."

Elton disappeared from the speakers like Marty had disappeared out the door of his home, and Marty bit his lip. "Rough ain't the word." He sipped the beer.

He had left his own life. It was what he wanted to do in his dreams but never dared to more than articulate during the fiercest of the past screaming fights.

This time he *had* left. He had passed the test. The test of dreams. The test for Sally's cosmic law. The cosmic judge had pronounced him free.

And Jan had done the same for him.

They were *free!*

Her cool nails dragged across his feverish cheek. "Poor Marty," she soothed him. "But you're yourself now, Marty. You see that, don't you?" Her hand clasped his in reassurance. "You're free of everything you didn't want. You're free of everything but me and you. Don't you see that, love? Now we can be together." She scooted her chair as close to his as she could get, her leg fitting perfectly against his. "We are together—just like we're the same person!"

Hope rose out of the sorrows flooding his heart, muffling the memories of Cissy and Will's playing voices, with even more finality than when he had closed that door and walked alone to his car. Then he was crushed by the bulging despair of the uncertainties.

Even so, its weight would not completely leave his chest. "Together . . ." He did his best to resurrect a smile. "Did you—did you tell your husband, Jan?"

"Husband?" She blinked and laughed casually, bringing his thumb to her lower lip. "I just made him up for you, Marty. I'm not married. I've never been married."

"You what?"

She rubbed his thumb up and down her lip, sucking it into her mouth, then dragging it out. Back in. Out. She licked it with the tip of her tongue. "I told you, Marty. I *know* you. You never would have taken me seriously if you hadn't believed I was married, and you would never give up your miserable slavery for me if you hadn't thought I was giving up my own for you." She leaned to him and brushed her lips to his. "I had to do it because I need you. I couldn't let your guilty conscience keep us apart."

"But . . ." It stalled every joyful emotion.

Jan had given up *nothing* for him, and he had given up his life. He had given up Leigh and his children. He'd shut that door with himself on the outside. He gnashed the loosened teeth and groaned.

"Don't look that way, Marty love. You needed me to give you confidence." Her sultry skin rubbed his enticingly. "Don't let my little untruth mislead you, darling. I do need you, and you *have* helped me."

Lying makes the world go round.

The waitress thumped his Bud bottle on the table and put the margarita glass before Jan. He waited until she was walking off before he nodded. "Yes, *you* . . . need *me,*" he mumbled, lifting the bottle. His fever grew hotter. He licked his lips, his adrenaline slipping away and giving in to the exhaustion he'd fought all day.

Jan's smile was consuming. "I told you we're alike, Marty, but you didn't believe me. I knew you weren't happy when I first saw you over there." She motioned to the corner table where he'd sat alone so long ago Saturday night. "I watched you for a long time, even though you didn't see me. I saw the failure in you when you got up to leave, and I felt it when you passed me. I knew it was time."

"Time for what?" he asked shakily, not able to think straight with everything running through his thoughts. Leigh, Will, and Cissy . . . and Jan.

She was sipping through the straw.

"Did you . . . did you have to lie to me, Jan?"

"Didn't I?"

He blushed, remembering Leigh's unhappy parting words and his flat reply. "How do you know me?"

"You did the right thing, Marty. Don't go getting cold feet now. Don't spoil this. It's too late to change things."

The emptiness he'd left would be even emptier if he returned now. She was right: It was too late. If he tried to go back to Leigh, it would only get worse. That short exchange had altered their lives as much as his first words of love. And even if he could go back, wasn't that what he had tried to escape in the first place? Wasn't he at last himself?

"You don't want to go back to the way it was, Marty," she whispered, reading his thoughts. "That's why you came here. That's why you took me back with you. You wanted to escape, Marty. You *have* escaped."

Willie Nelson's husky chords blasted the room, and he hid in its beating twang, his fingers fumbling a nonexistent guitar while he did his best to ignore the goosebumps coating his flesh. "But how did you know, Jan?" He tasted the thick texture of his own voice and swallowed. "How do you *know* me?"

"I just knew, okay? Isn't that enough?" She slid her glass away and nuzzled his neck, holding his hand with a tight grip that claimed him anew. "I wanted you bad, Marty." She sighed. "I *want* you so bad."

The gentle nibbles pushed feeling through him. Yes. It was okay. He had done it, and it was what he wanted. The details of what Jan told him now would make no difference to their future. "Well, it's over, anyway." He hugged her back, feeling a little better.

"Yes."

These had been ten years of a nightmare, right, Sally? And dreams did come true, right? Sometimes, for real. Martin did his best to seem confident. "So what's your real name, anyway?"

"I thought you liked my name."

"I do. I like its sound. But what about your last name? You never told me that."

"You never told me yours either, lover."

The Bud bottle shone darkly in the flashing lights as surrounding couples filled the dance floor for a starlight dance. He watched with disinterest. It was too late to do anything but go on. Too much had happened. Too much had been said. Life had changed for better or worse.

Only now he could be himself. "Paarman. Martin Alfred Paarman."

"I like it," Jan sighed, rubbing her palm over his slacks in the shadows, higher and higher.

"At least"—he fought to keep his voice level—"I won't have to change that."

Her knowing gaze caught his meaning. "Yes. Divorce is a lot like marriage. Starting a new life, with new opportunities."

"What's your last name, Jan?"

"I like yours, Marty."

"You can't have it yet." He tried not to grin. "What's your last name, now?"

Her hand worked his expanding crotch, and her eyes were far away. "Fancy."

"Fancy?"

"Fancy that?" She turned pink. "Don't laugh, Marty."

Controlling the urge, he shrugged. "Jan Fancy." He kept his face straight. "So all this is just because you want to change your name to Paarman?"

Her complexion paled, and her eyes grew large, and then she was smiling warmly again, drifting her hand back and forth along his zipper and dividing his attention. "Not just to change my name. Because I want *you,* Marty." Her lashes lowered, and her lower lip went puffy. Pouty. For a moment it was wrinkled and ancient like a corpse's, not quite hiding blackened teeth. "Don't you want me?" Her fingers lowered the zipper a notch.

The fearsome sight disappeared immediately, and he tried to pull himself together and forget he'd ever imagined such a horror, clearly brought on by the doubts he was trying to put to rest. "Yes." He leaned back and closed his eyes, forgetting the dancing men and women all around them, blocking out the music and their formless conversations, blocking the mirages of Leigh and her shocked hurt, of Cissy and Will wondering where their daddy had gone. He blocked everything but the gentle touch that was continuing to open his fly. Her lush voice was seducing him all over again.

"We should always be together, right, Marty?" She whispered a breath softly in his ear, her hand slipping between the zipper teeth and working past his slacks, stroking him. "Can we live together now? You can do what you want to now, you know. You don't need them. But I need. I just need to be with you . . . as much as I can."

Up and down. Up and down. Her fingers were quick with his need. He forgot the problems. Forgot Leigh and the kids. His hips moved with her under the table. This was why.

This was the reason.

She unbuckled his belt.

"Ya-hoo!" cried out a fat cowhand dressed in a fringe leather outfit that had never been past the outskirts of the city. And with that yell the noise of the bar crashed back into Martin as his pants loosened and her hands tugged at the elastic band of his underwear. *"Ya-hoo!"* The rebel yell got louder, matching Martin's feelings as her fingers crawled under his cotton shorts, jerking him gently. Back and forth. Up and down. Her palm was slick with his excitement.

The redneck song ended. Martin opened his mouth wide, his eyes even wider with a sudden bad feeling.

"Does that feel good?" she whispered.

The lights!

He bit his tongue to bring back full sobriety, sitting up and pushing her away as he pulled up the slacks and fastened them fast. "God damn, Jan—not in *here!*" He pushed her away with the shock of awakening from his dreamy stupor. He stared at the half-empty beer bottle on the table. "Shit, you'll get us *arrested.*"

Her face puckered, midway between disappointment and an apology. "I'm sorry, Marty. I'm just so excited. You're mine now, and I'm just so horny for you. I just want to be with you. I want you." Her voice was a whimper. "I need *you.* I need you so fucking bad."

Martin looked at his watch, thinking of Cissy and Will. But he was free now, and the night was his for what he wanted. They would be asleep in bed by now, anyway. Leigh might even be asleep, in a bed and home that were no longer his.

He had no home.

I need you, Marty.

No. He did have a home. Jan was his home.

"Do you want to go?" he asked Jan suddenly.

Her eyes lit up, and she beamed with pleasure. "I'm yours, handsome prince," she sighed.

At least he had someone to go with. Martin picked up the warm beer and took a swig, standing up. "Come on."

She reached for his hand, and they walked to the door like they had that first night when everything was different. He remembered it as another lifetime. He had been born again, as Oral Roberts would say, but in a different and better way that would release all his past hours into unending pleasure. "Where do you live?" he asked her.

"Nowhere until now." She bunched her shoulders and squeezed his knuckles. "Life alone isn't living, really, Marty. And I've been so alone except for those few times. . . ."

"Oh? What few times could those be?" He pushed open the door, and they went outside, brushing by a towering man and the two women he was escorting.

She smiled. "You'll think it's dumb."

"Oh, yeah?" A slight jealousy nudged him, but the smooth love of her voice drove it away. "Well, I ain't your teacher, babe, so you can tell me."

She was silent beside him as they walked. Tires squealed further up on the expressway, breaking the steady hum of engines.

"Jan?"

Her sigh was pleasure. "It was when I dreamed of you, Marty. Of being with you. I was all alone except for that."

"You *dreamed* of someone like me?"

They stopped, and she melted against him. Her arms went around his waist and held him fast. "Yes, but you were the one, because you're here now. I dreamed of *you,* Marty."

Dreams. She had dreamed and he had dreamed, and now their dreams were one. They were *real.* He laughed. What the hell difference did it make *how* since it was all real now?

"Yes. We're together now," she murmured. "Finally together. Connected."

. . . and the dream bone's connected to the real bones . . . Martin laughed hard. "Yeah, but where have you been staying, Jan?"

"I checked out of my room this afternoon, Marty."

It came together in his head so fast he wobbled with dizziness. "Your room. But we could have gone there last night instead of the motel, Jan. You should have told me."

"You still thought I was married, then, Marty. Remember? I'm sorry, but you were wavering so much, I just couldn't tell you yet."

He thought of the forty-dollar charge on his card. At least he wouldn't have to worry about Leigh's reaction when she saw the bill now. "Yeah."

"I checked out," she said again. "I thought we would be moving in together after we talked this morning."

His mouth worked in the knowledge of how close he had come to slipping, to not telling Leigh. If he had kept his mouth shut and stayed back at the house tonight, then Jan would still be inside the bar at their table, waiting, loving him so much and waiting.

With nowhere to go.

"What if I hadn't come here tonight, Jan?"

"I would have waited." She shrugged, bunching her shoulders again and lifting the flower print of her dress. "What else could I do, Marty? I couldn't *force* you to be with me. You wouldn't have been mine then. You had to make your decision, and I just would have come back every night until you *did* come in." She batted her eyes flirtatiously and pulled up on her hem, trailing a finger up the inside of her thigh. "But I knew you'd be here."

Staring at her legs, her thighs, his throat went tight. His pants went tight, too. He wanted to pull her dress back up when she let it drop. "What about your things?"

She tossed her head, sweeping the air with her locks. "I don't need them if I have you."

"But what about your car?"

She pointed, showing him the hazy stars flashing in the sky. "They're beautiful, aren't they, Marty?"

"Yes, but—"

"Okay. I took the bus. I walked, too, Marty. I don't have a car." She licked her lips, and her mouth glistened in the street light. "I don't have anything, really. But I don't need a car, or anything else if you're near. I don't need anything but you."

No car. Nothing. She had given up nothing for him because she had nothing. No husband. No family. Nothing. Aggravation boiled up inside him, creasing those thoughts on his forehead.

She stared into him like a lost child.

This had to be real; it was what he wanted. "What have you got, then?"

She flowed to him, caressing him, raising her face to his. Dreading his fears, he bent and kissed her, grabbing tight the magic she gave him all over again. He welcomed its floating presence and hoped it would drive away these hated questions.

A second passed. Her body was warm against him. His heart was beating faster. At last his arms moved around her.

The kiss went on as voices rose and fell. Footsteps went by. Whispering. When his legs were sagging under the weight of his body the kiss finally ended. He felt more drunk than any beer could make him, but every doubt and question was far away. He grinned, but didn't know what for.

"I've got you, Marty, haven't I?" She leaned on his chest, making him support her. "Haven't I got you?"

He let himself nod.

"Say it, Marty, please?"

Leigh flashed in and out of his foggy thoughts, but he couldn't recall those good times here with Jan. It was like part of his brain had been sliced away and destroyed. Jan's warmth made him woozy and powerful at the same time. "You . . . you've got me, Jan." He didn't even think as the words she gave him slipped out. He only listened to them break the still night air.

"You're mine, then, aren't you, Marty?"

Denial suddenly tried to force itself into him, but her touch was strong and his grappling lust stronger. He needed *someone*. He was alone, without even a home! His past was a stranger to him.

But Jan wanted him. Badly.

He had no one else.

"I—I'm yours, Jan," he said, resisting the memory of Leigh's traps. "I'm yours."

She stood on her tiptoes and kissed him again, and her arms stayed around his neck. She laid her cheek on his shoulder, arousing him with her tongue and warm breath. "It's nice, Marty. It's nice to have someone, isn't it?"

"Yes."

"Marty, it's so nice. It's so nice to *be* someone."

It was nice. It was nice to be himself. It was nice to be with *her*.

22

The waterbed sloshed gently, and Martin felt a warm body against his. It made him secure, and he yawned happily, the orgy he'd performed with Jan bright in his thoughts. Her head nestled between his chin and shoulder, and her hand rested on his chest.

"I love you, Marty," came her whispered, husky voice. He turned over in the darkness, facing her, not needing the light to see her. He had memorized her body better than any homework assignment back in school. Her soft flesh was as much his as the skin covering his own body. He pushed down the sheet covering them and let his fingers slither down her side and across her stomach.

"I'm yours, Marty. I need you."

"I need you, too," he said in a voice still marred by sleep. He licked her neck and sniffed the soft wetness of her body.

Their lips met. He rolled on top of her.

"Please, Marty. Please don't ever leave me."

He started to reply but stopped the waiting words, recognizing a difference in her tone. The grogginess began to pass. He blinked, and pulled his trembling fingers away.

"Marty?"

He rolled to the edge of the mattress, moving against the bed's wave that tried to drive him back into her arms. He clutched the nightstand, clutched it frantically as he recognized the familiarity of her body and knew it was not Jan's, that the intimacy of this bed was only because it was so well known.

The lamp was there on the stand, and with a horror wrenching him, he twisted the switch so the flare of incandescent brilliance showed through the yellow-striped lampshade and drove the night from his vision.

But not the nightmare.

"Stay with me, Martin," begged the blond-headed woman who rose to kneel on the mattress beside him. Her bowed head shook back and forth, and he saw the tears streaming from her eyes. Her shudders made her sagging breasts flop on a baby-scarred stomach.

He screamed, trapped in a vertigo of endless falling . . . into a trap. No exit.

It was Leigh.

"Wake up, Marty!"

He was shivering, choking and spitting out the saliva running down his throat. "No!" he screamed. *"No!"* He fought the hands that grabbed him and held him down, afraid, wanting Jan, knowing that she had only been a final torment of trickery from Leigh.

"Marty!"

He caught his breath. He knew his eyes were wild, and he was still jittery with the tremors that wouldn't stop. But they eased now as he knew the voice was not Leigh's but Jan's.

Leigh was a nightmare. Jan was his dream.

Her supple body rolled against Martin now. She released his wrists and wiped his brow. "Are you all right?" Her eyes were soft and gazed at him with sympathy. "What's wrong, Marty?"

The sight of the battered dresser and the rest of the motel room—the same one where they'd stayed the night before—helped him relax. He was with Jan, after all, and the fright he endured wasn't real, only the last remaining fabric of Leigh's entrapping claws.

"Darling Marty." Jan leaned close and rubbed her cheek on his. "You were screaming. I was afraid. I—"

He shook his head, not wanting to admit to the fears that jolted his rest, losing them completely in the sunlight that spilled through the drapes and across the floor. "Oh, Jesus, *what time is it?"* The very memory of Leigh shrank to nothing in the awareness of where he really was. And the continuing cost of this room hovered over him like an evil bird.

It was comparatively cheap, but it was still money being spent. Money he did not have. "I've *got* to get to work, Jan. God damn it, this is the third day! I can't keep spending money if I'm not making any!"

"That's sweet, Marty." She slid her lazy forefinger from his neck to his chest and drew his hand to hers, sliding it over her nipple, which soon stood up for his tongue.

"God damn it," he choked again, shoving her away despite her invitation. "There's nothing sweet about it. We have to have money in order to live, Jan. We've got to have money to get us a place to live."

"That *is* sweet," she insisted. "You're including me in your life, Marty. You *do* want me." Her fingers lifted his palm back onto the slope of her breast.

But he shuddered. With a resolve he wanted to refuse, he pulled his hand away once more and got out of the bed. "Jan, we can't just lie around and fuck all day."

"I know." Her eyes dropped sullenly. "But I can wish for that, can't I?"

We can't just lie around and fuck all day, Marty. He blushed, recalling those words Leigh had said to him and knowing he had spoken them just so to Jan. He kissed her an apology quickly, exorcising the memory. "I've got to get to work." He stretched, groaning at the pop of his bones. "Don't you have a job?"

Her eyes probed inside him. "I didn't think you really wanted me to have one."

Blood rushed hot into his face, but he didn't remember when they had talked about it. Maybe that first night when he'd been drunk? It was the most likely possibility, but why would he have said that then?

"Do you want me to divide my time between you and a job?"

"Well, maybe until we get ourselves started, Jan." But the words came out uneasily as he remembered saying them to Leigh years before. It seemed his past with her was even invading this attempt at a new life.

More than anything else, it was taking the job that had started the change in her and, along with her attention to Cissy and Will, had begun the process that had destroyed their marriage. Her job and their children had taken away from her relationship with him and finally ended it. "Maybe not," he sighed, grinding his back teeth and making financial calculations in his head.

"Can we make it on your salary?"

Martin reached for his shirt on the floor and began to pull it on thoughtfully. "Maybe. Maybe even with the alimony and child support. It'll be tight, though."

"I'll be tighter," she promised, squeezing her legs together. "I'll be as tight as you can take it, and I'll find us someplace to live. At a nice price, too. I can do that while you're working, Marty."

The pressure of this decision to forgo the possessions that had made the past years bearable raked him. But the grin on her face lightened that weight. "Yeah." He pulled up his pants. "Try to keep the rent under three hundred then, okay? Apartments can go at a pretty steep price. Keep it small."

She knelt on the bed and saluted him, twisting and jiggling with a sexy taunting. "I gotcha, boss!"

Boss. In charge. He liked that a lot. It drove the nightmare of waking up with Leigh further from his thoughts. "I'll go to my—*Leigh's* house and get some of the old furniture out of the garage for us, and the old waterbed." He buckled the trousers and patted the ungiving mattress. "I can't stand sleeping on this piece of shit."

"Who needs sleep?"

He smiled back, unable to hang onto the futilities with her there. He envied her optimism.

"Waterbeds are better for a lot of things."

"Yeah." He sat beside her and pulled his socks and shoes on, still cautious with his sore foot. It was healing slowly.

"I'll need some money."

Martin's eyebrows rose.

"For the apartment."

"Right." He finished tying the laces and fished out his wallet, finding six twenties and a ten. Folding them crisply, he tried to strike down a misgiving, then gave them to her.

Jan examined the bills with a faint smile. "Give me your work number, too, Marty, so I can tell you our new address."

"Yeah . . . okay." He stood back up and walked to the room's desk, finding motel paper and a pen. He printed the number with large legibility and handed it to her. "After I get the furniture we'll go grocery shopping."

She shook her head, opening her legs wide and then closing them, then spreading them again. "After you get the furniture, Marty, you'll be tired." She raised her right leg up and reached out to touch her toes, letting her tongue loll out of her mouth. "You'll take a hot bath while I do it, and then I'll cook you dinner."

Her willing manner pleased him. "I'd really like that. Thank you, Jan."

"Thank you, Marty. For everything." Her fingers were spread out over her pubic hair. "I need you, Marty. I love you."

He leaned across the bed and took her hand. "I'm glad you're here, Jan. I'm glad I met you." He bypassed the churning misgiving still trying to find a root in his gut. "I really need you, too, Jan."

"Really?" Her eyes flashed uncertainty.

"Really."

Sitting up, she placed her hands on his hips. She tugged him to her and forced him to lie back on the mattress, then covered him with her nakedness. "Then make love to me now, Marty. Fuck me hard and don't ever leave me. Be mine, always be mine."

Her desire swept him with earnestness. Jan was more than a match for all the second thoughts that still tried to creep in. She was something he craved. She gave him the knowledge of being desired and needed. Adored, even! She gave him purpose.

Leigh didn't need him and never had. She was only accustomed to the convenience of his being around to do the things she didn't want to do. That was all. She didn't need *him.*

"I love you, Jan." He hugged her in the reassuring way she had comforted him last night, and so many times before. Her name was like sweet honey in his mouth. "I will always be yours." Her grateful eyes made him secure all over again. "Always."

As the seconds passed too hastily he knew he could remain there with her forever, and when he once again forced himself to break away he matched her sigh of disappointment. But it kept their parting from turning bitter, and he was still sighing when he limped to the door. "I'll get a change of clothes at the house and get to work." He winked. "Don't forget to call me."

"Not in your wildest nightmares," she replied.

23

Martin hobbled through the wide hallway and stopped at the fifth door to the right of the elevator. He ran his hand over the imprint of the red triangular insignia on the white door. Dex Sales showed in raised golden letters in its center.

He took a deep breath, outlining his excuses one by one and keeping them in order. He opened the door.

"Hey, Marty!" exclaimed Cara, her eyes breaking wide as he stepped in. She watched his slow walk, not keeping the smile as he favored his right foot. "Geez, does it hurt bad?"

Wincing more than the pain required, he exaggerated the disability with a martyr's air. "Well, I couldn't make very good time if the building were burning down, know what I mean?" He put some pressure on his right foot and grunted, proving it really *did* hurt.

"I wouldn't have come in, myself." Cara shook her head.

Marty let his eyes pass the clock on the wall with unshown amusement. It was eleven-forty. "I was afraid you'd find out you all could get along without me. Couldn't afford for that to happen, right?" He leaned on her narrow desk and lowered his voice. "And to tell the truth, I can't afford not to be here."

"Don't worry about money," Cara told him. "They're going to pay you sick leave. I heard Sam talking about it to

Mike before I left last night. Hey, there's a load of messages on your desk, by the way."

"Great. Just what I was looking forward to." He sighed, feeling the mercy of Jan's philosophy that kept his world spinning neatly.

"It'll give you a chance to rest your foot. You'll spend the rest of the day calling everyone back." She giggled. "That'll teach you to run off and leave me like you did." Then her smile faded and her face got serious. Her voice dropped lower. "Hey, I called Leigh this morning to see how you were doing when you didn't show up on time."

Martin gulped. "Where? At home?"

"At work," Cara answered, still quietly. "What's the deal, Marty? She said you moved out." Her eyelashes fluttered curiously, echoing the empty look of her face. "Where were you yesterday? Really?"

He hesitated, not ready to talk about any of it yet to anyone else, then he fashioned another wink. "I told you what happened. The rest—" He gritted his teeth and shrugged, then winced, feeling the loose front teeth. Martin shut his mouth, raising his hand to his lips. A lower one was wobbling a little, too. "Shit."

"Are you okay?"

"Yeah. Yeah. Let me call some of those people back, Cara, and maybe we'll talk at a break, okay? I've got some catching up to do."

As she nodded her smile turned shy. "Apparently I do, too, huh? Go on and I'll bring you some coffee. But don't forget that you promised to tell me your secrets."

Martin just grinned and made a show of limping to the door across the hall. When he was inside, switching on the lights and pushing the door nearly shut, he released a heavy sigh, then leaned against the wall. After a moment he was breathing more easily, and he moved slowly to the chair behind the desk, sitting down carefully.

He rubbed his mouth. Opened it. The top front teeth were loose indeed. He clenched his fist, fingering the lower tooth with his other hand. It was loose, too.

"God damn it," he said. He would have to go to a dentist;

no way around it now. He might even have to get falsies, though that was an expense that would be hard to afford for a long while. "God damn," he cursed the rebel incisors. "If you were going to do this shit, why didn't you do it before?"

The teeth offered no explanation, and he continued to mutter.

At least he had Jan.

She made his world go round, not the lies! He grinned with caution and set back that thought to tell to her. His hands reached out to the memos and messages that waited in an accusing pile. "Damn," he whispered to that pressure that was added to everything else. He'd gone home, to Leigh's home—his ex-home—and showered quickly, then put on his suit. He'd been more an intruder than ever and felt a voyeur when he observed Leigh's underthings on the rumpled sheets of the bed. As he'd left he avoided glancing into Will's or Cissy's room. He was haunted by the memories there.

He got out as quickly as he could, no longer James Bond but a dirty, thieving burglar. He knew he no longer belonged there. Leigh was no longer his. Their relationship remained for a court of law only.

Martin closed his eyes regretfully and lowered his head over his desk at the thought of Cissy and Will. The sudden draining sobs and heartache the smashed him drove away the panic of his rotting teeth and soreness of his gums. In that sudden flash he knew he couldn't ever be the father he wanted to be. That life was no longer his. Everything and everyone had turned their backs to him.

Even his fucking teeth.

Everything and everyone but Jan Fancy.

A choking sob dragged itself out of his throat, and he cried, spilling the tears on his desk blotter as his body betrayed him with exhaustion. The finality tore his emotions in two. The past part of his existence was done with forever. He had burned down every bridge.

For Jan.

"Here you go," burst out Cara's high notes as she floated through the doorway and set a steaming mug on the desk near his face. The wet warmth cut a path to his cheeks, and he sat up, wiping his eyes.

"I thought you needed the caffeine to pick you up, Marty. It'll make you feel better, tiger." She sniffed the coffee's aroma and let her hand rest on his shoulder. "Free advice from Dr. Cara this time. You look downright awful, Marty. You really should stay home until you get better. But I'm impressed, I'll tell you that."

He blinked fast to stop the tears.

"Relax, Marty. It's okay. I like a man who cares enough to cry. Just take a drink of that stuff. I bet you'll sell all those callbacks at least one of our programs apiece!" She leaned on the desk with a wink. "I hope being up here will bring you up some anyhow, Marty. You really don't look so hot."

"Thanks loads." He snaked his hand out to the scalding porcelain, then pulled his fingers back fast. "I'll be hot if I drink *that,"* he snapped.

"I'm sorry. Hey, I'm just trying to help."

Her cheeks slumped.

"Thanks. I'll be okay. Thanks, Cara."

"But you really do look bad, Marty. Do you want to talk about it? You can start those callbacks later, you know." Her sweeping hand passed over the messages as though she were blessing them. "If you'll get whatever it is off your mind, you'll probably do a better job." She snickered. "And it'll do wonders for your complexion."

"What's wrong with that?"

"You're pale. You look like you need the nap Rip Van Winkle took. Leigh was pretty rough on you, huh?"

He rubbed his cheeks, wishing for a mirror. With Jan, he'd been tired but still felt great. But almost as soon as he was out that motel door the pains in his muscles had increased. He just hadn't noticed them before.

"Come on, Marty," Cara wheedled. "Give. What's going on?"

The skin of his face felt so dry it would flake off. "You just want a good story for your lunchtime gossip, don't you?"

"If I wanted that, I've already got it, Marty." Her finger

traced a fallen tear in a circle beside his hand. "But your secrets are always safe with me."

He knew how fast tales passed through the office when they were given to her. "Just like that time when Bob got drunk last Christmas and tried to pee on that dog, right?"

Cara's mouth twitched. "Did you try that, too, Marty?"

Their eyes locked for several moments, and he knew it would all come out soon anyway. He was past the point of hiding. Maybe his keeping this a secret was why he felt so bad and looked so bad. He wasn't completely free until he began to act it, right? If his new life had already begun, why hide it?

"You left her, didn't you?" Cara prodded.

Martin touched the mug and blew on its contents, then brought it to his lips. Despite the temperature, it was good to swallow and made him aware that he'd forgotten breakfast. No dinner last night, either. Only a beer.

As if the thought reminded his stomach, too, it growled noisily. "Are there any doughnuts left this morning?"

"You want one?"

His mouth watered. "Please. Jesus, I'm starved."

"Don't change the subject. I'll go get you a nice fat one filled with jelly if you'll talk. Did you and Leigh have a blowout?"

"That's coercion."

She smiled and nodded. "How about two doughnuts?"

Her offer made the hole in his belly grow. The story she wanted, edited for pornography, bubbled inside him. He would talk sooner or later, and he might as well get something for it. "Yeah. Yeah. We split up."

"Oh, yeah?" The green eyes widened, and she bent close. "What happened?"

He started to tell her, but the yawning emptiness of his belly sucked back the words like a greedy black hole. "Cara, the doughnut first."

"I won't tell anyone, Marty. I promised."

His tummy growled louder.

"Marty, you're never going to get that doughnut or get to

work if you don't tell me. Everyone else is out on appointments, and I'll stay here and bug you until you talk." She sat a hip on the end of his desk and showed him her leg. "Who knows, it could turn into something interesting for both of us."

He laughed. He had wanted her so much before, and he would have given anything to be hearing those words only last Saturday afternoon. Back in that time before Jan. Saturday B.J. It made him giggle like a teenager. Saturday B.J.B.J.: Saturday Before Jan's Blow Job. He snorted, too, relishing in the knowledge he would never feel that unquenched desire again. Jan wanted him and would give him anything.

"What the hell," he said, wanting that doughnut. "It's something that's been happening for a long time, Cara."

Her eyes dropped to his shoe. "Did she hurt your foot?"

"It has nothing to do with my foot getting hurt." But he could not forget how he had broken that goblet in his haste to return to Jan. He suddenly remembered that Leigh had bought it during their honeymoon. Actually, *he* had bought it for *her*. She had put it there on the credenza and always insisted it should stay there, as though she knew what would one day happen. In a way, wasn't it her revenge?

Cara was disappointed. "Oh." Then the sly bright flame was back. "Another woman?"

"It doesn't have to be—" He stopped short, unable to deny Jan. It would all be known soon, anyway. He and Leigh had gone too far yesterday. Humpty Dumpty had had his great fall. "Yes. Sort of."

"Well?"

"Yes. It was another woman."

Cara's eyes twinkled. "I thought that was it. I could tell by the way Leigh sounded when I asked her about you." She leaned down again, letting her neckline droop so he could see the bra that barely held in her breasts. "Is she pretty?"

"Very."

Straightening, she tugged her dress higher to show her lower thigh. She batted her eyelashes. "As pretty as me?"

It made him want to laugh out loud, but he resisted. "Yes."

That made her frown, and she changed her stance to one of rigidity. "Oh, yeah? Well, when do we get to meet her? God, where did *you* meet her, Marty? I thought you were wrapped up in those brats of yours."

"I just met her, like anyone meets anybody else."

But that was hardly the truth. He folded his hands over his stomach and began to regret that he'd let Cara bring him into this conversation. A bitter acid replaced his hunger as he thought of Cissy and Will. Didn't he still love them just as much? Did his moving out like he did change that?

"Are you staying with her?"

His eyebrows met in a withered frown. "Yeah. She's getting us an apartment today. Hey, what about that doughnut? I've got to get busy and get caught up."

"Yeah . . . okay." A distance painted her features. "Weird, Marty. I never figured you for sudden decisions like this. Life in the fast lane, huh?"

He took a long sip of the coffee and welcomed back the pang of hunger. "It's not so sudden, Cara. I told you that. Hell, it just happened that I met the right person. She . . . it's like she knows me. It's like she's known me a long time."

Cara walked to the door. "No wonder you look so ragged out. I never figured you for a swinger, Marty." She cackled. "I'll get that doughnut and let you get to it. You can tell me more later."

He touched one of his tingling teeth again, wobbling it in its socket with a dull ache. "Yeah . . . okay."

She went out, and the door shut as she pulled it behind her. That pinch in his gums and the throbbing of his hunger was real, and what had happened, and happened suddenly, was just as real.

Tonight he would be setting up house with Jan. It surged into a strange elation, like the time he'd gone over to his best friend's house in junior high and only his friend's big sister had been home. She had given him his first fuck. It had been magic.

At the same time, it was an elation tinged with regret.

"It's like graduation," he told himself in the silent room. "It's just like graduation from high school or college." He held the thought. "Leaving a part of yourself behind you for bigger and better things. For a new world." The idea blunted the pains and made him grin. He heard the familar intonation of Captain Kirk: "*. . . to explore new worlds and civilizations . . . to boldy go where no man has gone before . . .*"

"Yeah," Martin breathed. "Beam me down, Scotty. Let's hope we've found Utopia."

When Cara brought in the doughnuts he was reading the first message and picking up his phone.

24

Martin's stomach ached as he walked out of the office, but he was satisfied even so. He'd done well today. In spite of his late start he had managed to make all his calls, and had answered new ones by skipping lunch and breaks. He only missed two prospective clients, and lined up demonstrations with every one of the others.

"You sure stayed busy," Cara said in his ear when she caught up to him, matching his slow steps to the elevator. "You didn't even take coffee with me."

Martin bunched his shoulders, barely limping in the revival blossoming in his senses. He felt like a new man. Jan's man. "I got a helluva lot done. I may forgo my breaks from now on."

Cara didn't smile at his careless good nature. "I wanted to hear more about this new girlfriend, Marty."

"What?" He chuckled, taking out a cigarette. "Don't tell me you already ran dry on gossip."

"Marty—"

They stopped in front of the elevator together and waited.

"I didn't tell anyone about you," she said. She nudged him and her dress rustled softly. "It's *our* secret, Marty. But I thought you might want to take me out for a drink."

"So you can hear it all?" A smugness was affixing itself to

him. "Going to wait till you've got the sordid details before you gab, huh?"

"What sordid details?"

"Come off it, Cara."

The elevator door slid open, and they went in together, then were pushed close to each other as two businessmen and a woman moved in after them. The woman, in a suit similar to those of her male counterparts, was only different in her curves and the skirt that stopped at her knees. She glared at the unlit cigarette Martin stuck in his mouth.

"You can trust me, Marty," Cara wheedled. "I thought we could have a drink, you know? And if you wanted to talk . . ."

Her breath lapped at his chin, but its sweetness was suddenly saccharine. "I'm a real good listener," she went on, "and if you're not going to be married anymore, I don't mind you taking me out."

"You're too late, Cara." He slumped against the metal wall. Her words only made him think of Jan, made him glad Cara hadn't said them to him before. He might never have met Jan if she had.

"You're really serious about her?"

Jan was waiting for him, and when he got to her she would make up for all the meals he had missed. She would pacify his grumbling belly with the big dinner she'd promised, then give him dessert.

He chuckled.

Cara squinted. "I told you I hadn't told anyone anything. I even mentioned to Sam how you came in hurting like you did, and I made it out to be worse. I told him you worked your ass off without taking even one break."

He watched the floor numbers as they descended.

"Marty."

"Well, it's the truth, isn't it?" He thought of the sound of Jan's sweet voice when she'd called around three, and took the slip of paper he'd copied his new address on from his pocket, fondling it.

"What's that?" Cara tried to look at the scrap as the elevator came to a stop.

"My new home."

"Oh, yeah? Someplace nice?" She said it aloofly. "I wish you'd take me for a drink first, Marty. I think you need to talk." She brought her fingers to his cheek as the doors slid open.

He flinched. The pressure of her touch stung, right against his gums.

The other passengers filed out onto the marble lobby floor, but Cara held him back. "So where are you going now?"

It was none of her business, but he no longer cared. "To Leigh's to get my stuff."

"You're really going all the way, then?"

"All the way," he returned flatly, pushing past her.

Cara grabbed his hand, stopping him. Her red hair hung loosely on her forehead, emphasizing her eyes. They were small, tight pinpricks of annoyance that challenged his disinterest.

She didn't like hearing the rejections she'd always stopped him with coming back at her.

"I gotta go, Cara."

"When did you meet this woman, Marty?"

He chewed his tongue, teetering between lie and truth, but decided the truth sounded more unbelievable than anything he could make up. "Saturday night."

The anticipated rejection of his truth fizzled behind her pupils. "A long courtship, huh? And she's pretty, so you made it with her, and now you're going to divorce Leigh. . . ."

"Something like that."

Genuine concern wrinkled her face and startled him. "If that's not just bullshit, then you're a very stupid man, Marty. Did you at least use some kind of protection?"

"What?"

"Protection, you dumb ass. God, where the hell have you been? One-night stands are invitations to AIDS. Disease, Marty. VD."

"No." He shook his head at the idea, which had never even crossed his mind. "I know she doesn't have—"

"Unless you were there when she took her exam, there's no way you could know. I know these things, Marty. I have ten guys trying to take me to bed every week, and even as careful as I am, it's a dangerous game."

"No. It's—she's safe. I know."

Cara rolled her eyes. "I hope you're right, Marty. Because I really do like you. I hope you're right and that when this thing breaks off with her she doesn't give you some kind of going-away gift." Her hand smoothed his, and she stood right in front of him as others entered the elevator behind them. "I've always liked you, Marty, and sometimes I wonder what you'd be like. In bed, you know. Sometimes I've wished you weren't married."

The words meant nothing to him now. "I've got to be going, Cara."

She gripped his sleeve. "Marty, are you sure you know what you're doing? You don't even know her! I mean, you don't even know me, and we met two years ago."

"That's where you're wrong, Cara." He laughed, his confidence building despite her battle to betray him with doubts. "She's just like me. She told me so. We just seem to know about each other without ever saying a word. She's just like me. She's my dream"—he broke off in a chuckle—"she's my dream come true."

The elevator bell buzzed again, and others brushed by them. One man jostled Cara, but she didn't seem to notice. Her high eyebrow rose still more. "You mean like she's saying you're *psychic* to each other? Are you kidding? Don't fall for it, Marty. It's the oldest trick in the book. Guys use that line to pick me up all the—"

"No." Jan was real, and what they felt together was real. It was like meeting a twin who wasn't related. He walked to the doors that led to the parking lot, "It's not a trick. It's real, Cara. It's *real!*" He lowered his voice, seeing her still at his side. "I know exactly what I'm doing, and I'm doing it for me, just as you did when you broke up with your husband."

Cara held out her hand, reaching to him, but stopped where she was.

After a moment he stopped, too.

Her face jerked. "It's . . . it's not exactly like I said it, Marty. It—it's not such a bed of roses—"

"Maybe not for *you,*" he called back. "See you tomorrow." He turned away from her confounded stare and went on, feeling her darting eyes at his back. Then he was out the door and headed for his car. He looked at the address he still held with a buoyancy, wanting to go there now, only barely able to keep in mind the things he needed to do first. He had to get his clothes and fill up the car with furniture before returning to Jan. He would have to make at least two trips tonight so they would be more comfortable and wouldn't be stuck sleeping on the floor.

But then he would slip back into Jan's arms. Tomorrow he could get whatever else he wanted.

After a good night's rest with Jan.

Martin reached his Lynx and got inside, glad the car was a wagon, even if a tiny one. He knew Leigh would never let him use the Town and Country for his plans.

He turned the key and revved the motor like a teenager, blasting off into the street and on to his various destinations, the address of his new home repeating in his head as he whispered it to himself.

25

The miles between the office and the brick house went by in record time, but when he was there Martin pulled into the driveway with reluctance. Shivers slithered up his spine at the sight of Leigh's car, and he wondered how she had managed to pick up the children and beat him here. He warded off the dream of waking in her arms and believing she was Jan.

He didn't want to see her, and especially not the kids—not yet—

He didn't want to sleep on the floor tonight, either.

So Martin got out, bracing himself by blotting out the reminiscences that hung over the familar yard. His eyes wandered to the spot on the lawn where he'd made love to Jan Sunday night, already so long ago. He took it as his strength. He wanted Jan, and she wanted him, and he would do this for *them*.

"Daddy!" Cissy cried, banging open the front door and pumping her short legs to him. "Where were you, Daddy? We miss you!"

She bumped into him, crushing herself into his vacant stomach and stretching her arms as far around his waist as she could. He didn't—*couldn't*—speak, and he reached down to disengage himself from his daughter as tenderly as he was able to, wanting to hurry away.

She shoved her face back into his stomach, and it growled.

Cissy grinned at the noise, showing where one of her bottom teeth had fallen out. "Sounds like you got a tiger in your tank!"

Touching one of his wiggly teeth at her mouth's reminder, Martin swallowed, then sighed, picked her up, and carried her into the house, not listening to her chatter. Desperately, he shut it out, and put her down in the front hall as soon as they were in. "Where—where's Will?" he asked tensely.

She put her hands behind her back. "He's in his room. He's *upset,*" Cissy explained seriously, her eyebrows slippery worms. "He thinks you don't love us anymore."

The flat sentence drove a cold spike into his spine. "Of course I do. Of course I still love you, Cis. Nothing will ever change that." He licked at his teeth gently, wondering if it was true. While he did still feel love for both children, it seemed as though he now felt that kinship distantly, as with his own father and mother. He loved them, but that love's proximity was somehow different from before.

But it was only because there was so much on his mind right now. He had to adjust to it all first.

"Mommy says you're leaving 'cause you've got a new girlfriend and you don't want to live with us anymore."

"She said that?" Martin's brow creased, building anger. It was not nearly so simple. Leigh had never told Cissy or Will of her traps, of how she had snared him. "Well, that's not exactly right, Cis. I'll always love you and Will. I—I'm just moving out because I can't live with your mommy anymore. It's hard to explain, Cis, but it doesn't change *us.* I want you and Will to come over to be with me whenever Mommy will let you."

Cissy looked at the floor. "Yeah . . . that's what the teacher said when I told her. And the baby-sitter, too." She stuck out her lower lip. "But I wish you and Mommy weren't so mad at each other. I want you both to be here." She went back to the hall, staring at him with eyes that all at once became just like her mother's, knotting that same deadly noose. "Will does, too."

He gulped, hating how Leigh had somehow passed this on to her, and knowing that without him around it would get worse. "I—sometimes these things just happen, honey. Things happen—sometimes things change."

"The baby-sitter said *that,* too." Her eyes seemed dilated as she peered up at him. "Mrs. Murrow, you know? She said that's what happened with her first husband."

"Yeah."

"She said men couldn't be trusted, Daddy."

"She did, did she?"

Cissy took a step back and cringed as though she knew she shouldn't have said it. He tried his best not to show the aggravation he felt. He remembered Lisa Murrow and the time she had come on to him, telling him she was a daddy-sitter, too, but he had recoiled.

She smelled bad, too. Not like Jan.

"Daddy . . ."

"Mrs. Murrow is a bitter woman, Cis," he said. "Don't pay any attention to what she says."

"That's what Mommy said, too."

That surprised him, but he wouldn't allow the feeling of gratitude to Leigh to remain.

"Will Mommy get married to someone else, Daddy? Will he live with us?" She reached her hand into his.

His vocal cords locked, and he stared through the living room while he worked them. "Maybe." Martin did his best to smile cheerfully. "Then you'll have two daddys and two mommys. You'll get more presents on your birthday. And at Christmas."

"Oh." Her eyes held him for a long time, and she finally let go of his thumb and turned away. "I'll tell Will you're here, Daddy. He wants you. He . . . misses you." She sniffed, hiding her expression. "He cried last night after you left . . . like a *baby.*"

Opening his mouth, Martin started to say something, but his throat caught, and he waited too long. Her steps plodded away from him, then the bedroom door opened and closed again.

"Don't let her con you, Martin. She cried, too." Leigh stepped out of the kitchen, followed by the smell of roast. She had already changed out of her dress, which surprised him, and was wearing a Six Flags over Texas T-shirt and jeans. Her lips were trembling somewhere between a smile and uncertainty. "How . . . was your day?"

"How'd you get home so early?"

"I didn't go to work today, Martin." She spread her fingers out and stared at the nails wistfully. They were splintered—ragged and chewed. "I just didn't feel like it, and the children really needed me to be with them."

"Cissy said she talked to the sitter."

"I dropped them by for a little while after she got out of school this afternoon so I could be alone. I"—she dropped her gaze to the floor—"I needed to think."

Her obvious desire to speak with him didn't lessen his urgency to get back to Jan. His stomach was growling, and he wanted to eat the meal she was preparing.

But he was free of Leigh now, even if she was still held captive by the same delusions with which she had so long held him down. He shook his head, then slowed down because of the past they'd shared. It was a waste of time, but he gave her the occasion her self-imprisonment craved. Like Cara, she'd had her chance, and it was only now, at the prospect of his loss, that she wanted to set things straight. "What did you think about, Leigh?"

"A lot of things." She nodded at the couch. "Can you—do you want to sit down?"

"Just for a minute," he agreed, charitably giving her the opportunity she'd never given him. But he chose the easy chair across from her. He crossed his legs, holding in a grunt when his bones creaked like an old man's.

Leigh watched him, hesitated, then sat down on the couch. She sighed, then took a deep breath. "You—you're right that I've been concentrating too hard on my job, Marty. I haven't been spending enough time with *you.*" She reached out to straighten the photos he'd placed together on the coffee table, his own still missing conspiciously. "I haven't spent enough time with Will or Cissy, either. It's just—" She screwed up her eyes as if to cry, then broke into another loud sigh. "It's just that I'm trying so hard to get us everything we need and want. The bills have been so difficult. I didn't tell you because I didn't want you to worry, and I thought we'd catch up quicker than this. I didn't want us to do without the things we wanted." Her face pleaded with him. "I didn't mean for you to think I was ignoring you, Marty. I . . . love you."

The needling words hurt, stabbing him deep for several moments. But he masochistically enjoyed the pain, then found a sadism in his pleasure at her frustrated agony. She was like a hunter whose prey was escaping before her eyes, and she was using the very sticks and stones on the ground to try and stop him. But the words weren't even that.

Like the nursery rhyme said, words could never hurt him!

"We have so many good things, Marty. God, I know I try to act like Superlady and make it seem like I can handle everything by myself, but sometimes I just need to know that I've got someone behind me, backing me up. Even if I don't show it, I need to know you're there, Marty. I *need* that. I don't want you to think that I work at my job so hard because I love it." Her hands fidgeted over the roller coaster decorating her T-shirt, and she shook her head. "It's okay. The job isn't bad, but I work hard because I love *you.* Damn it, I do it because I love my family and I want us to have as much as we can."

Hot and nauseous anger took root in his gnawing stomach at this final decoy. He had learned her tricks as hard lessons through the years. Could it all change so quickly as she wanted him now to believe, especially when the opportunity of his life was waiting only a few miles away? "You should have talked to me about it, Leigh. You should have said something when there was still time, before—" He clenched a fist. "It's just too damn late."

"I'm telling you now, Marty."

The decision that he thought—believed—was already

irrevocably made loomed before him once more, bringing back all his doubts like a recurring nightmare. "What do you want to do about it, Leigh?"

"I—I thought about us all day, Marty. I thought about when we were first starting out, and the promises we made to each other." Her blue eyes blinked, and the tears glittered. "I . . . want you to come back home, Marty. I want us to try it again. We'll need to talk more, and I'll have to work it out so I can be home more. The children need a mother *and* a father."

All that he had ever wanted her to be was in this desperate promise. She was offering him what he should have had from the beginning as she clutched wildly to retain her hold. It was tantalizing, invigorating; it puffed him with importance to know he wasn't yet banished from the life they'd shared, that he could go on with her now in the way he'd always wanted.

Her eyes were hopeful, and his resolve wavered.

"Please, Marty."

But what about Jan? Starting over with Leigh would mean telling Jan that he'd lied to her and didn't love her enough to sacrifice everything for the joys she wanted to bring him.

And that he wanted to have. He would have to go to her in that empty apartment she'd rented this afternoon and tell her it was over before it even began.

It'll be hard, Marty.

Jan's tender voice pounded his heart.

It was hard. It was the decision that had been so difficult last night, and it was bulldozing his weakening resolve once more. It was the choice between the ten years of captivity and a new shackling he could only guess at, or Jan and freedom.

"Marty, when we were first married we made promises to each other. You and I. We promised each other we would never get a divorce."

"Yes." He concentrated on Jan, remembering her ways and her body: the way her breasts felt as he chewed them, her muscular pussy milking his hard cock. "I remember. And I remember we promised that we would never have the problems we've already had, too." Leigh or Jan. Jan or Leigh. A brand new life or the same old one with maybe some changes for the better, or maybe for the worse. Was it better to forget ten years that had gone wrong, or to try and make them right? His heart wrenched in his chest.

What were the odds?

"We can change things, Marty. We can overcome our problems. When we first met you told me we could overcome *anything.*" She got down on her knees and laid her face against his leg, running a finger down his calf.

"We were young then, Leigh." He closed his eyes and searched until he saw that memory, and her as he had seen her then.

He knew now he had married someone else. The longer they stayed with each other, the more he didn't even know her. They were nothing alike. If they ever had been, she had changed, and changed drastically.

"Shit happens, Leigh. We only knew the things we wanted to show each other. I kept secrets and you kept secrets. We never"—he choked out the misery and sadness of what they had lost—"really got to understand each other as we should have."

"Marty, we've spent over ten years together. *Ten* years. We know each other better than anyone else does even if we have kept secrets. We—we can make it work."

Her hand stretched out and stopped midway to his. It was a small space, but he knew it was one that might always be there. They could never be one the way he had discovered with Jan. Not of one flesh.

Jan knew him in the truest meaning of the phrase. From those first minutes together and slipping into that long, beautiful first night. He had burned for her, wanting her, and his obsession increased with each minute she was near. Their short separation, ghastly with his fear of never finding her again, showed what his choice must be. In these short days with very little conversation she had proved herself as Leigh never had.

They were alike.

"Please, Marty. Can't we try?"

Could he refuse Jan and always wonder? Would that be fair to her, or to Leigh? Would it be fair to him?

Leigh scooted between his legs, reaching the rest of the distance to take his hands in hers as she knelt there in front of him, begging. "Don't we owe it to ourselves to try? Don't we owe it to Cissy and Will?"

Her threatening overload spilled in those last pleas, relaying the worn flypaper for him to stick to while each word attacked the freedom he had finally rediscovered with Jan. His hand hung limp in Leigh's, and he bit his lip. "I'm tired of trying," he breathed.

The bedroom door in the hall opened, and Will and Cissy came out to stand silently. He saw them as the unbending bars of Leigh's rebuilt prison. For him. Just for him.

"I'll try for both us." Leigh squeezed his fingers.

Shutting his eyes to his children, Martin resurrected his incredible loathing for Leigh. He knew she was only torturing him and taking away the precious minutes of his life while Jan was waiting, wondering where he was. She might be worried that he had changed his mind. He shuddered, bitter at how it worked. He shook off her clasp. "I'm too damn tired, Leigh."

"No, Marty. It's never too late. Jerry Halverson, my minister, told me he would talk to you . . . talk to us both. He—he can help us get it right! H-he—"

"Leave your God and fucking church out of this, Leigh! I don't go to church, and I'm sure as hell not going to start now! Leave this God shit out of it. This is between you and me! I'm tired!" He jerked her to her feet and pushed past her. "I'm too fucking tired of all of your shit!"

"Daddy?"

Leigh turned with him. The children were cowering back in the doorway, their faces lined with torment. Leigh looked from them to Martin. "Marty, please—don't do this with Cissy and Will—"

"Why the fuck not?" He sneered at the two of them now, but only for a moment. It made his empty stomach twist and brought him close to actually throwing up. He covered his damp mouth and stalked to the kitchen, then to the door in there that led out into the garage.

"What are you doing?"

The screen slammed behind him, and he flipped on the light, seeing and smelling all the cardboard boxes along the side of the wall. Their contents had never found a place in the home. Almost everything out there was his.

Of course. He felt a sour humor, sniffing the musty smell. At least it would be easy to move. Then he saw the old sofa and unfinished table from their first house. The beanbag chairs in need of repair. The chipped table lamps . . . He remembered when all they'd had together was each other and their love. It had seemed to promise a future.

Martin swallowed hard. "I'm going to finally get this junk out of your way, Leigh!" he shouted back. "I'm taking this old furniture." He remembered the way she'd just wanted to dump it all and was now glad he'd put his foot down. Somehow he had known that he would need it one day.

It was destiny.

"Daddy?" said Will.

Something in his son's voice made him turn to the reddened eyes that even now made him guilty and sick. It was the hardest now. He had to get through these horrible minutes, then it *had* to ease away.

He was free.

But as Cara had reminded him a few days ago, *nothing* was free. Not even, he was learning, freedom itself. Because he was paying for that cherished condition dearly and was only surviving because he understood that each new agony spurred him closer to it.

"Daddy?"

"What the hell do you want, Will?"

A hesitation.

"Can . . . you play with me? Daddy . . . with my spacemen? I—I want—"

They were trying to break him down. Martin saw that through the furious hatred of the pressure billowing in his heart. "I showed you how to play with those damn things by your self!"

Will's mouth went loose. Tears rolled onto his pink cheeks. *"You . . . don't . . . love . . . me!"* the little boy shrieked, doubling over and trembling. "You . . . *don't!"*

Martin did his best to keep his voice even. He shook his head, wanting to feel pity for his son, but he didn't. "Will—hey, stop that crap! Daddy's busy now, okay? Just play by yourself tonight."

Will stared, his eyes white and big, his features stretched into an old man's wrinkles. "B-but won't you . . . ever . . . play with m-me again, Daddy?"

The nausea grew stronger. He clenched his jaw as the hostility dissipated and left him watching the tormented and crying little boy. He felt ashamed and filthy, like a bully who had just bloodied a baby's nose for no reason other than to reassure himself of his superior strength. "I'm sorry, Will. We—we'll play this weekend, okay? You can bring some of your stuff over to my new place. I promise, we'll play then—"

Will turned and ran back into the hall, his little feet plopping ridiculously.

"You . . . you hurt his feelings, Daddy."

Cissy's voice echoed in his ears. His vision blurred, and his teeth burned hot, kicking their raw pain into his brain. "I—"

But Cissy was gone, too.

Leigh's strained tone slapped him. "Sometimes you're a *bastard,* Martin."

The truth was out in that chastising, and her anger showed at last, replacing the false love of her lure, showing him how close he had come to a life sentence . . . to a death sentence.

"Fuck you, too," he snarled, going down the steps noisily with the relief of this latest 007 escape. He used the washing machine to hold himself up, gulping the stale air and emptying his brain of everything, thinking only of Jan. She waited patiently for him, loving him, wanting him to be himself and to be happy—

She washed his thoughts clean as he found what he wanted. He moved fast now, stacking his choices at the garage door. He had to get back to her. She was waiting. She needed him, and he had promised himself to her. She was his, not Leigh. She was his, and he was hers.

And the children?

He slugged the wall with fierce anger, cracking the plaster-board and blasting his face with dust that made him cough. It was so fucking hard.

But he had to hurry, and did, not even noticing when one of his teeth dropped onto the cement floor.

26

The crumbling brick walls of the apartment house leaned tiredly between two elderly warehouses, looking like a derelict unable to hold himself up. The once-ornate building overlooked a carpet of broken glass and soggy paper carpetting the sidewalk. The scene was silent but for two or three air-conditioning window units that dotted the upper windows. Their whines rattled the night, and the rest of the windows stood wide open, revealing an occasional passing inhabitant pushing out into the muggy, late summer air.

Matching that building's faded address to the one scrawled on the paper in his fist, Martin wrinkled his nose and tongued the gap in his mouth where a tooth had finally worked itself out. It annoyed him, but he knew it could be replaced. He could replace all his fucking teeth with shiny new ones that couldn't decay, just like he was replacing his rotted old life with his new one with Jan.

Forgetting the humiliating betrayal of his own body, he put the piece of paper back into his pocket and turned his head this way and that. He was in an older, dying part of the city where he'd never been. It was filled with outcasts who only existed in his life heretofore via the evening news and headlines. They provided a sort of kinship, though, and he saw himself in the faces he passed in the car. They were as imprisoned by life and its system as he'd been, unfortunates who didn't know what they wanted any better than their jailers uptown. They had been driven here because they could not compete, and because they had given up. They wanted, but not hard enough.

Martin twisted the Lynx's wheel around until the car crept into a crowded parking lot, and he peered at the dusty furniture stacked behind and beside him when he reversed into a space. He shut off the engine and got out, scraping his door against the dented Chevy pickup next to him.

"Daddy?"

Will's voice repeated in his thoughts, and he held his head, his fingers deep in the flesh of his face. It drove out the pleas of his son. He sighed, sniffing deep the raw breeze that was rank with the surroundings. He could smell hot used oil and ripe banana peels. His nose wrinkled, and he looked at his watch, then lifted the old waterbed sheets off the front seat and slammed his door, enjoying its crashing echo in the cranking night hums of north downtown.

"I'm free," he whispered to himself, turning his feet to the apartment house and hearing something like potato chips crunch beneath his feet. "God damn, I'm *free!*"

O brave new world, where no man has ever gone before . . . and the flowers bloom like madness in the spring. . . .

Moments crept by while he forced his bad foot through the parking lot's gum-ridden maze. The old junkers left only inches between themselves for his path, and he tore his shirt and snagged his slacks as he plowed his way to the apartment doors on the bottom floor. Door 18 beckoned with its numbers loose and tarnished, but Martin relished a long breath of the sweetly putrid air as he touched the knob.

The door creaked open to dim light, and he exhaled, then stepped inside.

The front room's mildew aroma mixed with the atmosphere outside to make his lungs raw. He limped to the open window with a gasp, leaning against a faded wall that peeled its dying paint under his fingernails. When he could breathe again he turned back, stilling the sickness violating his stomach in the relief that he had eaten so little. His eyes widened at the desiccated environment that rivaled its exterior gloom, going from the front room's watermarked paneling to the carpet that was black with stain, its ragged holes patched ineptly. His nose wrinkled again. "Good God."

"Marty?"

Crushing the bedsheets under an arm, he shifted and saw her at the warped door to another room, her body seductively hidden by a tigh midriff T-shirt and frayed cutoffs that stopped at the crest of her legs. She rubbed her crotch and grinned, posing against the wall with her other hand poised on her hip. Despite his disappointment he managed a smile. "Hi, beautiful."

She shook her limp hair, then displayed a dirty palm. "Not hardly. I've been trying to get this filthy place cleaned up." She wiped her forehead, streaking it, then walked around the pieces of glass on the floor, the pert swing of her breasts emphasized by their bralessness. "This afternoon I figured it must be better than it looked. I'm not so sure now. When I get groceries I'm going to buy a ton of disinfectant."

Opening his arms to her, he shrugged, not daring to agree. "It's not so bad."

"Really?" She was honestly hopeful. "Did I do okay, Marty? I . . . I've never done anything like this by myself before."

Overlooking the hours of back-breaking exertion the place needed just to be livable, he hugged her, finding the calm relaxation only her touch seemed to give him. "You did okay, Jan."

She waggled her nose, sniffing. "It sure stinks, doesn't it?"

"It just needs to be aired out good."

They kissed then, and he poured every emotional tension into it, groping her sweaty body roughly. He smothered her, chewing the tongue she offered into his mouth, then he grunted when she drew it back breathlessly. "Shit, Marty. I must stink as bad as this place does. Are you that glad to see me?"

"You bet." The ghastly confines faded into the glow of being so near to her, and knowing that he always would be.

We have met reality and it is ours! It is our dream. It smelled too awful in here to be anything other than real.

"It's still tough over there, huh?"

The memories were mercifully fading fast, but he nodded for effect. "That bad," he agreed.

"You must be starved, too."

The reminder of his long fast made his stomach bellow, even in the unappetizing surroundings of the air's decay. He blushed, stepping back.

"You sound hungry." She pointed at the kitchen nook in the corner, and he saw that her afternoon's efforts had at least dented its filth to passably clean. She smiled. "I started scrubbing in there first so I could fix you dinner. I'll get a quick shower now and buy some groceries while you lie down."

"No." He didn't want to be apart from her tonight after what he'd gone through. "That—that wouldn't be fair, not after you've been slaving in here."

Unbuttoning the tight cutoffs, she rolled them down to her knees and let them drop to the carpet, exposing her naked thighs and the black bushy hair that sprang out between them. Martin gulped, assailed by a familiar stiffening need.

She removed her shirt, standing bare. "It's the way it has to be, Marty. You need rest so you can work tomorrow." Her tongue poked out between her lips. "Because you sure as hell won't get any sleep tonight. Not if I can help it."

Her readiness to please him in spite of her hard work here pumped new strength into his veins. "I want us to be together for all of tonight, Jan. Besides, you'll need help carrying the grocery sacks from the car." He went to her and rested a hand on her damp skin. "I'll help you take your shower, too."

"Oh, yeah?" Her face became sly. "Going to make sure I get this icky smell off, huh? You going to wash my back, big man?"

"Whatever you want."

"No. Whatever *you* want tonight, my love. This is your

night of freedom." She began unbuttoning his shirt as his stomach roared more powerfully. A giggle trickled between her lips, growing while she stroked his chest and tickled him. She slipped off his shirt during another stomach rumble. "I guess you don't need to work up an appetite, huh?"

He chuckled with her. "I can start with you as my appetizer."

Her fingers unbuckled his belt smoothly and opened his slacks. She bent to her knees to lower them down his hairy legs. "This is your night, Marty," she whispered huskily, dragging down the waistband of his undershorts to blow her hot breath over him. "In the coming days you may regret this and want to go back . . ."

Her slick tongue touched his inner thigh and slid up, bringing him the shudders he desired. He laid his hands on her shoulders as lightly as he could, trying to keep his stance steady. "I—I want you, Jan," he swore.

Her moist mouth drooled around him, moving up and down. She stopped. "I love you, Marty. I need you, but I'm not stupid. You want me now, but I know you'll want to go back sometimes. I know you still love your wife."

He thought back to Leigh's promises tonight—the words he'd wanted her to say for so long. He had somehow gathered the strength to throw them back at her without a moment's consideration. He thought of her hurt face. She'd been crushed and broken by his rejection, betrayed.

But he didn't love her anymore. It was over, and he was out. He gasped as Jan's mouth closed over him again, up and down, back and forth . . . slowly.

A minute that was too short passed as he savored what she was doing to him—something Leigh never did. Despite the promises of change, he doubted she would do it now.

"There is still something holding you to her, Marty." Jan slurped, taking a wet breath before continuing. "I know it. I know you, remember? There is *something.*"

Her tongue flicked him, teasing him until he groaned and felt the pent-up anxieties dissolve into the lightning surge she coerced. "God . . . damn," he wheezed, trying to bring her back, wanting her to finish, wanting to release it all into her.

"Marty, I want you. I need all of you. I need you to be mine."

He frowned, craving this release more than he had ever wanted anything before. Needing her. Needing the freedom he had in her. "Please," he whined.

Jan's fingers pinched the tender skin and caressed him.

"It's Cissy . . . and Will." He sighed with hoarse frustration. "I have to—"

Jan's lips chewed him in slow rhythm, raking him gently with her teeth. "Do you want them more than me?"

He closed his eyes, trying to shut away Will's recurring pleas. "I—but I want them to come here to be with us sometimes, Jan. They're mine, too—they're my kids."

Her warm hand still worked him, keeping him at a level near frenzy. "They want you only for what you give them, Marty. They live off you." She paused. "They can't give back to you like I can."

Parasites. Though she didn't say it, he felt the implication in her tone and knew its chill in his heart. "But . . ."

Jan's mouth was slick around him again, squeezed him faster and faster. Up and down, back and forth. Squeeze . . . in and out, back and forth.

They would always be his, no matter what, wouldn't they? No matter what he said? No matter what he told her, nothing could ever change that, could it?

So why did it matter what he told her? "I—I'm yours, Jan." He forced the words out. "I'm yours. My life is *yours.*"

Squeeze.

Her lips turned up in a curious smile, at last satisfied, and maddeningly, she pulled away once more. "Yes, and you will make our new life, Marty. You have me, and I have you. I need you, dear heart, and now that I have you I can offer you everything you ever desired. We are as one, more than you and Leigh ever were."

"Yes," he begged. "Yes, please—"

She opened her mouth for him at last, and he shoved

inside fiercely, bucking his hips into her face and shoulder so hard he almost knocked her over. He synchronized himself to her mouth as the slobbery gurgle of her throat timed his explosion. She brought him to the joyous end that drove everything else from his brain. She gave him her submission with a tender force that overpowered him until only the two of them existed in the world they had created.

27

The air was crisp, but tinged with sulfur. Martin gasped, eyeing the gray stone of the fireplace and the newspapers stacked on the hearth. He sucked in a deep mouthful of the air with a growing recognition of his surroundings, not remembering what had brought him here.

He couldn't remember coming back here.

The house was dark and slumbering, and only the cracks between the curtains let in any light at all. But they were enough to give him glimpses, and he knew where he was. With wide eyes he stared at the outlines of the photographs of the children and Leigh on the coffee table, squinting as their glass coverings shimmered in the faint reflection of the outside glow. He stood very still.

Parting the thick fog that covered his murky, vague memories, he bit his thumb hard enough to draw blood. He had to keep himself from screaming into the silent house he'd called home so long.

It wasn't home now. He tossed his head to each side, feeling a dribble of sweat on his forehead. He had rejected this. He had left it all. His home was with Jan!

Had he come here in his sleep?

Impossible as it seemed, it was the only explanation. With

all the crazy things in this fast week, and as tired as he was, he must have come here out of habit.

Ice coated his stomach, forming stalactites.

He must have driven his car in his sleep.

"How?" he croaked, struggling to find his bearings. He held out his hands, shuffling ahead and reaching for where the front door was, but he bumped into a chair. "Ummph." He muffled his cry, stumbling in the slow pain that made him wince and stagger ahead. Martin bit his lip breathlessly and saw the front door through his eyelashes. He grabbed the knob, pulling it open.

But not to the front yard.

Leigh was sprawled lazily on the bed amid tangled sheets, naked, panting harshly. He fought panic, shrinking back when her surprised eyes looked up at him, then dropped with a low moan. He watched disbelievingly as her long, pale fingers gripped the wrists of the woman who knelt between her outstretched legs. The vision thudded into his brain. He tried to back out, but his legs buckled under him, and he crumpled to the floor.

"Daddy!" shrieked Cissy, appearing beside him in the blackness. Her taut, pale face melted and disfigured like the doll she had once left out under a hot sun. She reached out to him. "Daddy!"

Martin wanted to meet her little hand with his, shrinking from the fear and terror consuming her as it became his own. He knew her alien loneliness but could not raise his hand. He could not move.

"Please, Daddy?" her wobbly voice wailed.

The words he wanted wouldn't form in his mouth. They changed into others on his very tongue. "Not yours," he heard himself saying, unable to stop those syllables as his soul turned to ice.

"Play with me, Daddy . . . please?" begged Will on the other side of him. "Please?" His small hands held out the broken Darth Vader with entreaty, and again Martin tried to reach out, though his arms were bound with invisible chains.

They were not his children. He had rejected them. The heavy chain stopping his arms was his need of Jan.

If he rejected her . . .

"Please?" The voice echoed in his mind endlessly, joining Cissy's high whine, but he could touch neither of them. He could not even talk.

He could not reject *her.* Jan brought him back to himself. Cissy and Will wanted to imprison him.

"You don't belong here," sang Leigh's breathless whisper from the bed, and he jerked his face back to stare at her, seeing her gaunt, whitewashed face and its vague smile while the naked woman between her legs made lapping noises and caressed her breasts.

"Why . . . who?"

The sound choked itself off in his throat as the woman lifted her face from Leigh and turned to him silently, her face and lips red with Leigh's shiny blood, a nearly emotionless satisfaction dripping from her wet smile.

It was Jan.

28

Screaming, Martin bolted from the bedsheets as though snatched up by a giant. His arms flailed wildly in the nightmarish vision still lingering in his eyes like the afterimage of a flashbulb. He panted wildly and tried to stand up on the sloshing bed. But he swayed, could not find a direction in dizziness, and fell over the bedside to the floor, smashing his screeching foot on the carpet.

"No!"

The foot screamed under him, and green flares bounced through him crazily, vibrating new pain. The next shriek burned his throat raw, spreading its fire to collide with the humid, putrid air thick around his sweat-slick body. He got his foot into the clear and huddled over it, holding his other leg to his chest, his teeth chattering. Nausea pumped him, and he drooled uncontrollably. Then he suddenly vomited out the spicy spaghetti dinner Jan had made him. His belly tossed and twisted again at the sour odor that increased, and at the sight of the half-digested wormlike noodles covered in sauce. Desperately he tightened his abdominal muscles and clenched his teeth to hold the next surge in.

"Daddy!" The voices rang in and out, over and over.

"No . . . no . . . NO!"

"Marty—wake up!" Her cool hands smoothed his neck, and she slipped off the bed, kneeling on the floor beside him and cradling him in her arms. "Wake up, Marty!"

Their previous unions flowed through her fingers, and he trembled, staring into her frightened face that was unblemished by the dream blood. She held him tight to her warm breasts, and her honey-scented hair brushed his face, overcoming the sulfur from his dreams and the stale taint that made him shudder. "J-Jan?" he stammered.

"Yes. Yes . . . I'm here, Marty." She spoke to him as though he were a child, holding him that way, too, but it reassured him against the darkness of the room that was loud in his own mind. Slowly, it faded under her fingertips.

But Martin continued to clutch her tight, even though he knew it must be hurting her. She grunted but said nothing.

"Oh . . . Jan."

"Was it a dream?" her soft voice asked.

"Yeah." He swallowed, wanting her to drive it all away from him, needing her.

"I'm here, Marty. Everything's okay now. We're together."

He leaned against her for a minute that seemed an eternity, finally finding a steadiness as his heartbeat slowed. He reached for her face with apology. "I . . . I'm sorry."

"It's all right," she told him smoothly. "I understand how hard it's been for you, Marty. I know that—I know you, remember? I understand." Her fingers smoothed the damp hair against his head. "Are you okay now? Do you want me to get you a drink of water?"

"I . . . I'm exhausted." His body was heavy and so empty. He could not think. He wanted, but he didn't know what.

"It took a lot out of you to do what you did. Most people could never turn their backs on everything they've been like you did, Marty. It took a lot."

"Yeah."

She bent and kissed his forehead, and he sighed with that

tingle, then smiled, glad she was there to close off the horrible nightmare. He managed a feeble smile.

"Let me get you a drink."

Reaching out as she got to her feet, he cringed. "I . . . need you, Jan. I need you. Don't leave . . . please?"

She stood above him. Her faced showed the satisfaction he'd seen in her dream image. Even with the shadows. He swallowed.

"I'll just get you a drink, Marty. You need some water. Your voice is so hoarse." She patted his head. "Don't worry a bit. I'll take care of you. I think it's so nice that you need me, too. Don't worry. I won't ever leave you, Marty. I can't. You're mine now. We're together."

His lips were trembling silently. "Together," he whispered. "I love you so much, Jan." He gulped, "I *am* yours."

"Yes," she sighed. "You're mine. I waited a long time for you. I'll be everything to you if you'll let me. I'll always take care of you, Marty. Always."

The solemn velvet tone of her voice entranced him, and he relaxed, watching the form of her lithe body slither gracefully through the bedroom door and into the tiny hall soundlessly. He memorized the delicate roll of her buttocks and concentrated on those movements as she disappeared from his sight.

He needed her.

"That's right," Martin whispered to himself, stretching out his arm toward the door as if to pull her back. His eyelids sagged, and he studied her in his memory, not wanting his weakness. He knew the fast pace and emotional depletion of the last hours had more than caught up to him. He had sacrificed much to be with her. He'd given up his home and Leigh, if she had ever truly been his. Most of all, despite his inner denial, he knew he'd given up Cissy and Will. They were rapidly receding in the fog of his dreams.

But he was too tired to contemplate all this now, far too tired to change what he'd done. He knew he could change everything back when he was stronger, if that was what he wanted. Only a matter of hours had passed, and though he had firmly closed the door on his old life, he was certain he could force it back open when he was stronger.

He needed Jan for that, though. His confusion and the difficult decisions he'd already made caused this crushing weakness. Only a time of peace and Jan's attention would nurse back his abilities.

Then he would talk with Will . . . and Cissy. But not until he was better. He would not let them see him like this. He needed to rest and regain himself, and to let the excitement Jan instilled in him wear until he could renew and continue those other responsibilities.

He lifted himself on shivering elbows, gritting his sore teeth. His other front tooth fell onto the filthy carpet, and the front bottom one dropped out after.

"Sh-shit!" he cried. He drooled and caught his breath as air filled the open sockets. It was a bizarre pain, as if someone was slicing frigid razor knives into his gums, in and out.

He picked up one of the teeth and tried to fit it back. He pressed it against the next tooth but jerked his fingers back when that one wiggled, too. "My—my God—Jesus!" He stared blankly at the small white piece of bone and enamel in his palm—a piece of himself. He gripped it between his thumb and fingers and saw that it was blackened, its root rotted away.

It scared him. "No," he gasped. He wished he had gone to see the dentist more often these past years. His teeth were rotting inside his mouth, falling out. He had to get to a fucking dentist!

The empty sockets stung like open sores, but his body ached in other places, too. His eyesight was blurry more and more often these past hours. Tears welled up and blurred his eyes again now as sharp nails dug into his stomach and made him drop his head to his knees.

He was too fucking sick to go anywhere!

Thank God for Jan. She would help him. The sound of the water faucet in the kitchen reminded him that he wasn't as horribly alone as it seemed. She would take care of him and make him vital once more. She had brought him to his pleasure and meaning at last, just in time, giving him salvation at the very moment the toll of his imprisonment became destruction.

Jan fulfilled his life and would save his life.

29

When the alarm exploded in Martin's ears he tried to roll over and block it out, feeling as though he'd only just lain down. "God damn," he whimpered, cracking open his eyelids and shivering from the unwarmed waterbed's chill. His stomach was empty, but the memory of waking up last night brought back his nausea and made him reject all thoughts of eating. He stared around blearily, focusing as well as he could on the ripples that disfigured the yellowed ceiling.

"Hey, hot dick." Jan stood beside the bed, already dressed in tight shorts and a halter top. "Time to get up, sleepy-head." She leaned down for a kiss. "Time to get to work."

"Y-yeah," he grunted, and he took the hand she offered, rising to meet her open mouth. But even that brief electricity wouldn't discharge his lethargy.

She frowned when he didn't respond, then pulled him upright and to his feet. He felt his knees wobble. "Ouch."

She took his hand and helped him, pouting and looking him up and down with raised eyebrows. "You okay, Marty? What's wrong, love?"

He shook his head, so weakened by the continued illness that he could barely speak. "I . . . I'm all right. My stomach just feels funny." He glanced at the three boxes of clothes and personal items he'd brought back last night, then turned to the alarm clock. He would have to hurry. "I just wish I'd thought to buy some aspirin and Alka-Seltzer."

Jan patted his bottom playfully. "No prob, big guy. I told you I'd take care of you, didn't I? I did pick some of that stuff up, and I got up early this morning to start arranging things so this place would look better to you. I put the medicine right there in the bathroom." She laid the back of her hand on his forehead. "No fever, but I'll get you an aspirin anyway. Ready for breakfast?"

"Ugh," he choked, feeling the blood drain from his face at the very idea. "Just something for my stomach, I think."

"Scrambled Alka-Seltzer over easy?"

Martin wasn't in the mood for jokes and just shivered. "Can you get it for me while I get dressed?"

Unaffected, she waltzed to the bathroom, bouncing her breasts and ass slinkily. He saw, but this time he was unaffected, too, and bent to the cardboard box he'd hurriedly packed his business clothes in.

He frowned, ignoring her cheerful whistle as she opened a cabinet and turned on the water. The suits and shirts were wrinkled, and he regretted being so sloppy as he drew out a checkered coat to smooth it. He wished he'd taken the time to unpack before they'd gone to bed. He had just been so eager, so fucking eager.

To be eager fucking.

Another sour belch boiled his stomach berserkly, but he swallowed the saliva that came up his throat, hauling out a pair of blue slacks to lay on the bed. He tangled with dizziness when he sat down on the floor to drag on a pair of socks. Standing again, he couldn't remember when getting into his clothing had been such a battle, and he longed to get back into bed and try to sleep this off. It was as though he was harboring a terrible, sickening hangover from a long drunk.

"Here you are, Marty," Jan called out, emerging from the bathroom with a glass of fizzing water. She pressed the wet container into his palm, running her fingers over the back of his hand, helping him lift it to his mouth. "That'll help settle you down. I probably spiced up that spaghetti too much last night."

Tasting the heavy meal's final existence on his foul breath, he hoped she was right. At least her diagnosis made sense. Eating such a greasy dinner late at night on top of his stomach's bordering hysteria must have done it. He had known better than to have that second helping but had craved to fill his empty body with its temptation, just as he so wanted to fill his empty life with her. Yes, indeed, and his half-crazed feeding had probably caused that nightmare as well.

Martin gulped down the bubbly water, wincing at its aftertaste, then allowed her to help him back to his feet. She assisted him with the slacks, too, and then knelt to tie his shoes. He used her head to hold himself steady as she knelt at the laces, trying to reclaim strength. He hoped he would feel better once he got to work.

"There you go." She grinned, then pushed her face to his pants and nibbled through its fabric. Martin belched and groaned, feeling anything but sexy. He was actually relieved when she moved away and got back up. "You look damn snazzy," she told him.

"I wish I felt that good. I don't think I'll feel much like moving anything tonight."

"Poor Marty. But that's okay." She took his hand with a gentle caress, spreading her fingers over his. "Hey. She didn't change the locks yet, did she, Marty?"

His head was splitting in the fire and smoke that obscured so much of his thought. "Who? What?"

"The door locks," Jan replied, picking a shirt for him and holding it up to his chest. "The door locks to your house, silly."

He stopped another belch and shook his head.

The gas stopped at his teeth and reversed itself. He blushed at a fart.

It was bad, like a backed-up sewer.

"It stinks bad enough in here without you adding to it, Marty." Jan giggled, fanning the air away. Then she held out his right arm and slipped it into a sleeve, bringing the shirt around his back to get his left arm in the opposite sleeve. "I can take you to work and move the things myself if you want me to, you know."

"I—" The warmth of Jan's simple willingness to help with everything struck him in its opposition to Leigh's attitude, and he welcomed it. "No," he finally told her. "Somebody might think you were stealing. The neighbors are busybodies and know us pretty well." He belched again, painfully, and failed to resist another damp fart. He was barely able to keep back the rebellion in his stomach. "Sorry," he said, "but maybe I'll feel better tonight."

"I wish we could get it all during the day when no one's there, though, Marty. Being back in that dungeon tore you up pretty bad last night. I can tell."

"I've already missed too much work." Even if Cara was right and the company was going to pay him for the time he'd had off, the boss would frown at his missing today. It reminded him of the teeth already missing and the others enlisted in his body's revolution. It would take money to replace them—in George Harrison's words, "a whole lotta spending money."

Martin knew he had to work.

Jan put her arms around him. "You said you went at it hard yesterday, though. Just call in and tell your boss you charged in too quickly and that you've had a relapse. Tell him you feel a lot worse today. You may as well, since they're paying you for sick leave. And you'll feel a lot better once we get all this done with, Marty."

He knew it was true. His anxiety last weekend that Leigh would find him out, and then that he might never see Jan again, had realigned and magnified. Now he was afraid that something else might happen to break up this new life. That and the spaghetti were making him ill. Maybe the worry was somehow even making his teeth loosen! He and Jan needed so many things, and one of the most important was to finish setting up the apartment so it looked and felt permanent rather than temporary. He and Jan needed to be comfortable, and then all the frenzied worry pulling him apart would dissipate.

There would be other loose ends, to be sure. He had to initiate his divorce from Leigh and then plan his marriage to Jan. He refused to contemplate those entanglements now, only wanting to know that they were man and wife. It was already true in spirit, but he needed to achieve that reality legally.

He would feel a lot better once everything was moved and the place tidied up. It would give him the sense of belonging he still lacked, despite Jan, and would cauterize the still-bleeding, messy dismemberment of his life. That wound would scab sooner without his constant picking at it, and only a faint scar would show.

"Don't you think it's a good idea?"

Martin nodded at last and started to look around for a phone, then remembered that they hadn't had time to get one. That would need to be done, too. "Yeah," he agreed, praying that there would be no repercussions at work over this. But then, he had gotten a lot done yesterday, and if he went in tomorrow and worked as hard, there would be little reason for raised eyebrows. This week was the first time in nearly a year and a half that he'd even been late to the office.

"Good." She sounded relieved. "I don't know why, Marty, but until we can really start to live together—I mean with all the things you need here so you won't keep going back there—I'm just afraid you might change your mind, that you might go back . . . to her."

Leigh. Could he go back now even if he wanted to? Would she take him back after he'd rejected her again last night? In his sleep he'd dreamed that maybe she would, but could he stand it? Could she really change even if she wanted to? Did her offers mean anything? He shook his head. Losing Jan wasn't worth the chance. All Leigh had that he wanted was Cissy and Will, and he was too ill to give them the patience he'd have to. "I won't go back, Jan. Don't you worry about that. I won't go back ever."

Her eyes twinkled. "We'll need to find a lawyer for your divorce, then."

The time had come for that to be done, jettisoning the indecision and ridding the threats to his freedom forever.

Then it would be truly over. Truly . . . truly, no longer unruly. Out with the bad air, in with the good. Out with this sickness, to live life as he should! Martin stared at the wall, knowing that his past life was really over. Over and done with . . . over and out, and he'd already begun anew. Once the unraveling threads were all severed he could pick up the pieces and go on without looking back. It was the frustration and this new invisible prison of all the necessary nitpicking that made him ill. Not even the spaghetti had done the damage. Only the frustration and, quoth the raven, nothing more! Peace and salvation were at hand, and the faster he could finish it all, the better he would feel.

He took Jan's left hand in both of his and squeezed it. "I'll call a lawyer I know today, then I'll talk to Sam and straighten everything out at work, and we can go to the house and get what we need to fix this place up." He looked around and saw the things Jan had already done this morning: sweeping the front room carpet and scrubbing the kitchen out again. He knew they could have it looking better than he had first believed by tonight. It would be a load off his mind.

"I think you'll feel a whole lot better once we're finished," she said, inching forward to lick his chin.

It made him feel cheerful already. "So do I." He started taking off his unbuttoned shirt again. "I'll change into something old, okay?"

She shook her head and gave him a promising glance, helping him. "I'll do it. I'm very good at taking your clothes off, Marty. I enjoy it . . . and I think you'll enjoy it, too."

Her cool, gentle fingers unfastened his pants, and he felt her hands brush his naked flesh, rubbing his belly and overpowering the looming nausea. Then she dropped lower, pushing her nose into his hair. Again? Yes. But wasn't this what he wanted? Wasn't this part of the reason he was here and had chosen her? James Bond wouldn't complain, would he? The sick feeling was retreating now, as though she had taken it from him. He felt himself growing hard, sliding between her lips.

He needed her. Repeating it over and over inside, he let

her help him lie back on the bed to finish tugging off the slacks. Her throat captured him and worked him powerfully, just as it had last night. Her name sang in his thoughts with the lust she brought him . . . the pleasure . . . consuming him . . .

Time stood still, and he let her lead him and manipulate him, losing his problems and pain in her domination.

"Are you mine?" she whispered in wet, muffled words as he neared his final spasm.

"I . . . I'm yours, Jan. I—I'll always be yours."

Her eyes smiled contentedly. "You'll always be mine," she agreed breathlessly, and she tongued him, drooling her saliva down his ass.

Martin gasped as his body became her instrument again. She made him breathe harder and harder. Made his heart thud faster. He was filled with the ecstasy only she could bring. He was hers. He moaned happily as she brought his climax and he entered into the familiar laziness of gratification, knowing that more was in store for him . . .

. . . as they lived happily ever after.

30

Sam answered the phone instead of Cara when Martin called, and he accepted Martin's excuses almost casually. Although Martin didn't ask, he knew Cara had been spreading her gossip about his situation. Sam was too understanding and didn't even ask about his foot.

Sam knew.

But Sam had gone through his own divorce a couple of years ago. Martin felt certain he understood. He assured Sam that tomorrow he would be back at work and that things were finally beginning to settle down.

They were already settling down, and his illness was dissipating with the action he was taking. He and Jan drove to Leigh's to move everything he wanted to take. He broke down and rented a U-Haul, and he even made time to call a lawyer, though he managed to put that off until last. His divorce from Leigh was officially begun, and unofficially finalized with all the things he took, which was everything he really wanted.

Except for Cissy and Will. Martin swallowed.

He laid on the divan and stared at "Three's Company," rerunning on the tiny color TV he had brought from the bedroom he'd shared with Leigh. Jan shuffled through the apartment quietly, straightening his high school bowling trophies and putting other of his mementos up. Two's company, he told himself, but wished there was a third member to help with their labors. The exertion of lifting and moving furniture had tired him, but as Jan had predicted, he was feeling much better.

He felt at home.

"How's it looking, hon?"

"Great," Martin told her honestly. He picked up his beer from the floor, following a sip of it with a lie: "I wish you'd let me help."

"You're tired . . . and your foot still hurts."

He relaxed still more, having known that would be her reply before he ever spoke. "I'm just not used to it, Jan. Back ho—uh, back with Leigh, she would sit and tell me what to do, and *I'd* have to do it."

Jan shook her head. "It's a hell of a lot easier for me to just do it if I want it done a certain way. Besides, this is the first time I've ever been able to do anything like this. On my own, I mean. I kind of enjoy it." Her deep, luscious eyes connected to his in spite of the separating space. "Of course, I want you to like it, too, Marty, and I know I should be asking you how you want things, but then"—her gaze was dreamy and confident—"but then we like the same things, don't we? Especially since we're alike."

Taking in her placement of the furniture and the dusty paint-by-number oil landscapes, he found he did agree with the way she did it, and he knew he'd have done it that way himself, given the choice. He smiled, not showing his momentary unease at the way their minds matched so closely. How could she guess he would have done it like this? Was she truly so much like he was? Did they really have that much in common?

"Like it?"

Martin forced a James Bond grin. "You're astounding, Moneypenny."

Jan patted the big old La-Z-Boy he'd barely been able to lift onto the truck earlier, and then only with considerable help from her. Years ago Leigh had made him put it in the garage because of what she called its "ratty" condition.

But it was damn comfortable.

Jan had pushed and shoved it into the apartment, rejecting his help, and now it rested imposingly at the room's center like a throne, distanced by a couple of feet from the couch where he sat now. It faced the TV casually, awaiting its first guest in years.

"I like the way it looks," said Jan, admiring it. "It belongs there. A kind of centerpiece." She chuckled. "A center of peace."

Martin grinned. "I would have put it there, too."

"I know." Stretching, she plodded to the chair and brushed off its cushions, then crooked her finger in invitation. "Want to break it in with me?"

The worn gray cotton covering the chair invited him as well, and he grunted, sitting up. It was big and would hold them both without any trouble. "Sure." He stood up and stretched, joining her, and sat with her as she giggled. They both leaned back, and the chair spread out for them, the footrest raising their legs into the air.

"I knew you'd go for this."

The distraction of her easy familiarity with his likes badgered him again. "How did you know? Do I talk in my sleep or something?"

Her laughter was high and bubbly, almost vulgar. It made him shiver despite the comfort of her body and the almost-forgotten coziness of the chair. "I told you, Marty. I just know. I know better every day. I can feel it myself now. I know." Her eyes were distant all at once but returned as she lay her head on his shoulder. "I want you," came her husky whisper.

But he was still uneasy, and his own chuckles hid his questions. When her body snuggled nearer he wondered how often he'd had her already since they'd met only days ago, and if that was all that this was really about.

Days. He knew he'd already made love to her more than he had to Leigh in the whole last year of their life together. It was something he'd dreamed of more and more as time trickled on and the troubles increased.

Having someone like Jan. He had dreamed of her hard,

like Sally had said he must, and had believed in her despite every onslaught, and she was here. She was his.

"You're mine, Marty."

She was his and he was hers, and he knew it was so true. She unbuttoned his shirt with her nimble fingers.

He closed his eyes and enjoyed it blissfully, knowing he finally had it all. She claimed him. Even if Leigh no longer did. Even if no one else ever would. She claimed him, and he was hers. "Yes," he drawled. "And you're mine."

"Always," she promised. "You don't need anyone else, Marty. I am yours. You need me."

"Yes," he sighed.

Their bodies melded though their clothes were still on. He didn't want to stop himself from drifting into the pleasure of her memory. She had come to mean so much to him. Everything, almost. Jan gave him comfort and fulfillment. He would never want to be without her.

"Don't ever leave me," said Martin, feeling the warm, supple skin of her stomach with his fingertips.

Her earnest eyes stared into his, and he saw the light of their lives twinkling there. "Never for long, my love. You're a part of me. You'll always be near me. I know that. I'll always be near you, too, and I'll always come home to you."

The assurance brought him the expected joy. He opened his mouth, and her lips met his as quickly, parting as her tongue rushed to meet his, filling the gaps left by his teeth. Martin quivered with that sting, then melted with her temptation. Her breasts rubbed over him and she opened their clothes, pulling them off and discarding them over the side of the chair. Carefully she positioned herself on top of him and slid down until their hips connected and he pushed inside. Her legs bent in front of her and around his arms, pinning him in. They finally rested on his shoulders, not letting him move as she began pushing up and down. He was in and almost out, up and down. It was almost as though he were some inanimate rocking horse. A dildo—a *fucking* horse! A thing she was using for gratification.

It was as he'd used her in the beginning, and he liked it, knowing it was a game.

Her heavy panting wet his ear, and she dripped saliva on his cheek with louder and louder moans. He panted, too, breathing harder and listening to the thuds of his heart. They were alike. They were the same.

He grunted with her as the excitement mounted, destroying any thought not of her. Other considerations crumbled in the force of their physical, emotional, and mental union as they again became one, pleasing each other perfectly. He was in her and part of her, and she was part of him, surrounding him and inside him, too, closer than anyone had ever come.

Closer. Closer . . .

Hours later Martin woke up in bed beside her at the noise of his own growling stomach. Forcing open his foamy eyes, he acknowledged those rumbles inside with the concern of having forgotten to eat dinner once more. The very notion made him blush to himself. While they'd been moving he had bypassed lunch in the fear of reanimating his illness. He'd been so overwhelmed by the menu of sex Jan had served him from dinnertime on, he'd forgotten that hunger. With a startled wheeze he knew he hadn't had breakfast, either.

He'd been sick then, but it was no wonder his stomach had begun to growl again. Growling loud to impel him to break through the weak lethargy he felt. Martin dropped a leg over the side of the bed obediently, trying to keep himself from throwing up something that wasn't there. He gasped through a vertigo that overwhelmed him. Crying out, he dropped back down to the sheets, feeling boiling, crushing sickness again.

His stomach screeched, but he wanted to vomit at the very idea of eating or drinking.

"God damn," he wheezed, folding his arms around his middle tightly, trying to squeeze out the discomforting pain gurgling inside. He struck out mindlessly and grabbed Jan's shoulder, a sudden spasm making him dig his trembling fingers into her flesh.

Without a word Jan rolled close and held him with tender

passion, showing understanding eyes in the clock's faint glow. She reached out to him with those dark orbs, pulling him against her naked body as calm hands did their work.

"I . . ." He struggled, wanting to tell her how bizarre and peculiar he felt.

How weak, how *empty.*

"It's all right, honey," she cooed. "It'll get better. You're free now. The memories will fade."

He shook his head violently, believing that for once she didn't know. She thought he was agitated by his separation from Cissy and Will. He groaned with guilty horror, realizing how thoroughly he had forgotten his children, how his self-concern for his eating and everything else had completely driven them from his thoughts!

"God," Martin grunted, hating himself, forgetting hunger now as its importance was drowned in the unthinking betrayal of his children. "Oh, God damn," he said bitterly. That was the whole problem. His appetite had disintegrated, and his stomach had been bombarded by his rejection of the responsibility he owed them. He had imprisoned them as surely as Leigh had, releasing them like too-heavy baggage in his screaming escape.

He'd helped build their prison, and had left them, and that ultimate understanding was draining him.

Jan's moist lips found his, and he let her kiss him, scarcely knowing it and drawing little pleasure from that gift.

"Don't fret so, Martin. You'll feel better."

But how could he feel better until he did something about it? Tears waterlogged his eyelashes, and he could not bear the knowledge of what he'd done. "C-Cissy," he whined. "Will—"

"Tomorrow," she said softly. "You can call them. Maybe invite them to come over when you're better. It will solve everything, Martin. *Tomorrow.*"

The ache in his soul pounded him but eased to slow bumps at her suggestion. "T-tomorrow." He lay back down as she sat on her heels and watched over him. "Yeah."

Jan shook her head sadly, scooting closer. "I don't like to see you so upset, Marty. Can I do anything? What can I do to make it better?" She bent to touch his lips firmly, signaling him with her rolling tongue.

The understanding awakened him some, and the gnawing need in his gut sighed and retreated like a dog with its tail between its legs. An impossible excitement and desire swept through him, and he put his arms around her when she pushed against him slowly. He moved with her, hard once more. Panting . . . *wanting—*

"Again?" She laughed mildly, then straddled his body, burying his length deep inside her. Her eyes still twinkled. "You're not going to be in any shape for work in the morning, you know that?"

The concrete reality of his job jarred him, and, sensing the overload that consideration would bring, he pushed it quickly away. He didn't want to go back to the office until he worked this all out. The very thought of going back while feeling this way threatened him anew with sickness. "I . . . I can't work tomorrow," he gasped.

Her face displayed no anger or disappointment, only a careful study. "You're not well," she agreed with his unsaid thoughts. "Maybe I should take a job for a while, huh? Until you're better, I mean. Would that be best?"

A steady drone captivated his mind, and her offer creased his smile with an unwilling relief. She was so caring and considerate. So understanding. She ambushed every difficulty before it grew, and all for him. He sighed as her curly bush rubbed his tight skin.

"I'll go out first thing in the morning," she told him without regret. "Until you're better, Marty. I'll get a job and make us enough to live on until then. Don't you worry, okay?"

He wondered what sort of a job she might get, what she was qualified for. It startled him as he found himself wondering what sorts of jobs she'd had before. He knew nothing about her.

He hadn't had time to learn those things about her.

There was no time now, either. The damp, smooth pressure of her thighs slid over his and she fitted herself over him as though they'd been made together, her muscles like his own hand, knowing what to squeeze and when. It was far better than his own hand.

The sensations took him away from his failures, giving him the energy he was without. Up and down . . . in and out—She was helping him, giving him life. She cared for him and took care of him like no one else ever had or would. Leigh had never cared like Jan did. If she weren't with him now . . .

But that terror was too much to contemplate.

They made love endlessly, and he felt her surrounding him, giving herself to him, and bringing him to a peak they'd only neared before. She gave him so much, and she accepted him as he was, even now, weak and losing his teeth like an old man.

"You're mine, Marty," she claimed him again. "All mine. I'll take care of you."

He smiled and nodded, huffing too hard in his ecstasy to reply. He felt the coming orgasm with the pleasure he knew only in her.

Everything else was unreal and cruel, even the fading memories of Cissy and Will . . . and Leigh. Leigh especially. She would never offer herself so totally for him or give herself up so to him.

But Jan did. Jan made him hers. In spite of all these new troubles he confronted her with, she did not refuse him.

She wanted him and needed him, and she was his.

And he was hers.

31

All mine."

Martin lay back on sheets slicked by the sweat and juices he and Jan created time and again. He swelled inside her once more, shutting his exhausted eyes. She slid up and down him, freeing him from the nightmares of his past with each stroke she helped him make. She was his freedom, and only she could repair him and make him the way he should be. Only she could make him well.

"Y-yes," he croaked, breathing in her musk while her body heaved up and down, bathing his burning brow with the sweet breeze of their union.

Martin watched the ecstasy spread onto her face over and over, shining her pink cheeks with a film of sweat that dropped onto him from her swaying auburn locks. He inhaled their pleasure until it overwhelmed him with power and his eyelids fell unwillingly closed. But when he could open them once more, though the room was still dark, he could see daylight huddling behind the torn window shades.

He panted, and his tongue lathered sticky saliva down his chin. Jan's love was what he needed, what he'd gone so long without.

You're mine, Marty.

But she was no longer in bed beside him.

He was alone.

Alone and weakened by the tormenting nightmares that merged and pitched his brain in sleep. He'd had dreams more ghastly and consuming than that past night's vision of Leigh . . . and Jan between her blood-soaked thighs.

Dreams, one after another. Sometimes he dreamed that he awoke and Jan was gone, like she was now. It was unreal, like watching himself on film as he slid off the wrinkled sheets onto the floor, staggering through the unfamiliar apartment, empty with hunger. He wandered back and forth, discovering the cans of food with labels his weary eyes could no longer decipher. But he was too weak to open them. He gnawed at their tops hungrily and sagged, dropping a can when another tooth fell out during the attempt.

Then at last he found a bag of potato chips on the counter and managed to tear it open. Sweating under the exertion, he made a crunchy repast that tasted too much like cardboard on his tongue. He spit it out with a sour belch, nearly retching.

He needed Jan.

"J-Jan." He struggled, listening to the whisper of that hoarse tone float in his mind. He knew beyond a doubt that this was another hellish dream brought on by the high temperature of sickness.

"Jan!" He sat up in bed once again.

Maybe she had gone out to find a job. He opened his eyes to the empty bedroom of the apartment, slicing his glance from the discolored ceiling to the tattered brown curtains and peeling wall paint.

All alone.

"It's not exactly like I said it, Marty," said a familiar voice. He saw the shadowy outline of a business-skirted woman step near to the bed's side.

Marty squinted as he tried to force his tired and aching eyes to focus. Not daring to believe . . .

"It's not such a bed of roses, Marty," Cara whispered, unbuttoning her ruffled top and stripping it off to show him the body he once longed for. She bent close so he could see the slender bikini lines molded onto her tan body when she unbuckled her bra, her nipples huge and standing out, and he looked into eyes as green as the outfit she discarded, feeling the wisps of her fluffy red hair on his cheek.

He tried to raise himself but slipped as the water in the mattress sloshed. His hand darted to her, fingers outstretched.

She wasn't there.

Sweat dribbled down his forehead and into his foggy eyes. "G-God . . . damn!" he shrieked, making his aching molars sting. He shut his eyes quickly and was sick. He was hallucinating and lying in his own watery vomit.

"Daddy?"

Will's voice blasted in his ears, but he knew it wasn't real, and when it repeated, joined by Cissy, he squished his eyelids tighter.

They were a dream. They weren't real! Maybe his whole life . . . was a dream! He burrowed into the damp bedsheets, hiding.

"Marty?"

It was Leigh now. Her voice and memory penetrated him so deeply; she clung to his subconscious as tightly as she had clung to his life! He wanted freedom, but her entrapments clutched him powerfully.

Leigh was at his side. He could see her where Cara had stood. Her puffy face was strong but ashen, pained and sad above her quivering lower lip. She was still wearing the Six Flags T-shirt and holding out her left hand, its wedding band glowing on her finger. "Martin," she gasped.

"L-Leigh?" He lifted the heavy sheets and blankets, rank with his sweat and the onslaught of sex they bore. He tried to raise his hand to meet her fingers, startled that he could barely make a twitch. "I . . . I—"

Their fingertips nearly touched, and the wedding band burned a hot, blinding red before it disappeared.

She faded from sight.

"You're *mine,* Marty." Jan smiled, suddenly in the bed beside him, moving between him and the lost image of Leigh. Jan kissed him and poked her tongue far into his throat, grabbing his hands to make him tug off her red blouse. Then she jerked away and smothered her bare breasts onto his stubbled cheeks. She wrapped her long legs firmly around his, pushing her pelvis into his abdomen to seek him harshly. Almost dreading it, he felt himself stiffen and arch to meet her . . . inside her. Her thighs squeezed and loosened, squeezed. She pulled him in deep.

"Leigh," he gasped, still reaching to where she had been at the bedside, to the ring's glow that faded from his very memory.

"I love you." It was Leigh's voice, but Leigh was not there.

Jan drooled above his face, bucking against him, forcing him deeper and deeper inside her secret cavern, pushing so close that their flesh seemed to merge, to grow together as one.

"I love you, Marty," whispered Leigh's distant cry.

But Jan's fingers stroked his inner thighs, her long nails making him sigh as they probed his balls. She squeezed and forced his needs out and into herself.

They grew together.

For a brief instant he tried to pull back, and screamed when he felt his body rip away from hers, felt his flesh tear as though he were wrenching a wet finger from the frozen metal wall of a freezer. Tears dimmed his eyes, and he screeched frantically at the hot, dark blood pooling on his stomach.

"You're *mine,* Marty," soothed Jan, enveloping him and growing over him, covering the ripped, agonized flesh with her own. "All mine. You need *me.* You always needed *me."*

He choked, closed his eyes. Sobbed. He lay in the silent darkness for a long time. Another dream. When he opened his eyes again, he knew that.

It was all a nightmare, and Leigh only came to him in his dreams to steal him back. She came to trick him and burgle his mind, to steal him away from Jan and the true love he had finally found. Leigh tried to steal him from her with lies and promises.

"No, God, *no!"* He wanted Jan. Martin needed her and needed to awaken from these fevers that plagued him so viciously. He needed to be well . . . to live with Jan as he craved!

And then after restless, endless hours of fitful slumber, Jan was there. Really there. Beside him on the bed, rousing him from the hallucinations of nightmare as she made him harden and rise into the sheath of love she kept solely for him.

Though the frantic visions of his sleep were near-eternities of hell, he knew he must endure them until he was finally well once more. The freedom of his life with Jan would make it all worthwhile.

He was himself, and nearly free of Leigh's imprisonment. Jan told him so. Told him he was nearer freedom every day.

Through foggy eyes and a consciousness that barely knew the moment, he saw Jan's lanky hair and soothing gaze. She laid her hand on his hot face, wiping away the heavy drops that seeped out of his pores. "I need you," he mumbled. "You . . . you're m-my life . . . Jan."

"Don't worry." She breathed the whisper. "You'll be better soon."

He helped her wipe his burning, sweaty face.

"Don't worry, darling," she repeated. "I have you. I'll take care of you."

He felt her encase him and shoved his body into hers as hard as he could, surrounded by her fire that was able to empower the furnace inside him. His head lolled as he tried to nod the frenzied agreement he felt.

She smiled.

They kissed.

32

Mushy-headed, Martin saw the glare of the sun through his eyelids and tugged at the sheets, turning with an effort to the empty space beside him.

Empty, like in his constant dreams.

Was this a dream, too?

He pinched the loose flesh of his arm as hard as his trembling fingers could, digging in his nails, then wincing at the knife of pain until he was gagging. Choking spit back down and wheezing, he looked at the bed's emptiness once more.

Jan was not there. He tried to call to her with a dry throat, only to hear the wretched whine he made. He tried again anxiously: "Ja . . . an—"

The mildew- and puke-reeking apartment was silent and felt as empty as the spot beside him. Then he started, knowing the bright sunlight and the slant of their rays proved the time as late morning. He forced himself up in the bed with a clenched mouth and slid to the floor, but his legs buckled underneath him. "God fucking damn!" he gasped at a high pitch, clamping his hands onto the sideboards while his knees dropped with a wretched blast of fire to the discolored carpet. His legs went numb, and he could barely keep conscious with the waves flying through him at crazy speed and unwarned navagations.

"J-Jan," he finally whispered, fighting to reclaim his voice.

No answer.

Martin stared back through the door and its hallway beyond, listening because he could do nothing else.

Listening harder to . . .

nothing.

"Fuck it," he grumbled, grabbing the sideboard of the bed and dragging himself up on legs that still felt nothing. He shuddered in his own debilitation. A sense of déjà vu enveloped his senses, but he tried to beat back the feeling that this had happened before, that this awakening had happened many times before.

No! Dreams! Just fucking nightmares!

But he wasn't dreaming now.

He was deathly sick and knew from the sight of his gaunt, shiny-gray body that he had been so for days. No déjà vu. No dream or nightmare or mysterious law of the cosmos. He had no idea if it had been one day or a week, because each was just the same, and he always came to consciousness believing that it was the first day of illness when he awoke.

He forgot the days of empty nothingness, of hot illness and icy hallucinations.

And then there were the nights, when Jan finally came home to him. Those nocturnal meetings invigorated him with an instant vibrancy, as though he'd only dreamed the day's hell in a nightmarish sleep.

"Jan!" he tried to scream with all his might, and cringed at the hissing noise that came out, and how his vocal chords strained in rippling flame at the effort.

Frustration and its panic suddenly struggled for control. His skin felt as though it would burst apart trying to hold the battle in. He shook, unable to stop. Unable to restrain either emotion as his grip on the sideboard slackened and he fell back onto the stinking floor with wild gags and gasps. He couldn't even move! Lying motionless, he felt only the tears that streaked and burned down the sides of his face to soak him. The spasms became more powerful, and each breath tasted like acid on his raw tongue.

Martin knew he was dying.

The futility of his life weighed down on him, and he saw the waste of his years . . . the death he had lived for so long finally catching him here after those fruitless hours spent in a last-minute attempt to break free. His teeth were all loose and rotten now. Six had fallen out. His bones creaked and groaned with each movement. His skin stretched over them like centuries-old cloth.

"I . . . I'm dying," he choked, raising his head and withered hands, then burying his face into those flaking, sweaty palms, feeling the wisps of hair clinging to a bald head.

God damn! But his voice would not obey, and he croaked stupidly as he struggled back onto his hands and knees, then pulled on the bedsheet. It ripped, and the sound of its tearing fabric rang in his ears until he clutched the moving mattress that shifted like a storm-ridden ocean. Holding tight, he squinted to focus on the scattered pile of his brown-gray hair on the pillow's rumpled case.

He was sickened all over and felt so damn weak. He only wanted the life he'd so recently regained, and that life was poisoned by the past from which Leigh would not release him. Yet somehow he almost wanted to climb back onto the water-filled mattress and lie there as he had during the days before . . . days he couldn't remember. Waiting for Jan.

For life.

His feverish sight took in the room, and he saw everything as he would have placed it, and then he had to stop, wanting to drop into some kind of peace. The peace of death. He wanted peace. He wanted more.

He wanted—

At least he was dying at home. His true home.

Jan.

Martin lay quietly and shut his eyes, listening to his heart grow weaker and weaker. Feeling his chest tremble more and more slightly. Bumpa-bumpa . . . bumpa. Bumpa. Bum . . . pa. Bum—

He listened to it stop.

"What the hell are you doing down there?"

Disbelieving, Martin ripped open crusty eyelids and turned up to see her standing before him, the white gold bracelets on her wrists clinking when she rested her hands on her hips. Her eyes glittered brightly with a peculiar amusement.

He drew in a breath, shivering with the cold of his limbs, and stretched out a hand to her foot. It was covered by shiny leather high-heeled shoes. He saw the plain gray suit and matching skirt that uselessly tried to hide her figure. The skirt's high slit hid nothing at all when she moved her leg to the side. He saw the gartered stockings underneath and looked up into the bare taco lips of her sex.

Ready to eat—

He wasn't dead.

"What the hell are you doing on the floor, Marty?" she asked, her mouth twisted by the gentle curves of a smile.

"I . . . I fell." He cackled foolishly, feeling foolish and knowing he looked foolish. Hot blood pumped into his face as he found his voice easily now. "I . . . I wanted . . . to eat. I haven't . . . eaten . . . for a long time . . . Jan. I'm w-weak."

Her eyebrows twitched. "Are you hungry?"

Not for food. He knew he should be and was surprised that he wasn't. He wanted *her*.

But he had to eat real food for strength! He nibbled his lip, licking its blood. Chewed harshly. "I . . . I *need* to *eat.*"

She laughed. "Okay, okay. Well, get up off the floor, silly."

He tried to raise an arm. It was like a child trying to lift a railroad tie. He grunted and couldn't even wipe away the beads of sweat that poured from his forehead like rainwater. "I—I can't. I need . . . help, Jan. P-please?"

She bent down and looked into his eyes, displaying the naked breasts he'd slobbered for as her shirt fell open. "You're fine, Marty. You're doing just fine."

Her breasts jiggled, and the brown nipples danced.

He *wanted.*

But he was dying! "Damn it, I need a d-d-doctor!"

Looking past him, she backed across the floor, sitting on the La-Z-Boy's taunting center of peace. "Okay, already, but listen to this first. I've only been working five days, right?"

It felt and looked as though the walls of the room were closing in around him. The smelling, stinking room. He sniffed but caught only the scent of lemon Lysol and fresh paint. As startled as he could be in his state, he stared around the room. It looked fresh and clean.

"Hey, I've only been working five days, right?"

"I . . . I don't know. Can't . . . remember."

"Typical male." She sniggered. "Can't even remember to brush your teeth."

He reached up to the empty sockets in his gums but stopped again, trying to follow his earlier train of thought, though it was chugging away down the winding tracks of his battered mind faster and faster. "No," he whined. "This room—"

"Looks a lot better, doesn't it, Marty? I asked the manager to fix it up. Real sweetly, you know what I mean? He's a tough old bastard, not a sugar like you." She tittered. "But he's bald like you are, honey."

Marty flinched; his jaw dropped low. "When?"

"Oh, two days ago, I guess. You probably never even knew he was here, huh? I told him to keep quiet 'cause you were so puny. He's going to take care of the bedroom tomorrow."

"H-how?"

She fluttered her lashes. "I just asked him to, Marty. A woman knows how to do these things."

"J-Jan—"

"Anyway, listen to me, sweet cheeks. Only five days, and I've already been promoted, okay? Isn't it great! A damn good promotion, too. I'm the personal secretary for one of the execs now. You know, warming his lap and taking letters. It's just a little podunk advertising firm, but we all have to start somewhere, huh?"

"Doc . . . tor," he repeated, not understanding why she

wouldn't listen—why she was teasing him. "I need . . ." He shook again and suddenly remembered that he hadn't relieved himself all day and couldn't remember the last time he had.

He tried hard to move his hand again, and this time it jerked, trembling down to hold his balls. But even that pressure didn't revive the urge to take a piss. "Oh, Jesus . . ." He was alive, yes. But he wasn't living anywhere near normally. He tried to feel fear for his state.

He couldn't.

"I've made a helluva good impression with everyone, I think. It's a little tiny office, and I've already made friends with everybody. There's that real good-looking hunk I told you about yesterday, too. Built like a TV jock, know what I mean?" Her mouth leveled in sympathy then. "No, maybe you don't remember, love. You're getting so forgetful, but I guess that happens when you get old and sick, huh? Anyway, he's the top salesman . . . and baby, he is such a salesman! But so am I, and his eyes were all over me the whole day today. More than yesterday even. I've been brushing up against him every time I could since I started, and I've been listening to him. He's starting to tell me all the problems he has with his wife. He's been talking about it a little more every time we're alone, and today he touched me." Her teeth sparkled as her lips separated again. "Know what I mean, Marty? He sort of reminds me of you." She licked her lips. "It was kind of forward, but he asked me to go with him for a drink. 'Course, I've been kind of forward, too." She thrust out her pelvis for emphasis and giggled.

Martin grimaced, only half hearing the words of this nightmare that overshadowed any he'd ever endured. He was fucking dying . . . and fucking *hallucinating!* The smoke from the blaze frying his mind even disfigured her words and the sight of this slobbish apartment—

"But I couldn't do that to you, Marty. Could I? You need me. And I know you want me. You always want me, don't you, baby?" She glanced at the watch on her arm. "So I asked him here, okay? He'll be by soon."

The words weren't real! They were a nightmare dream he

didn't believe in, set on him by Leigh's evil prison magic to drag him back to her captive dungeon. *They weren't real.* They had to disappear . . . so ruled by the cosmic law! He was hallucinating—being driven insane!

"Poor Marty," Jan whispered, running her thumb across his sweaty face. "Poor, poor Marty. You look so pitiful. You've lost all your hair, too, handsome. You don't even have as much as the apartment manager now. And there's yucky old teeth all over this rug." She giggled again. "Your teeth, hot dick." She scooped one up and examined it like a jeweler with a diamond. "Yucky-yuck. Didn't your mommy teach you to throw away your trash?"

He wouldn't hear her, and she was only a formless shadow as she bent to the still-crusted carpet to pick up another yellow-brown molar. Kneeling beside him, she studied it, too. Her nose wrinkled, and she dropped them both into a wastebasket.

Clunk. Clunk.

"Jan. Please! I . . . I want to go . . . to . . . the bathroom. Jan . . ."

Tilting her head to the side, she finally looked concerned. "Oh, dear, Marty. Do you really need to?"

He gritted the teeth that were remaining and screamed in his tiny shrieking yelp when two more fell down his throat. The scream became a choking gag, and colors surrounded him insanely. Yellow, red, and green.

Green the shade of Will's tiny Star Wars monster.

The teeth crawled down his throat and away from his windpipe, and he screamed again. Uncontrollably. Not believing . . . *not fucking believing! Fuck you, cosmic law! I ain't believing!* "I . . . fuck . . . I haven't been able to shit or piss all day!"

A slow grin returned to her painted lips, and she touched his head, patting it as if he were her dog. Then she stood, taking his hand and lifting him up easily. Easily . . . queasily, thought Martin, and he clawed at her clothes to keep on his hollow legs. His feet were hollow, too, and he held tight to keep from falling.

"Don't be so eager, Marty." She took his arms to steady him. "Down, boy. You'll muss me and tear my dress."

She held him secure, but he felt woozy, and his knees lurched. Wobbly. He gratefully let her drag him across the gritty floor back into the bedroom and to the little bathroom at its rear, gagging from the reek of the fermented urine that still stained its floor.

The manager will fix up the bedroom and all tomorrow.

She lifted the cracked toilet lid and helped him sit down on the cold, crisp porcelain. He winced as he saw the scaly pale skin hanging and flaking off his naked legs. *Leprosy!* But he didn't care anymore. He wanted someone . . . anyone! "I n-need . . . t-to call m-my k-k-kids," he stuttered, trying to push something out of his bladder or bowels. Even painful, burning diarrhea.

Anything!

But now he couldn't even push out a fart.

"God. G-God damn," he cried.

"Can't go, huh?" Sympathy glowed once more in her black pupils. But it was cold, and completely different from what she'd been like these past shapeless nights.

"But . . . G-God d-damn—I need t-to fuck . . . ing *t-try!*" His throat grated raspily, and he tried to chew his tongue for more saliva. "C-can you g-get me a g-guh-glass of . . . wa . . . ter?"

"Yeah." She turned to the sink and took a slimy plastic cup off the floor, then filled it and handed it to him.

Martin didn't care that its inside was filled by dirt and rust, and his trembling hands clasped it.

She stood very close. Her body heat warmed him, and she let her hand slide down his naked back, bring back a familiar tingle. His penis quivered as he tried not to admire her or desire her. He didn't want the impossible, astonishing surge in his loins. He sobbed, wrinkling his face so much that flakes of its dry flesh fell onto his skinny knees.

"I really look good, huh?" She stepped to the side and faced the sink, admiring herself in the medicine chest mirror. "I think all the guys at the office thought so, too."

Then the doorbell chimed.

"Jan," he gasped.

Looking down, she stared at him for a moment and winked. "We're together, at least, right, Marty? I won't be long. You're mine, remember? All mine." She helped him bring the cup the rest of the way to his lips, and the tasteless fluid wet his mouth as he lapped it thirstily—

And scalded the tender membranes of his throat.

Choking, he tried to repel it, dragging away from her. A pitched noise splattered from him.

She shrugged, setting the cup back on the sink without expression.

"Jan—" He wheezed. "J-Jan!" He was gagging as she slipped out the door, and it swung slow behind her, clicking loudly as it shut.

The water was undrinkable, but he wasn't thirsty.

No.

He only wanted to be! He *wanted* to be thirsty. He *needed* to be thirsty. Dear God, he wanted—He needed—

Through the door he heard her walking. Heard the front door creak open. Her flighty words were muffled. They were swallowed by the nasal bass of a man.

What the hell was happening? What was happening to him? Why was he like this?

The voices continued, still muffled but becoming clearer as Jan invited the man inside and shut the door loudly behind him. Martin tried to pick out what was being said. Jan's giggles and gleeful chuckles were clear. They were followed by a man's wheedling tones and an occasional deep laugh.

Then nothing.

Martin sat there immobile, forgetting why he was there. A biting loneliness more crushing than any disaster warped every thought. "Jan," he whimpered. "Jan!" he wailed, but the cry was only in his brain. His voice would not come. He was listening to nothing. Jan's giggles and the masculine voice came nearer. Martin was held in a tornado of confusion and loss.

What the hell was she doing?

Who was she with—*why?* Where was *he? Who* was he?

"I . . . I'm M-Martin," he whispered, the words turning to sharp spears in his throat.

"Just a second, Glen," Jan was saying, right outside. Then the door opened, and she was beside him. She smiled at the mirror, took off her jacket, and brought a tube of lipstick out of the creaky medicine cabinet to freshen the color of her lips.

Martin tried to touch her. To reach out and touch her. His arms stayed still at his sides.

"I'm waiting out here, hot buns," reminded the husky voice, and there was a teasing tap on the door. "I want that surprise you promised me, remember? A warm, juicy, *tight* surprise!"

Sighing, she glanced down at Martin and pursed her lips with a pleasant pucker. "They're all like that, aren't they, darlin'? Always wanting to get something for nothing." And she giggled. "He thinks he's using me, you know? But that's exactly what I'm doing to him. He's our first conquest, huh? We know all the tricks now, don't we, Marty?"

But he couldn't reply, and just stared dazedly when she brushed back her out-of-place hair. She turned back to the door, twisting the knob and opening it. He saw the half-dressed man a foot or so back and watched him take her in his arms.

He was tall and muscular. Short blond hair and cleft chin. His chest was wide.

Martin seethed with jealousy.

The man pressed her face to his and began to unbutton her blouse as they kissed.

Martin stared as the covering slipped off and the man dropped it on the floor. Jan kissed him back furiously, and he saw the saliva mix on their faces. The man's fingers dragged up her skirt, and he whistled, then began unbuckling his slacks. They dropped to his shoes as Martin gaped, no longer able to feel anything but frustration. He couldn't move—could only stare and stare and stare and watch the big man strip off her clothes, fondle her body, and push her to the mattress, crouching between her raised knees until they rolled out of his sight.

But not out of his hearing.

Martin's bitterness grew with the noise of their wet kisses and cries, and then the sound of the rippling waterbed as they fell onto it. It sloshed as their moans came faster and faster. The headboard bumped in noisy rhythm into the wall, as it had with him and Jan just last night.

And the night before.

The sound of their pleasure burst in happy shrieks.

Martin was weaker. A red ball of hate consumed him.

It had lasted forever.

The torment nearly castrated him, scalding what remained of his mind. Each noise echoed inside him louder and louder until he finally heard their conversation again.

". . . maybe tomorrow at lunch?" the man said.

"Maybe. Maybe I'll give you dessert after lunch, huh?"

He chuckled brusquely, and she squealed. Martin imagined the man thrusting his fingers into a cunt filled with lust.

A moment later he heard the front door open and close, and again he had forgotten where he was. He had forgotten all but Jan and his own lust for her.

"Hi." Her soft voice spilled over him when she reappeared at the doorway, smiling sheepishly, as though he was a cop who'd caught her smoking grass. "Sorry about that."

"What . . . the hell . . . were— You f-fucked him, Jan! You fucked him while I was right . . . *here!* You m-made me sit . . . in here and *listen!*" He struggled with all the things he wanted to scream at her. "A-and I . . . I'm sick! Fuh-fucking sick! I thought . . . you l-loved me!"

She touched his fingers one by one, then put her hands on his shoulders and lifted him from the toilet seat. The bones of his knees shrieked, but then she smoothed her palm over them, making the pain disappear. She let him lean on her and walked him to the bed. "We've got all weekend, Marty. Today is Friday." She nodded at the bedstand clock, and he saw it was after midnight. "Was Friday, anyhow. But we've got the whole night tonight. We're alone now."

"B-but"—his voice caught—"who—"

"Just a guy," she assurred him, showing a twisted smile. "The world is full of them, tiger."

"But . . . you love m-me!"

"Always. Always, Marty. Like you always loved me. But it didn't stop you from fucking around, did it? You even got married!"

He allowed her to help him into bed and position him, too weak to resist if he wanted to. *Did he want to?*

His thoughts flailed. "I—I didn't know you . . . when I got married. You weren't there."

"I've always been inside you, handsome. Always. I was always there in the back of your mind. But you used me. At first it was good because you wanted me so bad, but then you only wanted me when you couldn't have anyone else." Her face darkened above him, and she climbed into the squishy bed with him. He stared, finally noticing that she was clad only in a stringy pair of panties and one of his T-shirts.

"You used me as a comfort against Leigh and anything else that bothered you, and you never gave anything back anymore. But when it got so bad for you, you came back to me. You were with me so often, Marty, especially when Cara would tease and tease you and would never follow through. I learned how to take from you without you even knowing it. You used me so much, and each time I became more real. I got to know you so well."

Martin's mouth gaped wide, but he couldn't speak now; he could only listen in hated silence.

"Leigh was gone, and the kids were on your nerves, Marty. The girls at the bars laughed at you. No one cared but me, and Marty, the funny thing is, I didn't care, either. *You* didn't even care. You just wanted out so bad. You wanted me so bad, but I wasn't quite real then. Only when you invited me . . ." Jan's breath was warm in his face, and she licked him, her hand rubbing down his stomach to grope for his balls.

It made him unbelievably hard.

"You wanted so bad to believe Leigh was fucking around on that trip when you had to stay home and take care of the kids—and you hated them all. You wanted out so badly. You wanted me to be there so badly. And then you wanted me to stay—to be with you all the time. You didn't care about anything else. Not even that warped old guitar! It was all expendable if you could just keep me with you, fucking me all the time. It was everything to you. Nothing else mattered."

"I," he croaked, but more words would not form.

"I. Yes. *I,* Marty. *I* was so important. You traded it all for this. You made me and gave it all to me."

"I . . ." It was the only word his lips would form, and he repeated it over and over.

"Yes. I. You. *You* wanted *me.* You can say that."

"I—I—I—I want . . . you."

"Again."

"I want . . . you."

She smiled, her lips wet for him. "Always?"

"Y-yes. I—I want you. Always."

"And I'm beautiful, aren't I, Marty?" She gazed at the wide mirror on the chest of drawers.

"Beau . . . tiful." He looked into the mirror with her, seeing her reflection as she lay back and opened her legs to it.

But he was not with her.

"I—"

"No, Marty. *I.*"

She was alone on the bed in the mirror. He could not see himself. He wanted his heart to hammer incessantly until it shattered with the remnants of shock he still felt in his mind.

Wanted.

He wanted.

"You want *me,* Marty."

He could not stop his own words. "I—I want you, Jan."

"I'll have you always, Marty. Any time I want you or need you." Her giggle turned haughty. "But I'll never again need or want you like you do me, darlin'. You're just where I want you now. My figment. You can't disbelieve in this dream because you're part of it, darlin'. You started it, and I'll never let you be anything else."

Figment.

"I'm you, Marty. I'm what you made. The flesh of your flesh." Her lips were taut as she turned them up in a grimace that was the terrifying parody of a smile. "I'm the very flesh of your mind, darling. The succubus of your soul and everything you ever wanted, and wanted me to be." She stroked her standing breasts with long nails, sliding those nails forward, making him flinch when they entered her skin and spat out small drops of blood.

The shiny red dribbles spread, running down past her navel.

Martin had opened his mouth wide, and the raw air picked at his toothless gums without mercy. But he could make no sound. He could not even breathe.

Her sharp nails dug deeper into her flesh, and she grunted, slicing a line from her brown nipples to each armpit. Then down her sides to the tender swell of her hips. The blood drooled out the even lines, marking each incision, and Jan crouched down and forced the nails downward still. Down to her knees.

Further. All the way to her feet.

"N-no! M-my . . . God!"

Blood gorged each deep cut, dribbling slowly out.

"Want to unzip me now, Marty?" cackled her high voice as it gurgled and changed, lowering. Becoming colder. Vile. The sound of a thousand spiders crawling through the unlit room you're about to enter.

His tongue was a solid icicle inside his stuffy mouth.

Both her hands reached up to the long slash splitting her right side, and he wanted to gag when she pulled the oozing flesh apart, opening a hole that revealed her dark, steaming truth. She tugged harder, widening the gash, ripping it up to the skin of her shoulders.

It hung loose in pulpy, dripping clumps.

Martin's eyes were wide, too, staring into the horror beyond even the insanity that had struck him down. Jan pulled the ripping flesh away from her back. Away from her breasts and tummy. The shredded and slimy layer of skin shone with her tanned pinkness, and she dropped it to the carpet with squishy splats. She tore off her outer shell the way a magician would remove a paper suit.

He saw Jan's loving chestnut eyes pop out, hanging by the thin tethering of stringy veins. Their absence revealed yellow orbs that glowed, underlined by blackened circles that merged into a flattened green nose above gnashing gray teeth. Her mishapen baboon head dropped from a squatty neck that tapered into shrunken, bony shoulders and flabby breasts that rotted on a bloated, distended stomach.

She lay on the bed and spread skinny thighs. They tapered into awful scarred legs that met at the pulsating, dripping hole of a gangrenous vagina that slobbered hungrily for his prick.

"Now fuck me, Marty," the ghastly voice commanded. *"Fuck me good.* That worthless shit didn't know how to do it like you can. Fuck me the best you can, and I'll stay the night with you. Give me what I want, and maybe we'll do it again in the morning."

Her pus-ridden body stank of long death as it slid on top of him, and he gasped at its weighty heaviness, felt her mesh her bristly pubic hair into his as her rough scabs scraped across his flesh. She drooled and panted, her grasping fingers caressing his limp penis until it was unwillingly hard. She forced it into the wet folds of her icy vagina.

He cringed, closing his eyes tight and holding his breath so he wouldn't smell her dead stink, then he felt the power of the reunion he'd craved before and was now forced into. It made him move with her, pushing into her timidly at first, and then deeper and deeper, surging into the power of an orgasm that would bring him his only meaning now.

"Fuck me, Marty."

He did his best.